Peng

That Uncertain Feeling

Kingsley Amis, who was born in South London in 1922, was educated at the City of London School and St John's College, Oxford. At one time he was a university lecturer, a keen reader of science fiction and a jazz enthusiast. His novels include *Lucky Jim* (1954), *Take A Girl Like You* (1960), *The Anti-Death League* (1966), *Ending Up* (1974), *The Alteration* (1976, winner of the John W. Campbell Memorial Award), *Jake's Thing* (1978), *Russian Hide-and-Seek* (1980) and *Stanley and the Women* (1984). Among his other publications are *New Maps of Hell*, a survey of science fiction (1960), *The James Bond Dossier* (1965), *Colonel Sun*, a James Bond adventure (1968, under the pseudonym of Robert Markham), *Rudyard Kipling and his World* (1975) and *The Golden Age of Science Fiction* (1981). He published his *Collected Poems* in 1979 and his *Collected Short Stories* in 1980. He has written ephemerally on politics, education, language, films, television and drink. Kingsley Amis was awarded the CBE in 1981.

KINGSLEY AMIS

That Uncertain Feeling

Penguin Books

Penguin Books Ltd, Harmondsworth, Middlesex, England
Viking Penguin Inc., 40 West 23rd Street, New York, New York 10010, U.S.A.
Penguin Books Australia Ltd, Ringwood, Victoria, Australia
Penguin Books Canada Ltd, 2801 John Street, Markham, Ontario, Canada L3R 1B4
Penguin Books (N.Z.) Ltd, 182–190 Wairau Road, Auckland 10, New Zealand

First published by Gollancz 1955
Published in Penguin Books 1985

Made and printed in Great Britain by
Richard Clay (The Chaucer Press) Ltd,
Bungay, Suffolk
Typeset in Baskerville

To

HILLY

ONE

"THE BEVAN TICKET," I said, "has expired, and will have to be renewed."

The middle-aged woman put a hand to her mitre-like hat and frowned across the counter at me. After some time, she said: "Mrs. Bevan said she just wanted one like the one she had out last time."

I was used to this sort of thing, as indeed to every sort of thing that could go on here. "The Bevan ticket," I repeated in the same tone, or lack of one, "has expired, and will have to be renewed."

My gaze, slightly filmed by afternoon drowsiness, swam round the square, high room, fixing idly on the etching, or daguerreotype, or whatever it was, of Lord Beaconsfield's face which hung over the Hobbies and Handicrafts Section. Lord Beaconsfield had had some connexion with the founding of the Library, which took place a long time ago. At the moment his likeness was glowing in a cloudy beam of late spring sunshine, and looked as if it wanted to be sick but knew that this would be wrong. I nodded imperceptibly to it.

"She couldn't get in herself this afternoon, you see, Mr. Lewis," the woman was saying; "she's had to go down the Food Office because of her boy, so I said I'd take her book and change it while I was changing mine, like. Quite often I do it for her."

I allowed a pause to elapse. From the dozen or so other borrowers present came sounds that had grown familiar to me; the squeaking of shoe-leather, a fairly loud grumble of voices, the thud of a book replaced on the wrong shelf or dropped. Quite a long way away to my left a date-stamp thumped intermittently. I wetted the ring finger of my right hand and smoothed the place next to the parting where my hair was just beginning to go. Then I swayed my long thin body over the rows of tickets, taking my time about bringing my face nearer the woman's. My face is a round and rubicund one, and a girl I once knew used to say it looked cheerful, but that was before I got this job. Anyway, I now moved it forward, making a great effort not to blink my eyes, which are grey. They began to smart a little, but I've often thought that not blinking them makes me look more formidable, and I could do with that. It doesn't seem to work when I try it in the mirror, but you couldn't expect it to, I suppose. I stood facing this woman, keeping absolutely still, as if I were waiting for her to scream or faint. Nothing happened apart from the collapse of a loaded shelf in the Geography Section, which one of the other assistants was rearranging that day. Weighing my words, I said: "The Bevan ticket has expired, and will have to be renewed."

"But you've always let me do it in the past, Mr. Lewis. I've never had any difficulty about it before. And Mr. Jenkins, is it?—he always let me do it too."

"Mrs. Edwards," I said compassionately, "have you been listening to what I've been saying?"

She looked timidly down at her shopping-basket, which was stuffed with goodies for her luckless family. "No," she said.

Just then young Dilys Jones, a blonde girl of sixteen or seventeen, came into the Lending Department from the entrance-hall. Her face was flushed and she was picking at the buttons of her pink woollen cardigan. She said in some agitation: "Mr. Lewis, can I speak to you a minute?"

"Excuse me, Mrs. Edwards, will you please?" I waited until an expression of mature calm had had time to diffuse

8

itself over my face—I was on surer ground here, pretty certainly, than with the non-blinking trick—before I turned to Dilys. "Now, Dilys, what's the matter?"

"Please, Mr. Lewis, there's a lady come into Reference to make an inquiry and she've been terribly rude. Awful, she've been, Mr. Lewis, honest."

I moved another few feet away from Mrs. Edwards and dropped my voice. With people like Dilys, the term 'rude' tends to get used in situations where indecency, rather than insolence, is in question. "What on earth's she been doing?" I muttered.

"Terribly rude she was. Kept on asking me about a book about some old-fashioned thing, something about costumes or something, but I couldn't hear what she was saying really, and she kept going on and on at me, and she got proper insulting, man—Mr. Lewis, so I came and . . ."

"What sort of lady is she?"

"Aw, well-dressed like. Plenty of money, I'd say."

"Yes, I know the kind of lady."

"Used to having her own way, you know."

"Yes, I know. Why didn't you put Mr. Jenkins on to her?"

"Couldn't find him, sorry."

Dilys was good at not being able to find people, though she generally managed to get hold of me all right, as now. "Did you look in the cataloguing-room?" I asked. "Or round the Biography Section?"

I wondered for a moment why I was bothering to prolong this conversation. In the first place, no doubt, it was because Dilys was a girl, a fact not to be lightly set aside. In the second place, it was because she was on the right side of the line dividing the attractive from the rest. Nice, that. What was in the third place, if there was a place so numbered? Oh, the usual thing, presumably: when nothing's going on or likely to start going on, which is a lot of the time, I start practising certain poses and tones and phrases, for no very clear reason. Anyway, I often used to behave like that in those days—it's last year I'm talking of. There must have been something to do with vanity in it, but vanity, if you train it with enough devotion, can be the best defence against boredom.

So I stood there now all willowy, one lot of fingers drumming away like fury on the counter, until Dilys had at last stopped listing the main stages in her search for Ieuan Jenkins. I didn't mind helping her anyway, and said with quiet confidence: "Don't you worry, Dilys, now. I'll be glad to look after it for you," and, raising my voice to an official kind of tone: "Very well then, Miss Jones, if you'll attend to this lady here I'll see to that other matter immediately."

Trying to look preoccupied and earnest, and wishing the chief could see me looking it, I couldn't help feeling a glow of triumph at having got rid of Mrs. Edwards. I opened the counter and went out, grinning tensely now and slapping my shoes on the dark-brown hummocky lino. The place was starting to empty, thank God, as tea-time approached, thank God. Two slow old men came out of the Newspaper Room and turned towards the main doors. They looked poor as well as the rest of it, and so reminded me of how poor I was, especially for a man with a £6 11s. 5d. electricity bill to pay before the end of the month (discount 3s. 3d., but much too late for that now). Why had the Glamorganshire Electricity Board got to have that money before the end of the month? If they'd owed me money, I could wait, oh yes, I'd got plenty of time, see, no hurry about that at all. But whenever I owed them money they had to have it immediately, straight away, now. Why was that?

Distraction was at hand: a female student from the local University College crossed my path some yards ahead and my glance dropped involuntarily to her legs.

Then it climbed again, voluntarily, to the swing door of the Reference Department. I injected into my demeanour a purposeful air that owed a little, I confess, to the striding, sneering hero of that week's main feature at the Pavilion. You wanted to see me? Well, now's your big chance, lady. Siddown, will you? All right, shoot.

I put out my tongue at a painting of a former mayor, a tiny little wizened fiend of an auctioneer, which hung in the entrance-hall. Then the memory of Dilys's description made another and more genuine sneer twitch at my mouth. Well-dressed, eh? Not much difficulty then, eh, in picking her out from the other users of Aberdarcy Public Library. The colloquy with Mrs. Edwards had got me into exactly the right mood to deal with this person, whoever she might be.

Who she might be, and in addition who she was, remained obscure when I saw a woman of thirty or thirty-five swing round and face me with an impatient movement. She was standing by the counter behind which we filed some, but not by any means all, of the weekly reviews. Yes, I knew the kind of lady all right. "Can I help you?" I asked. I tried, successfully I think, to suggest how very unlikely, all things considered, this was. My lethargy had vanished, giving place to an alertness that seemed disproportionate in the circumstances. I felt nervous too.

She looked up at me quickly with wide dark eyes and checked whatever she'd been going to say. Her frown lifted. "Yes, I should think you probably can." Her voice, deep, educated and English, reinforced my suspicions of her. "It's really quite a simple matter."

I noticed now that she was attractive in a square-shouldered, taut-bloused way, with skin the colour of the top of the milk and hair the colour of tar. But I said with what I hoped was irritating deliberation: "I'll do my best, naturally. I thought I gathered a few moments ago, though, from what one of our junior assistants was telling me, that you'd encountered a certain amount of difficulty in establishing just what it is you need."

Hesitating again, she smiled, showing china-like teeth firmly clenched. "Well, I can see that must have been partly my fault. I just couldn't seem to make myself . . . Oh, by the way, my name's Elizabeth Gruffydd-Williams."

This was one of the biggest Aberdarcy names, and hearing it pronounced by one who owned it made me feel even less confident. But since it was clearly my political duty to seem unimpressed, I just nodded my head a little bit.

"My husband's on the Council, you know. Perhaps you've had some contact with him? He's on the Libraries Committee."

"No, I've never come across him."

"Oh, pity." I had to admire the way it didn't put her off. "Let's see, you're Mr. . . . ?"

"Lewis." I returned her stare.

"What I was actually looking for, Mr. Lewis, was a book or books on the history of costume, preferably with plenty of coloured illustrations. They've asked me to design the costumes for the next production of the Darcy Players." The mention of these, a local troupe of amateur actors keen as mustard on culture, wrung from me no cry of inarticulate wonder, in fact no sound at all. She went on: "The setting is medieval Wales, you see, and we want the things to be as authentic as we can get them, naturally." She put her head on one side so that a lock of the black hair, which she wore long, fell across the angle of her jaw, and a black pendant-earring swung to and fro. "I wonder if you have any suggestions, Mr. Lewis?"

I had one or two I could have brought up, but they had no immediate bearing on the matter in hand, so I

12

just said: "Wouldn't the University College Library be a more likely place to inquire, Mrs. Williams?" and wished I hadn't said it in my cut-glass, Cardiff-announcer accent.

"Yes, well theoretically of course I quite agree with you, but they were terribly tiresome about not letting . . ."

I let her ramble on; three years in this job had made me an adept at letting that happen. I thought for a bit about her air of authority, and wondered how recently it had been acquired. It derived from her husband's position, presumably, and the odds were that that too had been gained since the war. Still, that didn't matter, did it, now it was no longer true, thank God, that it took three generations to make a gentleman? I yawned, and, when the momentary deafness had passed, understood this gentlewoman to say that she'd have had to sign on for a three-year course at the College in order to borrow a book from its Library, which, as she put it, "would have been just too much."

This declaration, rounded off with a slight laugh, had come out with enough volume to make an unshaven, wild-eyed student look up from *Sight and Sound* and old Parry, a retired Grammar School master famed in his day for almost continuous pauses when conducting a class, lift his shaggy head and stare with emphatic bafflement at the SILENCE PLEASE notice above the periodical racks.

Very quietly indeed, I said: "I see. Had you thought of trying the subject-catalogues here?"

"I'm ashamed to say I'm rather a fool with catalogues and all that kind of thing. I'd really been hoping to find someone here who might be prepared to help me out personally."

She looked suddenly up at me again from beneath her dark, rather thick eyebrows, and it occurred to me that it was rather silly, even though it might also be rather fun, to be hostile to this woman. Furthermore, I now realised, my hostility, such as it was, grew not out of any righteous feeling for Dilys, but merely from my familiar embarrassed defensiveness at talking to a member of the anglicised upper classes, a thing I'm supposed to have got out of now. I realised too that it was no use hiding from myself the fact that I quite liked the look of this particular member of those classes, especially the daunting carriage of her head, complete with the earrings, and the hair of course, and the set of her shoulders in the black tailor-made costume or whatever it was. I decided to stop being the Pavilion hero, or at least to see what I could do with him in another aspect. .

Screwing up my eyes a little, I said: "Well, I wouldn't mind having a go at that. Between ourselves, though, I warn you I'm not much of a catalogue expert either. Would you mind waiting a moment while I go and have a look?" I dropped the Cardiff announcer too and used the pure Welsh 'o' in 'moment' and 'go'.

"Not in the least; thank you very much."

We eyed each other for another second or two, before I went out. Yes, I thought to myself, very fine indeed; no question at all about that. Strong and active, good at leisured pastimes like tennis and golf instead of just joining in them to conform, probably a furiously reckless car-driver. Some things about her appearance and mannerisms seemed to indicate that a certain basic human activity never entered her thoughts, others that it never left them. Perhaps they were really the same things all the time. I reflected, as sometimes before, that women were a thing in themselves that had made a profound and not easily forgotten impression on me. Well, that was life, wasn't it? Yes, and it was also true that this little representative of that noteworthy sex was a little devil when she was roused, no doubt. That'll do, Lewis, that'll do, thank you. Give it a rest, can't you, Lewis? There could hardly be more and better reasons why I shouldn't let my thoughts wander, or rather sprint, in that direction. And besides, in the last few weeks I'd been enjoying myself no end, practising the role of the truly strong man, the man superior to things like sex. Oh, and money too, of course.

The subject-index gave nothing of any conceivable use under *Kostyoom*, *Dres* or *Kloadhing* (the reason for its being in 'reformed' spelling is something I still hope to lay bare some day), except for a history of underclothing which might help to soften the rigours of an evening duty or two. But, wait a minute, I was superior to that kind of thing. I firmly refrained from making a note of the shelf-mark, and began humming like a fool to drive the catalogue page-number out of my head.

Back in the Reference Department, I found the woman frowning short-sightedly over *The New Statesman*. Too vain for glasses, I decided as I made my report, and found all my suspicions reviving when she said "Oh dear" with a dropping, ladylike inflexion.

"Well, what's the next step?" she went on. "If there is one."

"Yes, there is one. We can go and see Mr. Jenkins."

"And who might Mr. Jenkins be?"

"What he is, among other things, is the man who sees to the inter-library exchange system. We can find out from him if we can get hold of something you might want from somewhere else."

"Somewhere else?" She pronounced it 'somehwere', like an elocutionist.

"Somewhere else, yes. From another library."

"Ah, that sounds a bit more hopeful, doesn't it?"

"Along here."

"It's very good of you to go to all this trouble."

"Oh, I wouldn't say that."

"Why not? Why wouldn't you say that?"

"It's nicer doing this than being on the lending counter."

She laughed and said "Mm" several times, indicating complete familiarity with the miseries of being on the lending counter, then began to walk with tapping high-heels along the gloomy corridor I had brought her to. She looked about with the irritated wonder of one being shown a very ancient and boring ruin. We came to two adjacent doors. One of these led to a room ostensibly dedicated to book-repairs, but nobody used to do very much of that in my time, and the place was actually three-parts full of junk, the peculiar detritus, almost but never quite totally useless, thrown up by a large public library. I opened the other door and went in. This was where Jenkins catalogued the non-fiction. Nobody had been cataloguing the fiction since the outbreak of war, and after the war nothing had happened to make starting again seem desirable. Here too, there was plenty of junk, much of it powdered with dust and plaster, but no Jenkins. I found that I was glad about that.

Mrs. Gruffydd-Williams had followed me in. Although her expression didn't change, I could tell that the room seemed squalid to her, as it did to me seeing it through her eyes. I felt ashamed, as if the place were my bedroom, and said challengingly: "He's not here."

Looking into the corners, she agreed, and edged past a rusty cabinet. "Do you work in here, Mr. Lewis?"

"No, thank God," I said with emotion. "This is the cataloguing-room. I'm nothing to do with that."

"Why 'thank God'? Is it such an unpleasant job?"

"Well, no, I wouldn't put it quite like that, but . . . we've been up against a lot of difficulties, one way and another."

"I'm sorry to hear that. Shortage of staff principally, I imagine?"

"Well, no, not so much that at all . . ." When I tried to define these difficulties, which I'd grown to think of as a kind of immemorial and irremediable heritage, I found that they tended to recede into a kind of Celtic mist—which is where a lot of things of that sort are to be presumed hidden. But I soon forgot all about that, though I went on talking, when I realised how close to this woman the smallness and littered state of the room forced me to stand. I had one elbow on top of the rusty cabinet and she was leaning against the edge of a table with her arms spread behind her. When she asked a question I noticed that she spoke with her teeth together but with her lips moving very freely. This gave her voice a harsh resonant quality which I thought suited her looks.

There we were, then, started on one of those conversations which vanish from the mind before they're even over. After a minute or so, she moved her hands back a little on the table-top so that her body and thighs were in a straight line. I felt an old and hateful excitement beginning to stir in me, the kind which, although mingled with apprehension, has the property of soon casting off any hateful ingredient. In the preceding few years I'd spent a good deal of time and energy in courting and avoiding that excitement. At the moment it was limited by the shame I felt in my ill-fitting tweed suit. This had apparently been made to measure for an under-nourished gorilla, with immense shoulders, long arms and a tiny abdomen. That morning, moreover, I'd noticed a curious pink stain on one trouser-leg—my knee it was, waiting for a chance to run for a bus or something and force its way through to the light of day.

The woman listened to me coolly. She was no doubt merely engaged in concealing the boredom she must feel. In a Councillor's wife, just as in an assistant librarian, the efficient concealment of that emotion wasn't an unexpected skill. The only thing, in fact, which was at all out of the ordinary, which came anywhere near justifying the half-shuffle I made towards her under the pretence of easing my stance, was the way she was leaning on the table. And if she really was bored, why didn't she go away? I repeated this query to myself when she moved again, this time pulling her shoulders back. Dear, dear. I wanted to shut my eyes: there are some things a man doesn't like to see. Was this attitude merely a habit of hers, something she didn't notice herself doing? Unlikely, in a woman of her age. I sweated a little, or at any rate felt convinced that I ought to, and started praying for and against an interruption.

This was at once provided. In the middle of a particularly vapid and halting sentence of mine about some particularly soporific, and indeed largely fictitious, detail of library organisation, the opening door rapped me admonitorily on the elbow. While I rubbed this and the woman grinned, a man in the late forties with a dark red face and thick lips came by degrees into the room. Every straight grey hair in his abundant crop seemed the same length, making his head look as if it belonged to a little furry animal or shaving-brush. Seeing a strange woman, he dropped his head and hunched his shoulders, then looked at me.

"Hallo, Ieuan," I said. "This is Mrs. Gruffydd-Williams. Mr. Jenkins."

While she nodded and smiled, Ieuan Jenkins moistened his lips audibly. "How do you do," he said in a hoarse high-pitched voice with a strong North Walian accent; not an imitation, but the way he habitually talked. "Well now . . . hallo, John," he added.

"This is really your department, Ieuan," I said, quickly deciding to withdraw from Mrs. Gruffydd-Williams and her inquiry. A patrol encountering a vastly superior enemy force should avoid contact and retire at once before suffering any casualties. "This lady has a query about a possible exchange. I told her you were the man to deal with it, eh? So I'll leave it to you to . . ."

"Don't go yet, John," Jenkins said in tones of entreaty. "Must have a word with you, old man . . ." He looked about as if he expected a sound-proof barrier to spring up round himself and me.

"Of course." I brought out a pencil and handed it and a pad to the woman. "If you could jot down the details while I . . ."

"Why, certainly," she said with obtruded charm, starting to write.

In the corridor, at the other end of which some sort of juvenile disturbance was going on, I said to Jenkins: "All right, Ieuan: shoot."

"I beg your pardon?"

It was one of his favourite things, pretending not to understand slang. Although English wasn't his mother-tongue he guarded it jealously against all innovations (which he stigmatised as 'incorrect') by letters to the South Wales press, and, once, to the *Observer*. Since I know a little about linguistics I often used to attack Jenkins on this point, and at any other time would have gone for him over the 'shoot' business, forced him to admit he knew what I meant. But I knew what he'd got me out here for, and wasn't looking forward to it, so I only said: "Sorry. What was it you wanted to talk to me about?"

He hunched himself up again. "About the job," he began submissively.

"The job? How do you mean?" It was gross time-gaining.

"Aw, John, you know perfectly well, boy. What else have we been talking about for the last month or more?" Submissiveness laid aside, his voice pealed down the re-echoing passage and mingled with the juvenile disturbance. He's always been a great one for the *hwyl*—you know, the old Welsh oratorical fire and the rest of it.

"Oh, you mean old Webster's job? What about it?" Webster, the Sub-Librarian, was going to Leicester as Chief Librarian in a few months, and the vacancy had recently been advertised.

After beginning to repeat my last phrase in a half-scream, Jenkins checked himself and turned liquid eyes on me. "All right, John," he said quietly; "no need to tell me if you don't want to. No need to discuss it at all."

"I'm sorry, Ieuan, I wasn't trying to shut you up. What do you want to know?"

"Just whether you've sent in an application for the post, or whether you intend to do so or not. You were going to think it over. You were going to let me know, if you recollect."

"Yes, I know, Ieuan. Well . . . I talked it over with Jean, and we decided that I should apply, because after all it's up to me to have a shot at anything that . . ."

"Yes yes. Quite so, John. Thank you."

"I mean I shouldn't be crabbing your chances, because with my lack of experience I'm not very likely to . . . "

"Say no more. That's all I wanted to know."

"I'm only putting in for it so as to show them I'm . . ."

"All right, John, all right, boy. I've heard all I . . ."

"Just for practice when . . ."

Jenkins raised his hand like one quelling applause. "I'm sorry," he said. "I don't like being a nuisance in this way. I get worried about it and make a fuss, I don't want to embarrass you. But you know how important that extra cash would be to me. Bear with me when I fly off the handle, won't you?"

"Well, of course, Ieuan, I absolutely understand. There's no need to feel . . ."

Long overdue, Mrs. Gruffydd-Williams came into view again from the cataloguing-room. "I've put down all the details I can think of, Mr. Jenkins," she said briskly in her clenched-teeth voice. "Including my address and telephone-number. Do get in touch with me, won't you? as soon as anything comes up. It is—rather important." Saying this with insulting mock-humility, she relinquished the pencilled sheet into his care.

"Righto, then, Mrs. . . . Thank you. Thank you, John. How's the wife?"

This question seemed so far off the point and so unnecessary—he and I had already exchanged words a couple of times that afternoon, and would no doubt exchange more before we parted—that I wondered whether he might have felt himself called upon to spoil what he might think were my chances with this woman. He was a great advocate of things like the sanctity of the home.

"She's very well, thank you, Ieuan," I said loudly and slowly, and added loudly and slowly: "So are both of the children."

"Good, good," he said. "Well, thank you." He nodded at the two of us and moved quickly away, shutting the door of his earth behind him.

The woman raised her black eyebrows at me as if in commentary upon the oddity of my colleagues.

"Everything satisfactory?" I asked.

"Well, I rather hope it will be."

We moved together towards the entrance-hall. I felt I was walking in an absurdly unnatural way, like a schoolboy on the stage for the first time in his life. Did I always swing my arms as if I were carrying a pair of empty buckets? Surely not. And what did I suppose I was going to say next?

Perhaps under the spell of the frenzy of gratitude just vented by Jenkins, she did some thanking as we halted in the entrance-hall. "It's been nice chatting to you," she went on. "I'll ring up next week, if I may, to find out what stage things have got to. Or would that be too soon?"

"No, I don't think so." Looking over her shoulder, I could see an enormous car, of amphisboenic appearance, parked at the kerb outside the entrance. It must be hers, the lucky little thing. There was a slight pause. "I'm sure we'll fix you up all right, Mrs. Williams. Good afternoon."

"Oh, goodbye, Mr. Lewis. Until next week."

"Yes, goodbye."

I watched her trot masterfully down the steps and approach her car, then I went back to the Lending Department. The obvious expensiveness of the car had managed, like most things that week, to remind me again of the electricity bill. It was very rude indeed to send me a Final Notice, all in red like that, as if they doubted my intention of paying at all. And how did they mean, Final Notice? I'd only had one other. Wasn't it 'incorrect', from the Jenkins point of view, to use Final except as the last of three or more? Perhaps I could fight them in court on that issue. Yes, if I didn't mind losing.

The encounter with Mrs. Thing-Williams had made it too late for me to slip out for a cup of tea. Life was returning to normal, I perceived, a perception substantially reinforced when, immediately inside the Lending arena, I found myself confronted by a woman who could have been, and perhaps actually was, the twin of Mrs. Edwards the Bevan ticket, and who, like her, 'knew' me. This one wore a smaller and less episcopalian hat. She said in a blurred voice: "Have you got a nice book, Mr. Lewis?"

"Hundreds of them," I said reassuringly, and pushed past one of the juniors to a set of shelves behind the counter. Though I was sincerely looking forward to the dialogue which now impended, it was rather terrible to know in such detail what lines it would follow.

On these shelves we kept about two hundred books of the kind technically known as romances. Most of them were ordinary 'light' romances, but a couple of dozen at one end made various untenable claims to literary merit. This two hundred, the composition of which changed only when rebinding necessitated the withdrawal of the odd volume and the calling-up of a reserve from the open shelves, used to supply the entire literary needs of half-a-dozen times the number of housewives, office girls, shop girls and schoolgirls. I sometimes wondered how this could be, and then how it had originally come about, and then what people had done before it came about, but now, after a long spell of duty, a debilitating encounter with a moneyed person and a missed tea, I only took down a book at random and handed it to the deutero-Mrs. Edwards.

"Have I read this one?" she began by asking—a popular query, this, and spoken in the tone of high-level business executive to confidential secretary.

"No," I said firmly.

After a searching, don't-lie-to-me glance, she turned over the pages doubtfully and inattentively, then stared hard at the lettering on the spine. "Who's it by?" she asked at length.

"A very good author."

"Not too light it isn't, I hope?"

Pursing my lips and drawing in my breath, I shook my head like a hanging judge. "Not a bit too light."

She fought back gamely: "Mm. Is it a good book?"

That finished her. Of all the questions borrowers could ask, this was my special favourite, and, in the clear insolent tones of Mrs. Gruffydd-Williams, I made my favourite answer: "You'll like it."

TWO

"WHAT SORT OF party is it going to be?" my wife asked.

"Drinking and talking, I expect," I said, tucking my shirt into the trousers of my blue serge suit. This shone here and there in a good light, but it wasn't a gorilla suit. "Bits of things to eat on sticks."

"A standing-up do, you mean?"

"Yes, I should think so."

"Didn't she say anything about it over the phone?"

"No, not much; she sounded in a bit of a hurry."

"I see." She went on brushing her hair for the moment. "Do you think there'll be many there?"

"No idea. I shouldn't be surprised."

"I expect they'll be all her classy friends, won't they?"

"Probably."

"Funny her asking us, really."

"Oh, I don't know."

But perhaps it was rather funny. Mention of Elizabeth Gruffydd-Williams's visit to the Library the previous week had drawn from my wife the information that she'd been at school with her. This wasn't all that funny in itself, because everybody always seems to know everybody else in Aberdarcy, despite its size, and although this woman was now out of our class she apparently hadn't always been so, having made what people in this part of the world still call a good marriage. What could justly be called funny was the promptness with which Mrs. Gruffydd-Williams, after I'd told her casually of this schooldays connexion, had come out with an invitation to this party. And then she'd rung off before I could tell her that her books, the reason for her having rung me up at all, hadn't come in yet. Yes, it was funny. In the intervening couple of days I'd thought a good deal about it, but now I only said:

"Well, you know, I expect she wants to show herself off as the great Aberdarcy hostess entertaining all the local big shots. For my benefit because I'm a man, and for yours because she wants to show how much better she's done for herself than you have since you were at school together. If I'd got all that money that'd be enough to make me invite two people to a party. And anyway, she hasn't got to pay for it herself."

"Clever, aren't you? I don't see why you've got to be like that about her. I think she was just being decent. These people are always throwing parties and things." She put her hairbrush down and began fixing earrings into, or on to, her ears.

"Come on, get a move on. Mrs. Jenkins'll be here in five minutes, and I don't want to have to talk. . . ."

"All right, I'm ready now. You're not."

"You don't look ready to me. I've only got to put my tie on."

"Easy enough for you. Who had to put the kids to bed?"

"Agreed." Hopping on the way, so as to draw the toe-caps of my shoes across my trouser-calves, I went to the mirror and tied my tie. It was cleaner than the others because I wore it rarely, not liking it; apparently made of hessian, it had been a Christmas present from Jean's mother.

"Don't start playing the fool there, will you?" Jean said.

"Playing the fool? Me? Why should I play the fool? How do you mean?"

She turned round on her stool—I'd retreated to get my jacket—and glared at me, as far as somebody of habitual and almost comical amiability of expression, at least

25

when animated, can be said to glare. "You know bloody well what I mean, now."

"I don't, honestly."

"Yes you do. I've seen you with these upper-class types. Showing off all the time, honest Joe making no bones about what he thinks of them, that's you."

"No it isn't, I never do that. You're making it all up."

"Yes you do. What about that Coll. dance when Prof. and the Principal and his wife came and talked to us? The way you went for Prinny's wife over the election. You and your amateur theatricals: Karl Marx bloody Lewis."

"I didn't think you could remember that far back."

"I can, though, and don't you forget it. I've seen you doing the same thing with that yachting lot in the Red Dragon. You know what I mean. I'm not standing for it to-night." Unwillingly, she started smiling. "I'll walk out on you, honest."

"All right, I won't say a word."

"Well, that'll be a bit of a change, I must say." She stood up. "Do I look all right?"

"Yes, of course, darling." Someone with such abundant dark-red hair, a small thin full-lipped face with large dark-fringed eyes, and a slender figure was bound to look all right, especially with careful make-up. It was saddening to remember how lustrous, as well as abundant, her hair had been before she'd had the children; to know how necessary that careful make-up was and how angular her hips and shoulders had become. But I didn't think of that as she stood there frowning and smiling, narrowing her eyes as always when staring at someone. Her face is one that I can never see without wanting to smile for one reason or another.

"Is the dress all right?" She turned right round, much too quickly for me to see the back. The front suggested that the best had been made out of something not very opulent.

"It's fine. Haven't you done something to it?"

"I've lowered the front a bit. Not too low, is it?"

"No, it's just right."

"You'd say if it wasn't, wouldn't you?"

"You bet I would. It's bloody fine, really."

She nodded, reassured by this use of her favourite word. "You look nice. You look very young."

"No, do I really?"

"Yes, I said you did."

"How do I?"

"I knew you were going to say that. I'll tell you how when you've gone down and brought up a clean nappy off the kitchen table and the rubber knickers on the rack over the stove for me, there's a good boy."

"Oh, why is it always me?"

"Don't shout, dull, you'll wake him up. Go on, now, and I don't want any of that swearing."

When I returned with the baby's stuff Jean was bending over the cot which stood in the far corner from the bed and was partly hidden from it by a kind of flying buttress common in this type of attic. As I approached, the baby drew in his breath with a grating but pleasantly drowsy sound, like a sawmill at work on a summer afternoon. I'd often had cause to resent his presence in this room, but it was hard to do so now, seeing him asleep in his recumbent-camel posture, one which recalled his mother's attitude in front of the fire on cold days. No creature, I thought, could be so vehemently asleep as he was now, his buttocks in the air, his face pushed over to one side by the pillow. Knowing better than to try and turn him on to his side, Jean drew the blanket up to his shoulders. "Let's go down," she said.

In our sitting-room on the floor below, she said to me: "Now you're to stick with me to-night, see? No wandering round seeing what you can pick up like you usually do."

"Oh, I don't usually do that, do I?"

"Well, no, not really, I suppose, but you won't to-night, will you, darling?"

"Why, can't you look after yourself?"

"Course I can, but I'll be nervous with all that crowd."

"All what crowd?"

"Aw, all the bloody horse-riders and yachters and golfers and aeroplane-fliers and what-not. You know 'em all right. I can never think what to say to those types."

"Neither can I."

"Don't lie, now. I've never seen you at a loss for a word with anyone."

"You'll probably see me at a loss for one to-night."

"I bet. But you'll stick to me, won't you?"

"Like a bloody leech, man."

"That's the spirit. What's keeping Mrs. Jenkins, I wonder?"

"Is she late?"

"Must be. Go and get the clock from the kitchen, will you?"

I went into the room next door and took the clock off the dresser. On its face was painted a scene of animal husbandry in the United States, with steers and lariat-casting cowboys. One of these, in the left foreground, twitched stiffly to and fro in the saddle in time with the loud, clacking tick, to which a dull thumping periodically added itself.

"What is it?"

"Quarter past."

"Isn't it fast to-day?"

"Don't think so. It was slow for the news at six."

"She is late, then. Not like her."

"No. Unless she's had one of her turns."

"She looked all right this morning out shopping. Still, they come on pretty suddenly when they do. You know, Ieuan really should get her to a specialist, John."

"He has, I told you. The chap couldn't find anything wrong with her."

28

"I mean another one."

"Well, he's got her name down, but you know how long that'll take, and he hasn't got the cash to jump the queue. Bloody marvellous Health Service the Tories have . . ."

Before I was fairly launched on my diatribe, a knocking was heard at the street door beneath our window. An uproar at once set in, consisting of the raucous barking of a dog and what Jean and I knew to be a human voice. Both dog and voice were the property of a Mrs. Davies, who lived with her husband and grown-up son in the lower half of the house. They weren't our landlords, a dispensation which had often cheered me. The house belonged in fact to an Englishwoman, a solicitor's widow, who was characterised by two desires: that we should have as little contact as possible with the furniture and pay the rent in cash.

"Here she is," Jean said. "You go, John."

"Oh no. Why is it always me?"

"I want to see Eira's tucked up. And you'd better get a move on or you'll have Mrs. Davies to deal with."

With an inarticulate cry I sprang out of the room. The voice from below started calling "Mr. Lewis" repeatedly as I hurried downstairs. "I'm coming, Mrs. Davies," I replied repeatedly, and very loudly, but to no avail. The arrival of visitors for us always troubled Mrs. Davies and I'd sometimes thought that she'd have preferred us to do without them.

In the passage-type hall the bowed shape of Mrs. Davies, holding a now whimpering dog by the collar, was barring the way not of Mrs. but of Ieuan Jenkins. My heart sank. "All right, Mrs. Davies; thank you," I said, and when the crone retreated towards her basement: "Hallo, Ieuan. Anything the matter? Coming up?"

"No, John, thank you, I can only stay a couple of moments. I'm afraid we shall have to disappoint you to-night."

"Nothing wrong at home, is there?"

"Nothing seriously wrong." He sighed, standing there hunched up under the light from the bare bulb. Passing his hand over his grey crop, he said: "The same old business, you know. But fortunately only mild this time. Still, I'm afraid any baby-minding is out of the question for the immediate future. I've sent her to bed. I'd help you out myself, but I don't like to leave her."

"Of course not. You're sure it's not serious?"

He half-turned away to kick idly at the skirting-board, his hands in his raincoat pockets. "No, it's not serious."

"Well, that's something, anyway. Anything either of us can do?"

"No thank you, John, it's nice of you, boy. I'm extremely sorry indeed to spoil your evening."

"That's all right, Ieuan. Neither of us were all that keen."

"It's nice of you. Well . . ."

"Give our love to Megan and tell her we hope she'll soon be better."

"Yes yes. Good night, then, Johnny. See you tomorrow morning."

His small figure retreated and the front door slammed, causing a valedictory flurry of barking from the basement.

Grimacing to myself, I ran athletically up the stairs.

"What's up?" Jean asked.

"Ieuan. We've had it."

"Bad, is she?"

"Yes, bad, that's what she is, bad. Yes, she's bad all right."

"Aw, come on now, John. How bad is she? Do you think I should go round?"

"No, I asked. No need to, anyway. There's nothing organically wrong with that woman. All mental, you know. Hysterical. Just for the fun of it."

"Don't be silly. I seem to remember you telling me on another occasion that hysterical stuff was just as real as the, what, physiological kind of business."

"No need to bring that up, is there?" I began pacing a little. "Well, I feel full of fun now. Really going to enjoy an evening at home. Just what I could do with."

"I didn't know you were so set on going."

"It isn't that," I said peevishly. "It's being all dressed up and no bloody place to go that gets me down."

"Look, John, I know it's a disappointment, but it isn't the end of the world. You could fetch some . . ."

"No, no, I know, it isn't the end of the world. I'm quite clear on that. But that's not what I'm talking about, see?"

"Look. You'll have to go along to the corner and phone 'em up and tell 'em we can't manage to . . ."

"Jesus wept."

"Wait a minute. You can pop into the General Picton and get a couple of flagons—cider for me—and we'll listen to the wireless. There's a play on, isn't there?"

"Yes, Maugham, I think. Well, I suppose we could. The cash situation isn't any too wonderful, though."

"Never mind, let's fill our boots. I'll pay for the cider. And try and get some crisps." She dug down the side of her chair for her purse and gave me a florin (cider), a sixpence (crisps), and three pennies for the phone. "There. Now get cracking or you'll miss the start of the play."

"Right. Thanks. I'm sorry I jumped my trolley just now. I was just fed up."

"I know. Off you go, now."

"Do I need my raincoat?"

"Up to you, that is."

"Yes, but do you think I'll need it?"

"Go on, I'm not your mam. Take it in case."

Wearing my raincoat I walked along towards the phone-box, having a look at the lights of Aberdarcy ranged above the bay and thinking about Mrs. Jenkins. The trouble was that I disliked her, or rather felt continuously unhappy in her presence, which isn't really much different for my money: you behave much the same whichever you call it. It was guilt at not feeling sorry for her that really bothered me, and seemed to touch off a much less logical guilt, at having cruelly applied for the senior job that Ieuan badly needed. Although he had by far the better chance I couldn't help feeling that I was conspiring to rob him of several extra pounds a week. Those pounds would in time pay for a specialist to investigate the blinding headaches, untouchable by ordinary analgesics and so far untraceable to any cause, that attacked his wife every few weeks. Those pounds could also be used for generally alleviating Mrs. Jenkins's lot, or alternatively for a regular crate of whisky for Ieuan to help him not to worry. Apart from brightening Library duty up no end, a chronically drunken colleague would be a far less dismaying companion than a chronically worried one.

I arrived at the phone-box, and, after clearing away the remnants of somebody's sandwiches, got going with the directory, started the dial whirring and heard the ringing tone gurgle a few times. After a click, a peculiar faint roaring became audible, like a distant football crowd. Above it I could distinguish female laughter and then a man's voice calling something. A bawl came in my ear: "Hullo-ullo-ullo."

"Hullo, is Mrs. Gruffydd-Williams there, please?"

"Is what? Is what? Quiet over there, for Christ's sake. Man here on the phone." Someone made a hooting noise. "Sorry, old boy, what do you want? You'll have to shout; bit of a disturbance here, I'm afraid. Never know what they'll be getting up to next. Rough types. Oh, do pipe down, Margot, this chap wants . . ."

"Is Mrs. Gruffydd-Williams there?" I bellowed.

"Jack Griffiths you want, do you? I'm afraid he's . . ."

"No, Mrs. Gruffydd-Williams."

"Oh, got you now, got you now, you want Elizabeth. It's for you, honey. Character on the wire says he wants to talk to Mrs. . . . Gruffydd . . . Williams. Think he means you?"

"Hullo," the Gruffydd-Williams woman said.

"Hullo. This is John Lewis."

"Who?"

"John Lewis. From the Library. You asked me and my wife to your party to-night, you remember. Well, I'm afraid we can't . . ."

The background noise had been swelling again and she now said: "Just a minute." Then I heard her yell in muffled but very powerful tones: "Shut up. Shut up. I'm on the phone. Shut up." The clamour was stilled. Then: "What was that about the party?"

"You kindly asked myself and my wife to . . ."

"Oh, did I? Well, if you say I did I must have done. What about it?"

"Nothing much about it, don't worry. We can't come and that's that. Sorry to draw you away from your guests."

"Here, wait a minute. You say you can't come?"

"That's right. We can't come because our sitter-in's ill and can't come, so we can't come, you see."

"Where do you live?"

"Cwmhyfryd. Mansel Road. What about it?"

"Mm, long way, isn't it? Can't you get another sitter?"

"What, at this time? Hardly."

"Oh, pity. Pity. Somebody ought to do something about it, oughtn't they?" She hung up at once.

I came stiffly out of the phone-box and crossed the road to the General Picton, thinking that you just couldn't do anything with people like that. Well, that was that, and there was quite a lot of consolation. It was as well to know who you were dealing with before, not after, you

33

got at all tied up with people, and in particular there was now little to regret in having missed the party.

After some delay, for which an apology was offered and accepted, the licensee of the General Picton sold me my drink with courtesy and in a strong Aberdarcy accent, twin stars of virtue. We exchanged repeated farewells and thanks rather in the Ieuan Jenkins style, and parted.

At home again, I'd switched the wireless on without getting an electric shock and was just opening the first flagon when a manic tattoo on the front door got Mrs. Davies's dog going again on his barking sequence. "I wonder who the hell that is," I said to Jean.

"Probably some pals of Ken's."

"That'll be it." Mrs. Davies's son, who worked the projectors at the Cwmhyfryd Coliseum, was an unflagging devotee of lewd company and had more than once woken our baby by conducting midnight singing, laughing or swearing sessions with other rough persons. These took place in the street just under our window, no doubt because Ken was reluctant that his friends and his mother should enter into social relations. When, as was now probably happening, a crowd of them turned up to take Ken off to a café or dance-hall on his free evening, they'd wait outside the door repeating blasphemies to one another until their mate emerged; then, after a short but intense tumult of greeting, they'd be off, cackling and screeching with hilarity. I was very afraid of them and always tried to be friendly to Ken.

I became aware that Mrs. Davies was calling not "Ken" (or rather "Kan") but "Mr. Lewis". Uneasily speculating, I went to the half-landing in time to hear a woman's voice saying loudly and in an English accent: "Since he does live here, perhaps you'll be good enough to get out of my way. Come on, Bill, we'll go up. Oh, hullo; made it at last, thank God."

The last sentence was addressed to me when the speaker

caught sight of me peering over the banisters. The lifting of her head brought her face into the light, but the style and content of her first sentence, apart from anything else, had already identified her as Mrs. Gruffydd-Williams. She looked quite formidable as she pushed angrily past a momentarily dumbfounded Mrs. Davies, and, followed by a tall, loping man I'd never seen before, advanced up the stairs towards me.

"Difficult place to find, this," she said, striding into our sitting-room and nodding to Jean. "Yes, I remember you all right. You've lost a lot of weight since the old days. Luckily I remembered you'd said Mansel Road or I don't see how we could have found you. This is Bill Evans, by the way. As it was we had to knock at four houses before we found anyone who'd even heard of you. And then that queer old trout," she added, turning to me. She was wearing an orange-reddish dress which gave her an air of ignorant wildness and freedom, like the drunken daughter of some man of learning. "She one of your family or something?"

"Who, the one downstairs?" I said woodenly. "No, she's called Mrs. Davies. She just happens to live there."

"Well, let's be off, shall we? You're behind the party as it is. And don't worry, Bill's used to looking after children, even small ones. He's had plenty of his own, haven't you, Bill? Very kind of old Bill to leave the party just when he was really beginning to enjoy himself and come down here with me, don't you think? I tried to get one of the girls, but Bill insisted it should be him, didn't you, Billy?"

The man, who had a very small head and a big moustache, met her eye for a moment and then looked suddenly away as if hearing his name called from a secret panel over the fireplace. I was almost certain I caught a smothered snigger from Elizabeth Gruffydd-Williams, who now said to Jean: "You really can trust

Bill, provided you give him all the necessaries, you know, any feeding-bottles and teddy-bears or whatever it is children want. Don't worry, now, he's a responsible chap."

Jean, who'd done nothing since their arrival but switch off the wireless, got up hesitantly and said: "Well, it's very kind of you, but I don't think I'd better. The kids don't know your friend and they . . . You go, John, I'll be all right here."

"What, now I've dragged Bill all this way? Come on, nothing to worry about. Time's getting on."

"Well . . . just for an hour, then. They don't usually wake up at this time." She put a finger in her mouth and pondered for a moment longer, then looked at the man. "I'll show you the stuff if you'll just . . ." He followed her silently out to the kitchen.

Grinning slightly, Mrs. Gruffydd-Williams watched him go. After looking round our sitting-room in a way that re-evoked my feelings on showing her the cataloguing-room at the Library, she perched precariously against the edge of the gate-leg table. "What do you pay for this, if you don't mind my asking?"

"Three guineas a week."

"Mm, know how to charge, don't they? Rents of furnished places are fantastically inflated in Aberdarcy. My husband's trying to do something about it."

"What?"

"How do you mean?"

"What can he do, I mean?"

"You'll have to ask him about that, I don't understand these things myself. Ah, here we are," she added as Jean and the man came out of the kitchen. "All set? Understand your instructions all right, Bill?"

As the three of us started moving off, Jean said to the man: "It's very kind of you to do this for us."

"Yes," I said; "thanks a lot."

He nodded and sat down gingerly in an armchair by the hearth.

"We shan't be long," I said to him from the doorway. "Oh, and by the way, do help yourself to some beer."

He spoke then, for the first and only time. "Ah, thank you very bloody much. That'll make all the difference in the world."

THREE

"OH, HERE'S SOMEBODY I want you to meet," Elizabeth Gruffydd-Williams said, handing more drinks to Jean and me.

Being wanted to meet people, and then meeting people, had been happening to us ever since arriving at the party. No sooner would I have painfully crunched into third gear with one conversation than the sudden enforced switch to another would leave me misfiring, stalling even, in front of a beady-eyed wholesale grocer or income-tax inspector's wife whom I'd been taken the length of the room to look at, or, rather more rarely, who'd been brought over to look at me. Quite apart from whether I wanted to look at them, why should they want to look at me? And I'd thought that this peripatetic method was more the thing for much starchier parties, those where the presence of elderly and/or official persons make compulsory circulation no more than humane. Anyway, it was hard to reconcile all this decorum with the awful yelling I'd heard over the phone. Well, that must have been the product of some isolated outbreak of violence or fatuity, a half-serious scuffle over a woman, say, or an imitation of Sir Winston Churchill. Manifestations of such an outbreak or of something or other still lingered:

an oldish man asleep with his head on the arm of a chair and his trousers covered with cigarette-ash; a youngish man seated upright on one of those *pouf* things, swallowing frequently with lips apart; a girl with the look of an exceptionally promising art-student, but in fact the current mistress of a dentist recently sued for removing the wrong tooth from the jaw of an estate-agent's daughter, sprawling over a cushion on the wood-block floor and trying to light a cigarette. The other people, however, and what a lot of them there were, were standing up to do their smoking and eating and drinking and talking and laughing, and were doing it without any very obtrusive animalism.

Noticing this I missed what Elizabeth said next, which I was sorry for when I saw the man she was now wanting Jean and me to meet. His mouth, which had all the mobility of a partly-collapsed inner-tube, was incompletely encircled by a brownish grime of stubble; his greying hair came horizontally out of his scalp and projected in two stiff, inorganic shelves over his ears; his eyes, long and heavily-lidded, glared a little. He was wearing a formal dark suit, which evidently caused him rancour, and his hands, like the hands of all the men I'd met that evening, were shaking. More important than any of this, I knew him: name, Gareth Probert; occupation, poetry-writing office worker.

"We're rather proud of this man just now," Elizabeth told Jean and me. After explaining who he was, she went on straight away to give a mixture of fact and conjecture about a book of poems Probert might be going to have published. The central or connecting theme of this work, it turned out, was an adolescent's discovery of the meaning of Wales. Quite soon Elizabeth was lavishing on its author flattery so gross and prolonged that I was afraid he mightn't like it. He seemed to like it.

During this I rehearsed mentally some of the highlights in his school career. In the school precincts themselves, there'd been the motor-horn in the French lesson (an interesting contrivance worked by friction and unscrewed from the door-frame of an armoured car appearing at a T.A. exhibition), the ferret, previously goaded to frenzy, introduced into the Masters' Common Room, and the terrorist organisation applying pubic ordeals by fire in the lavatories. Extra-murally, the two chief episodes were the partial destruction of Ernie Bevin's car, left parked outside some meeting, and the grenade-throwing caper among the rocks in Castle Bay. The grenades, pinched from a nearby camp, had been bakelite training models, but were capable of satisfactory wounding. Only two people, however, had been hurt; Probert himself and a great fat lout called Beynon, now the owner of a flourishing paper-bag business in the area. I'd heard from one of the others involved how Probert had managed to throw one of the grenades right into the hollow occupied by fatty Beynon, who'd tripped and sprained his ankle trying to get away before the bang. The grenade had been a dud. Probert had laughed so much that he'd fallen into a rock-pool, soaking his golfing-jacket and shirt, getting a big anemone in his ear and spraining his own ankle. I marvelled at the sensibility which could fuse these elements (together with others involving the violation of waitresses or dance-hall partners) into the orchestration of art.

"Well, Gareth," I said as soon as I could, "it's nice to think that I was with you some of the time when you must have been gathering the material for your book. Makes me feel in a way I can share some of the credit, if you know what I mean."

While Probert turned to Elizabeth as to an interpreter, she said: "Oh, you two know each other, do you?"

I laughed. "Why, Gareth and I have been pals for years. We were at school together, weren't we, old man?"

"I believe we were acquainted at one time. I must confess I fear I retain no very clear memory of it." He sounded like an actor pretending, with fair success on the whole, to be Owain Glyndwr in a play on the Welsh Children's Hour. Then his manner changed: wagging his hand at me in dismissal, he began smiling searchingly at Jean. "Good evening, Miss Hutchings. Long time no see, as they say." A fold had appeared in each of his grub-shaped eyelids.

Jean looked at him in the serious, measuring way that I rather like as a rule, though I failed to on this occasion. "Yes, well, I'm Mrs. Lewis now, you know."

"Yes, Gareth, you behold a married pair," Elizabeth said. "I'd have explained all that, given time." She smiled at me to show she bore no malice, which I thought was pretty cool after her uninterrupted thousand-word laudation of Probert.

"This is really extraordinary," Probert said, ignoring her. "My word, but this is strange. *Iesu mawr*, and who would have thought it?"

"I didn't know you knew each other," I said, trying not to sound nettled.

"A long time ago it was," Jean said. "We did History Final together at Coll."

"Must have been while I was doing my National Service," I said.

"Are you coming to see my play?" Probert asked Jean.

"Sounds exciting, Gareth," she said. "When's it coming off?"

"Yes, do come," Elizabeth said to me. "I told you something about it that day at the Library, you remember."

"Oh yes, that's right." I restrained my laughter. "The one about medieval Wales, is it? With the costumes you want to get as authentic as you can?"

"That's the one," Elizabeth said. "Here, your glass is empty. Let me get you another drink."

"Not for me, thanks," I said firmly. Jean also shook her head.

"Oh, I'm not having that. You're not ill, are you? You'd like another, wouldn't you, Gareth?"

"A big one"; then, to Jean again: "It's coming off at the beginning of next month. Out of the season, of course, but what would you? It's the only time we can get a decent theatre."

"Sounds exciting," Jean said for the second time, and blushed.

I covered this, as usual with this sort of thing, by asking a question about which I could hardly have felt less concern: "Is it in verse, this play of yours, Gareth?"

As Len Hutton might react to being asked if he took any interest in cricket, Probert said: "Yes. It is in verse."

"What, you mean all through?"

"Every word, Mr. Lewis."

"And what's it called?"

"*The Martyr*, if it's anything to you," Probert said in a monotone, drawing the words out a lot, as Elizabeth arrived with four fresh drinks.

"Here you are," she said rather loudly. "Go on, take them. I don't like people not drinking at my parties." Her teeth were more tightly clenched than usual and she was blinking a lot.

As I took the glass she held out to me, I felt a tweak of pity for Bill Evans, at this very moment giving my baby his bottle, probably, or reading my daughter Eira a story featuring Noddy and Big-Ears. Such, or worse, would be my fate if I ever became a victim of Elizabeth's. So just to myself, not out loud, I made two little vows: *one*, she wasn't going to make me drink (my stomach will never take more than a few), and *two*, as a sworn foe of the *bourgeoisie*, and especially the Aberdarcy *bourgeoisie*, and especially the anglicised Aberdarcy *bourgeoisie*, I'd see to it that I never came here again. The importance of this

41

was suddenly underlined by a movement of Elizabeth's as she bent, cigarette in mouth, to Probert's lighter; the orange-reddish dress was not only cut lower than Jean's, but discernibly to more purpose. I coughed, thinking that the time to pack that kind of thing in is before there's anything to pack in, and turned away to put down my untasted drink.

There was more talk about *The Martyr*, while I pondered on the possible advantages of abruptly insulting its author. Elizabeth and her pals ought to get satisfactorily annoyed if a lower-class nobody rounded on what they must regard as a cultural 'lion', even as mangy, undersized and generally shagged-out a lion as this. It was queer, or possibly not so queer, that this crowd should have picked up a scruff like Probert as their court poet. Earlier that day I'd been led by what must have been exceptional boredom to look into a book about Dr. Johnson, of all people, and I reflected now that here was a present-day version, possibly in a degraded form, of Johnson having a big time at Streatham, surrounded by fashionable devotees, with Elizabeth being Mrs. Thrale. Would Mr. Gruffydd-Williams (I hadn't seen him yet) turn out to be Thrale or that other chap, Piozzi was it, who sang in opera was it? These speculations entertained me, and made me feel rather intellectual too.

I looked up to see a diversion approaching, in the shape of two men of equal height and similar figure wearing informal clothes—pullover, pastel-shade trousers and suède shoes—that contrasted in several ways with my own lustrous serge. The elder, a man in his forties with a high nose and long upper lip that gave him a fastidious, measuring-up expression, carried a jug that I thought was probably silver; the younger, sandy-haired and protuberant-eyed, sparked repeatedly at a table-lighter that also seemed to be silver. There was at least one such lighter on every horizontal surface in the room.

"Anyone for a refill?" the elder man asked in a precise, rather ponderous voice.

Probert extended his glass in a ready, hairy hand. I thought of trying on the new arrivals a phrase I'd heard used by the W.E.A. Secretary in my home village: "Who are you, I presume?" Then I thought I'd better not.

Elizabeth now introduced the jug-man as her husband Vernon and the lighter-man as Paul Whetstone. Vernon Gruffydd-Williams, still pouring drinks, nodded with a deliberate amiability; he was clearly Thrale, not Piozzi; Whetstone, blowing out smoke and for some reason leaning backwards, shook hands with Jean without bending his arm.

To me, Whetstone looked insignificant but probably not harmless: was he homo, perhaps? Gruffydd-Williams, on the other hand, seemed to show more positive characteristics. The authoritative manner suited a man presumably possessed of a lot of authority; apart from his seat on the Council and on two or three of its committees, he had another and undoubtedly better one on the Board of the Cambrio-Sudanese Oil Association, whose refinery makes its own peculiar contribution to several cubic miles of air west of the town. And then, or rather first of all, there was his money.

"We were just talking about Gareth's play," Elizabeth said.

"Oh, fine," Whetstone said, sipping his drink.

Probert stared contemptuously at him, then said in a baleful tone: "We're still being badly hung up over the costumes."

"Oh? I'm sorry to hear that." This was Gruffydd-Williams, vigilantly nosing out inefficiency. "What seems to be the trouble?"

"Nothing has been done towards it, nothing at all," Probert went on. "Nothing at all can be done towards it until we get material of some kind to work from. I'm a

43

poet, not a designer of costumes, so I have to go elsewhere for the information I require. Elizabeth has been trying through the last month to get our Public Library to disgorge some books which could help us. But nothing of any sort has by now occurred. Nothing of any sort at all."

While I was admiring the non-Englishness, the air of being literally translated from the Welsh, of some of these linguistic forms, Elizabeth was explaining to her husband my connexion with the matter in hand. I felt his eyes shift appraisingly over to me. He was working out how far I was mixed up in the plot to keep Probert short of reading-matter.

Probert had been muttering on, making his intention clearer: "But of course trying to get the Library to do something is the same as expecting a corpse to get up and dance. What do they care? They can't even bother to get their shelves into proper alphabetical order."

This was a familiar charge. A little off balance at finding myself wanting to defend the place where I worked, even against a chap like this, I said: "If you were in that much of a hurry, you'd have done better to write to a bookseller for catalogues and order from him. If we haven't got a book in stock it may take some time to find out . . ."

"We tried that," Probert broke in impatiently; "we tried that. There was nothing at all in print that met our requirements. That's why we had to come to you. It was a last resource, believe me."

"It's rather difficult to get hold of a book when you've no idea of the title or author, because then the other libraries have got to go looking through everything in their catalogue that might . . ."

"Damn it, man," Probert said quietly, then paused until he'd got everyone's attention. "Damn it, man, it's your bloody job, isn't it? You don't want us to do it for you, surely to God? I'll wager there's little enough work gets done down there as it is."

The others in the group, except Gruffydd-Williams, shifted about like people suddenly feeling a cold wind. I said carefully: "Come on, now, Gareth, what about listening to the facts? You haven't answered them, you know."

"Oh, facts," Probert said scornfully. "Fellows like you can always trot out facts of one sort or another. You're so bogged down in your facts you've forgotten how to think."

There's nothing to beat an attack on facts for making me angry. With a sort of expanding lightness in my chest, I said: "Yes, I know, you prefer feelings, don't you? All right then, here's a feeling for you, boy. I feel you ought to stuff your . . ."

"Tell me," Gruffydd-Williams said loudly and close to my ear. "Tell me, now, how's the Adult Education side of things going? I heard the other day that the book-box system wasn't working too well these days." He drew me several feet away, his fingers tight on my elbow. "According to your chief, anyway. Do you have anything to do with that side of things?"

I cleared my throat. "Er . . . yes, a little. But it's mainly Mr. Jenkins's pigeon, that side of things."

"I see, yes. Now tell me, what's your impression of Jenkins? Confidentially, of course. He's put in for the Sub-Librarianship here, as you probably know. I always think the opinion of a colleague can be extremely valuable."

I was still thinking about Probert and facts *vs.* feelings, but managed to say: "Mr. Jenkins is an excellent man to work with, I can assure you. He . . ."

"Pleasant to deal with, you mean?"

"Oh yes, very. And he knows the Library inside out."

"Then it's your impression that he'd make a good second-in-command?"

"Very good indeed," I said, though I really thought, or thought I thought (rivalry muddles such thoughts)

45

that Jenkins was too much of a worrier, too soon down-cast or rattled, to do the senior job more than just adequately. Not that I, with my laziness, had any edge on him. "Yes, you couldn't go wrong there."

"I see." He looked up at Whetstone, who'd followed us away from the group and now stood uninterestedly smoking, with folded arms. "Sounds fair enough, doesn't it, Paulie? Got the gen now, haven't we? Ergh ergh ergh ergh." This was his laugh, a loud and guttural one. Quenching it, he turned to me again. "Don't seem to care much for our friend Gareth, do you?"

"No, that's right."

"You mustn't be too hard on him, you know."

"Why not?"

"Well . . . you know what these fellows are like. He's not a bad·sort of chap."

Here was a chance to do a bit of tail-twisting by proxy on the Gruffydd-Williamses' lion. "Oh, don't you think he is? I think he is rather a bad sort of chap."

"We've known him quite a long time, old boy," Whetstone said, narrowing his eyes.

"I'm sorry to hear that," I said politely.

"Well, if you don't mind my saying so," Whetstone was beginning, but Gruffydd-Williams cut him short:

"No, Paulie, let him say his piece. This interests me, I must say. Why do you think our poetical friend is a bad sort of chap?"

"He's rude," I said.

"And you don't think that being a poet entitles him to be a bit different from other people in that way?"

"On the contrary."

"I see. Have you anything to add to that?"

I cast about for something to add that would irreversibly establish me as 'impossible' in the eyes of the anglicised Aberdarcy *bourgeoisie*, that would see to it that I never came here again. I could see Elizabeth's orange-reddish dress out of the corner of my eye. I said: "Yes: I can't see why you invite a chap like that to your house."

"Oh, you can't see why I invite him to my house?"

"No."

"Right, now I'll tell you something. Neither can I. Got that? Neither can I. I'd have liked you to go on just now and tell him his fortune, only one has to remember one's obligations as O.C. party. Ergh ergh ergh ergh. Next time you just let him have it. Only make sure it's off the premises, okay? Bad sort of chap, can't see why I invite him to the ergh ergh ergh ergh. Oh ergh ergh ergh ergh. Oh bloody marvellous. Oh dear. Oh dear. Yes, Robbie, I know that look in your eye. Get it over with."

This last was addressed to a small man with a wine-coloured corduroy waistcoat, who'd approached on my other side and who now said in a high rapid voice: "Hope you don't mind a bit of shop, Griff. I went through the reports last night, and there's just one or two . . ." He led Gruffydd-Williams away. Whetstone followed him.

I turned away and surveyed the room. What was going on in it was the same as what had been going on in it when I arrived. If the R.A.F.-moustached man on my left wasn't telling the same story for the tenth time, his listeners were doing the same sort of laughing; the drink the dentist's mistress was lifting erratically to her mouth surely couldn't still be her first; the prices of second-hand sports cars were still being discussed behind me, droningly and in slow motion; they all held a replica of the glass and olive and cigarette they'd had from the word go. Should I break in in a renewed effort to be marked down as 'impossible', bawl a defence of the Welfare State, start undressing myself or the dentist's mistress, give the dentist a lovely piggy-back round the room, call for a toast to the North Korean Foreign Minister or Comrade Malenkov?

No. Like everything else, all that, now I'd failed so badly over the tail-twisting, was much too boring. How

47

could these people so much as move about, weighted down as they were in their Field Service Marching Order of boredom? But that wasn't quite fair, was it? No: if you actually had a sports car or a cabin-cruiser or fifty table-lighters, if you had the money, in short, to invite all these craps home, or to take a half-share in the dentist's mistress or even perhaps buy him out altogether, then you were all right. No: then *it* was all right. Because if you were all right—*rubbish*: if *it* was all right . . .

Losing my thread, I looked round for Jean. Probert was talking hard to her, with Elizabeth listening rather inattentively. She caught my glance and mouthed some phrase at me, pointing at Probert. No thanks, I thought; whatever it is, no thanks. I smiled and waved to her, then hurried out.

FOUR

IT WAS WONDERFUL in the lavatory. I made myself properly at home and had a good look at a curious and hence almost certainly French cartoon of what was apparently an anatomy lecture with two nude persons doing the demonstrating. "*Tiens*," I said.

I decided that a ten per cent exaggeration of Probert's present appearance would make it all right for him to exhibit himself as a 'wild man' for financial reward, provided he could contrive to evade arrest. Such a livelihood would be in his family tradition: hadn't one of his uncles been supposed to spend some weeks each summer starving in a barrel at a fair? And why did this Probert pretend to be so Welsh? I remembered that like me he'd been awarded nought for Welsh in School Certificate. Such a result, in that language, means an almost psychotic ignorance. It's standard practice, of course, with writers of Probert's allegiance to pretend to be wild valley babblers, woaded with pit-dirt and sheep-shit, thinking in Welsh the whole time and obsessed by terrible beauty, etc., but in fact they tend to come from comfortable middle-class homes, have a good urban education, never go near a lay preacher and couldn't even order a pint in Welsh, falling back, as Probert had done earlier in the evening, on things like the Welsh for big Jesus. (And don't tell me they can think in Welsh without knowing the language. Ever tried thinking in Bantu?)

Well, we'd have to be going soon to relieve Bill Evans, poor sod. But there'd have to be another couple of jousts, first, in the frightful pee-talking lists on the ground floor. Somebody now tried the door-handle. Sighing, I pulled the chain.

From the hall, the noise of the party was tremendous, reverting to the pitch, I guessed, that I'd heard over the phone. I stopped to admire a sort of infernal-colliery painting from the brush, or perhaps the trowel, of a fashionable Czech artist who'd settled in one of the Valley towns. Then I went in.

On my way to rejoin my wife at the far side I met my hostess. At the sight of her I felt my energy and intransigence rising. She'd had her eyebrows plucked, I noticed. Well, that wouldn't save her. I'd show her. I'd teach her. When I greeted her in a way that I associate, perhaps rightly, with the West-End stage, she asked me to have another drink. It couldn't matter now, I thought, and we went over to the table where the drinks were set out and where, unaccountably enough, the crowd was at its thinnest. She gave me another of those dreadful dehydrating Martini things. In it, on a little stick, was a little white onion, rich, as I knew from experience, in brine and concentrated nitric acid.

"Well, it's very nice to have you here," she said.

49

"Thanks. It's nice to be here."

"What was Vernon talking to you about?"

"Vernon? Oh. We were just having a chat about old Probert."

"Just as well you got pulled away when you did, wasn't it?"

"Well, yes, I suppose it was in a way. Pity in another way, though."

"Why, how do you mean?"

"Things were just beginning to warm up nicely, I thought."

She frowned slightly. "You've got to remember that Gareth isn't quite like other people."

"Yes, I know he is," I said, trying to suggest by my tone just where Probert's dissimilarity from his fellows might lie.

"Don't let's keep it up. It wasn't really very funny."

"Your husband thought it was."

"He thinks everything's funny," she said impatiently.

"Good."

She shook her head abruptly once, in negation or nervous tremor. "It was all rather unfortunate." She settled herself on the edge of the table just as she'd done in the cataloguing-room at the Library. It clearly was a habit after all; my vanity had been barking up the wrong tree about her, from the start. Thank God it hadn't taken me barking with it. All fantasy again.

"I hope you're not annoyed with me," I said.

"Of course I'm not." There was a pause; then her manner altered. Fixing her eyes on mine, she said: "Tell me something, John, will you?"

"Yes?"

"I don't want to pry into your private life."

"No."

She leant forward on the table-edge with the result that, but surely not in order that, I could have seen down the front of her dress if I'd looked. I didn't look. After what had begun to be a rather ludicrously-prolonged staring-match, she said: "You won't mind me asking this, will you, but are you putting in for the job at the Library when Webster goes in the autumn?"

I tried to conceal my surprise. "Well, yes, I haven't yet, but I am. What about it?"

"I was only wondering. You know my husband's on the Libraries Committee?"

"Yes, I did know. Why?"

"He asks my advice about a lot of things, you know." After a moment she lowered her head again and I admired her white parting. "I've been talking to Jean; I hope you don't mind. I've known her a long time. It'd make a lot of difference to you and her, I suppose, wouldn't it, if you managed to land that job? I mean, I don't know what you're pulling in now, but I imagine it can't be very . . ."

"No. Yes, there's no doubt it would make a difference."

"We might be able to help you there."

"What? How do you mean exactly?"

"Well, I don't suppose you know quite what you're up against, do you?"

"In what way? You mean what the competition's like?"

She gave a slight, impatient laugh. "Well, wouldn't it be a help, John, to know the kind of man the Committee want to appoint, and that kind of thing? The kind of questions they're apt to ask on these occasions, what they expect and so on?"

"Yes, I'm sure it would."

"I've heard Vernon say, oh, many a time, that the right man for a job has thrown it away by shooting some line or other, when he'd have been perfectly all right on his merits. They lay claim to all sorts of knowledge they haven't got, and couldn't have, just because they're afraid to admit there's anything they couldn't tackle. Well, naturally that puts people off."

"Yes, I suppose it would."

"Don't want that to happen this time, do we?"

"No." I recognised with fatigue the onset of a fresh enigma. Exactly what, for example, didn't we want to happen this time? And just how far were we supposed to have got towards identifying the right man for this job? Some sort of lobbying, some sort of log-rolling, seemed to be being offered. But it couldn't be, could it, not really, not to me? I knew theoretically, from hearing my father talk, that this sort of thing went on, but it was a shock, and an unpleasant one, to think that it might be going on here and now. Oh, nonsense, it couldn't be. "Oh, I quite agree," I said.

"Don't get the wrong idea about this, but I think I could help you. Being an old friend of Jean's, after all, you know."

"Yes. Well, that's extremely good of you."

"We must get together some time and have a chat about it."

"Good idea, I'd like to." I tried to catch sight of Jean.

"That's fine." Elizabeth smiled amiably, and it was as if she was telling me not to worry about the lobbying-enigma. Her face was rounder than I'd thought, with broad cheekbones and forehead, but its pallor made it look delicate when seen close to, and there was none of the toughness I'd detected at our first meeting. Her smile half faded, giving her an almost timorous air. Some of my uneasiness at the lobbying-enigma fell away. I smiled back. "Are you enjoying yourself to-night?" she asked.

"Good Lord, of course I am. What do you want me to do to prove it, a rope-dance?"

"No, that won't be needed. Unless you really feel you must."

"I haven't brought my ropes, otherwise I would."

"Do you know them?" she asked, dropping her voice.

I moved a little nearer, just to hear better, of course. "Eh? Sorry, do I know who?"

"No, I mean do you know the ropes. At this kind of do. I'm only asking because I certainly didn't at your age, I know."

Horror and derision at this trope went further to restore my confidence. Anyone who said things like that must be harmless. "Perhaps I don't," I said in a thick voice. "Why?"

"You looked a bit lost over there, I thought."

"Did I?"

"You must try not to mind Vernon; he likes making people feel out of things."

"Does he?"

"It may just be that you look very young. You do, you know. I think it must be something to do with the way your hair grows up away from your forehead like that."

I've several times been told something like this, occasionally, as earlier that evening, by Jean. I've also been told, not by Jean, that I have a look of 'innocence' to complement the one of youth. With both these valuable commodities, I felt, I'd recently been undergoing some deterioration of stock. Well, it was nice to be told again so soon that one of them, at least, retained some worth. Yes, and this would be a good time, I decided, to try out a new smile, featuring the lower lip and nostrils, which I'd been practising that week. Trying it out, I said: "Oh, you mustn't talk like that, you know, you make me feel such an infant."

It seemed to work all right: she leant a little further forward, and this time I did just peep down the front of her dress. What, I asked myself, could be the point in not? It looked very nice down there. She said, lifting her chin: "I certainly wouldn't want to do a thing like that. But then you're not an infant, are you, John?"

"No," I said, thinking of how it would sound over the wireless or look on the TV screen. "I'm not an infant."

"I knew you weren't one, I knew what you were like as soon as I set eyes on you."

"Well, er . . . what am I like then?"

"You're like me. You're one of my sort. Aren't you?"

"I don't know about . . . I mean, I suppose . . . I'm afraid so."

"I've got a feeling that you and I are going to get on very well together."

"I'm sure we are."

"In all sorts of ways."

"Mm."

Her breasts seemed to expand, and perhaps actually did, as she squared her shoulders in the way she'd done in the Library. She narrowed her eyes and her lips came away from her set teeth. There was no longer the slightest difficulty in thinking up an act which would finally label me as 'impossible' in the eyes of the anglicised Aberdarcy *bourgeoisie*. I wondered if this kind of woman would still be having this kind of effect on me when I'd reached the age of eighty, say. Fifty-four years was a long time to wait for a spot of peace and quiet. "I'm very much looking forward to having a . . . chat with you about the Library," she said emphatically.

"Yes, it would be nice."

"In fact, the sooner it happens the better as far as I'm concerned."

Could all this be true? Was all this what it sounded like? Of course it could and was. This kind of woman surely wouldn't run the risk of being misinterpreted in this particular direction. No; here at last was familiar ground. My mouth took over from my mind and said in a tone I couldn't have produced voluntarily: "We must fix it up." My face twisted itself into a shameful and ridiculous ogle.

"Yes, we must."

Oh no we mustn't, I thought with punctual, flaring panic, as soon as her words were out. That's just what we mustn't do, just what we mustn't fix up. Just who mustn't fix that up. I tried to say so, but before I could work out how, she'd said:

"I could ring you at the Library, couldn't I?"

"Well . . . it's rather . . . Someone else might answer the phone."

"Then I'll just ask for you, as I did the other day. No reason why I shouldn't, is there?"

"No, nobody would . . . No."

"Good. That's settled, then."

I thought briefly that she seemed a bit quick off the mark, then, speaking very fast and almost at random, said: "I haven't much free time, though, I'm afraid; I'm usually at home with my family, you see, that's how I spend pretty well all of my time when I'm not on Library duty at the . . . Library, so that I can't . . . That's really the position." Fixed it, I thought, or rather unfixed it.

Drawing a deep breath, and wishing I were pouring a nice cup of tea, I poured myself another drink from one of the silver jugs. A large piece of ice fell into my glass and the liquor splashed over my hand. That wasn't at all the way I'd intended to pour; it was devoid of grace, especially the pantherine sort I was favouring at that period. But that didn't matter, did it? Well done, Lewis, I said to myself; you've got the idea. A cool head you've got, Lewis, and bags of guts. Brains save sweat, Lewis, and sweat saves blood. I'll see the right people get to hear about this, Lewis. We like your sort. Oh, and just to be going on with, you can have a look at that history of underclothing you've been trying to forget about. I drank a toast to me.

She was looking at me blankly. "That's rather a nuisance," she said with that downward inflexion that remains so foreign to my ear. "Still, I hardly imagine you won't be able to afford the time for the discussion I've been talking about. I'll speak to my husband about it and let you know." She got down off the table-edge. "Here he comes now, by the way."

Gruffydd-Williams came up to us, followed by Whetstone, who gave me the glance of a great conductor introduced to a dancing xylophonist. Gruffydd-Williams smiled first at his wife, then at me. He looked intelligent and almost rabidly at ease. I thought his smile was saying: "Nothing you can do will surprise me." He seemed totally different from the man who'd had the ergh-ergh-ergh-ergh session with me about Probert. He said, with his voice this time: "Ah, all together again, eh? Come on, Paulie, replenish your stock. There are lots of very thirsty people about."

Just then the dentist approached and said something to Elizabeth, nodding towards his mistress, who was sitting on the arm of a chair. Her face was white and her expression suggested that she was even more radically mixed up inside, and even deeper down, than might usually have been guessed. I remembered an ex-neighbour of hers, an ambitious electrician who used the Library a lot, telling me that before the days of the dentist she was often to be seen going off to the Town Hall to collect the dole wearing an outfit that included bow-tie, jodhpurs and riding-boots. "Really used to upset me for the day, it did," he'd said to me.

I tried to picture this while I watched her lover and her hostess move off towards her, but another part of my mind was telling me that I'd managed in the last hour to make a fool of myself in more than one way. After hanging about for a bit while Whetstone, interposing his pullovered back, talked to Gruffydd-Williams, I went over to Jean. She was still with Probert, and chatting away, which was unusual for her at a gathering of any size. She stopped when she saw me coming.

56

FIVE

"Is Mrs. Gruffydd-Williams there, please?"

"Who's that speaking?"

"Lewis here, John Lewis."

"Who?"

"John Lewis."

"Oh yes?" The man at the other end of the line sounded like Gruffydd-Williams himself, but there was no recognition in his tone. When whoever it was added nothing, I said:

"I wanted to speak to Mrs. Gruffydd-Williams, please."

"Oh, did you? What was the name again?"

Yes, it was him all right. Was it his plan to make me alternate my own with his wife's name until I got cheesed off with it and hung up? I told him my name yet again as requested, going on: "I was at a party of yours the other week, you remember," then reflecting that that must now be several parties ago from his point of view, went on with: "Our wives were at school together."

"Oh yes," Gruffydd-Williams said, differently from before. He took a long time over it, starting and ending low down and raising the pitch in the middle. He implied, not only recognition, but a full knowledge of my past and an accurate forecast of my future. "Well, I'm afraid you're out of luck this time, my dear fellow. I imagine she's gone out somewhere. Anyway, she isn't here. I don't suppose I can be of any assistance myself?"

"Well no, I don't think so, really, thanks all the same," I said, in the hope of casually deflecting some of the irony that seemed to be lurking about. "She did ask me to get hold of her specifically, you see."

"Get hold of her what?"

"Specifically," I said in a quavering voice. "She wanted me to get in touch with her personally."

"Get in . . . Oh, I see. Yes?"

"Er, will she be in in the morning?"

"Before about eleven, yes. You'll have to excuse me now. Got to rush. Bye-bye to you."

No doubt an extraordinary meeting of the Cambrio-Sudanese Board was in session. I visualised Gruffydd-Williams, in burnous and sash as a compliment to his dusky colleagues, squatting on a tasselled cushion and, narghile at hand, talking in voluble Arabic about boring. Boring: quite funny, that. Time to be off home now; it had been a long day's work, aggravated by a visit from the dipsomaniac. This man, who used to look us up every couple of months, had leant against a cabinet displaying works on the Far East, with special reference to French Indo-China, and had proceeded to clap his hands and sing, singing louder for every tatter in his mortal dress and louder still for every time he'd been asked to leave. Finally, as usual, it had been left to me to throw him out. Then I'd had to stand all the way in the bus with a little boy staring at me.

I walked slowly, in strong early-evening sunshine, past some tennis courts, feeling rather relieved at having missed Elizabeth. The decision to ring her up had been taken by Jean, not me; it follows, pretty well, that the motive of the call had been economic, not amatory. While I stopped walking and looked bemusedly at two girls playing on the end court, I thought how good Jean was at making me do what she wanted. It was a power rarely used but capable of going like a cheese-wire through the successive strata of my indolence, caution, irritation, counter-suggestion, cries of "You do it" and hypochondria. I wished that I could be obstinate, or that people would at least give me credit for not being. They don't even notice.

The sun seemed hotter than ever, and sweat crept down my chest with a faint verminous tickling. A large brown dog ran up to me, his whole bearing demonstrating a mistaken certainty that I'd been waiting all day for just such a one as him. On my recommending his immediate departure, he gave an abrupt, crashing bark, like a rifle-shot on the sound-track of a film about British India, and, with the demeanour of one making a lightning change of plans, ran off with all his strength after an invalid-car that was just popping its way round a distant corner. His bark came faintly back to me through the humidity. I envied him his committed air.

A main feature of the twelve days or so since the Gruffydd-Williams party had been the dumbfounding invitation to tea. A letter, of all things, had been lying on the mat one morning when I went down to bring up the milk. It was to Jean, from Elizabeth. Jean was to take the children up at a stated time the following week (the day before yesterday, as it was now) and, over tea, to engage in 'a chat about old times' with her hostess. I've already mentioned the tenuity of these 'old times', assuming them to refer to shared experience at school and not, say, to the glories of Druidic Wales or the fauna of the Oligocene Age. And what, in any case, could have persuaded Elizabeth of their fitness for resuscitation in talk, especially with two young children there to coat her furnishings with jam? Was it all a cunning manœuvre for strengthening her connexion with me while allaying Jean's suspicions?

"Don't be a fool," I muttered aloud, just as one of the girls, returning a service into the net, raised a loud squall of laughter. "She just wanted a pal, that's all. She's lonely."

What? The tale of women Elizabeth could call on to chat to must run into four figures, let alone what she surely preferred, men to chat to. Well, then. So what was it all about? At the tea itself, she'd had a good deal to say about my prospects of getting the sub's job and her intention of 'seeing what she could do' about it, without making a single concrete revelation or suggestion. (Hence my attempt to ring her up just now.) She'd run Jean and the kids home afterwards and had come up and gossiped haltingly with us for nearly an hour without even mentioning the matter in front of me. So what was it all about? Well, to-morrow morning might show.

I looked more intently at the tennis-players. The one on the far side of the net had no claim on my attention beyond that of being a girl, but the one nearer me had some, even from behind. She had short shorts and well-shaped hips, and was bounding about very prettily, or so it seemed to me. It wasn't just that women were a thing that had made a profound impression on me; no, also to be taken into account was the fact that I found women attractive, especially attractive women. Now how had that come about? Just then the nearer girl turned and came to retrieve a ball, leaning forward directly in front of me to gather it. I wished she hadn't; the result was something that a member of the Watch Committee and myself would concur in not liking to see, though from different motives, one might hope. Why did I like women's breasts so much? I was clear on why I liked them, thanks, but why did I like them *so much*?

A tremendously loud noise started up behind me. For a moment I thought that the trumpets and horns of the B.B.C. Welsh Orchestra had mustered in the roadway and were starting to practise the *fortissimo* playing of simple chords. Then I knew that that couldn't be right; a car was blowing its hooter. I turned. It was an enormous car of amphisboenic appearance, at its wheel a woman with black hair done up on top and octagonal sunglasses. She was looking at me and grinning. "Hallo," she said, taking her thumb off the horn. "Seeing if you can pick up a few tips?"

I went over to her. "Hallo, Elizabeth," I said, not certain whether I was putting into or keeping out of my tone the shocked fury I felt. Here I was, trying to gather the strength to drub her out of my mind, and then life, the giggling fool, allowed a thing like this to happen. Seeing her in the morning, as planned, would somehow have been much less unmanning.

"You don't seem very pleased to see me," she said.

"Oh, but I am. It was just rather a surprise."

"A pleasant one, I hope?"

"What? Oh yes." I noticed that the hair seemed a shade blacker if anything and that, as usual, there were earrings with it. These, as usual, made me feel a bit afraid of her. "Yes, a very pleasant one."

"Oh, whacko. Look, I've been wanting to get hold of you. Are you doing anything for the moment? That is, apart from . . ." Grinning again, she gestured towards the tennis court.

"No," I said stiffly. "I was just on my way home."

"Fine. I'll give you a lift."

I went round the car, a move which took me a long way towards the opposite pavement, and got in beside her on the leather couch affair which ran across the whole width. As I remembered from my two rides in it on the night of the party, it smelt new, and I could now see that its gears were worked by a kind of conductor's baton attached to the steering-column. We at once began going rather too fast.

"What was it you wanted me for?" I asked.

"I say, I've just thought of something."

"What?"

"One or two of us thought of going out for a few drinks this evening, over Llansili way. There's a rather nice little country pub there we sometimes go to this time of the year. What about coming along, if you've nothing better to do?"

61

"What a wonderful idea; I'd love to." I meant this. The idea of going out, on a fine May evening, in a car, to enjoy myself, was a solemnity not easy to withstand. I'd read all but the editorial and correspondence sections of the new *Astounding Science Fiction*, and my only other possible mental pabulum was the Library copy of an American novel reputed to echo, though not of course to rival, the Henry James of the middle period. I'd have been quite keen to tackle this sort of thing even a year ago, but nowadays it seemed somehow uninviting. How lovely. A ride in a car. To a country pub. No need to keep worrying about not missing the bus back. Then another thought occurred to me and my glee subsided.

"Left here, isn't it?" she said.

"Yes—I don't think I . . ."

"How long will it take Jean to get ready?"

"Well, that's just it, you see. I'm afraid we shan't be able to come after all; I've just thought."

"Why not? Expecting some people?"

"No, it's just that we can't go out, not together, not as a rule anyway."

"Why not?"

Like most people, she was clearly bad at deducing, even from the most obvious facts, the conditions that determined other people's lives. I said in a neutral tone: "We have two young children, you see, and it's illegal to leave them unattended after dark."

"Oh, but surely there's someone who can pop in and keep an eye on them for you?"

"It isn't quite as easy as that, unfortunately. You have to know people reasonably well before you can start asking them to keep running in and out, and we haven't been living in that place very long."

"Oh, but surely you must have a regular sitter, someone you can give a few bob to whenever you want them.

How do you manage in the ordinary way? You must have some sort of system."

"Yes, we have. It consists mainly of not going out."

She threw the car aside at right angles so that I nearly had to prostrate myself at her feet among the various pedals, and answered in the same tone of courteous interest: "I say, you know, if you don't want to come to this do, just slip me the hint, will you? and I'll drop you at your doorstep right away. It'll be no trouble to me."

"No, I didn't mean I didn't want to come. I just meant I shouldn't be able to come."

"I'm sorry, I must be very dense. I'm afraid I don't quite see why you and Jean have both got to stay and look after the kids."

"It isn't that. The point is that as far as we can we don't go out separately. That's all."

"But how queer. You mean Jean's afraid to let . . ." She paused and changed gear, then said: "But don't you ever go out except together?"

"We did soon after we had Eira, but we never liked it much. We don't see anything of each other during the day, so we decided to be together in the evening as much as we could."

"I see; very laudable, I'm sure. But just once in a way won't make any difference, will it?"

I had a rude word ready to say to her, but suppressed it; she was giving me a lift, after all. It was all very awkward, not least because I did want to go on the drinking expedition. "No, of course not," I said. "We'll see what Jean has to say. She may be able to think of something." I had little hope of this, and indeed my spirits had fallen to the point where a special depressed feeling of mine, which I was getting quite a lot at that period, was making its entry. It combined rootless apprehension, indefinite restlessness and inactivating boredom, as if through the action of some carefully-dispensed tripartite drug. I'll be saying more about it later; just now I was reflecting that there was nothing attractive about it, nor had it the alternative merit of doing me good. It might all be something to do with the air or the water: Aberdarcy has the reputation of being 'relaxing'. As often before, a longing for strenuous manual work arose in me, then rapidly passed. I remembered that I must soon fill in and send off my income-tax claim form, and for these purposes would first have to find it.

With no more said, we pulled up at the house and approached it just as Ken Davies, groomed for a dance or similar depravity, came out of the front door. A human figure, perhaps a quarter life-size, was emblazoned on his tie. A very large number of glances were interchanged as we all sidled past one another on the narrow steps. I thought it best to leave him unintroduced, even unexplained.

I led Elizabeth through the half-light of the passage. Near the foot of the stairs I stumbled on something soft, a bundle of washing or corpse, and warned her about it. As I spoke, a raucous barking, interspersed with hysterical whining, started up in the basement. Mrs. Davies could be heard calling out: "Is that you, Haydn? Ken've gone on, just this minute. You just missed him. See you there, he said."

Ignoring this, I began climbing the stairs, where it was even darker. The baby could be heard crying from above. Elizabeth stumbled noisily over the bundle.

"Haydn, is that you, man?" Feet ascended the basement stairs. "Who's up there? Who is it? Who's in my house?"

"Only me, Mrs. Davies," I made myself call. "Just me and a friend."

"Oh, it's you, Mr. Lewis. Visitors, is it?"

"Yes, that's what it is, Mrs. Davies," I said, mounting.

"I don't want no noise, Mr. Lewis."

"Neither do I, Mrs. Davies."

"All right then, Mr. Lewis."

In our sitting-room we found the whole of my family assembled. The baby, his upper lip hidden behind his lower one, was sitting on the pot, crying steadily; Eira was crouching naked with her face in Jean's lap, singing as best she could; Jean, herself apparently wearing only a dressing-gown, was vigorously towelling Eira's hair. They'd clearly all been having a bath together, a favourite entertainment of theirs.

Around them was a multitude of objects, such as might, in a memory-test, be shown to spectators for one minute and then withdrawn. Apart from clothes, adult and juvenile, male and female, ironed, newly washed and fit to be washed, there were a half-eaten, browning apple, several broken biscuits, a plastic doll, the torso of a rubber doll, some children's books with pictures of clothed animals on the covers, a cup, a card of blue safety-pins, an orange with one of my pencils stuck into it, a bottle of cod-liver oil, a pair of plastic knickers, a lot of string un-wound from a ball, a tin of powder, a spoon, a wooden locomotive, some nappies in varying states, the defaced cover of my *Astounding Science Fiction*, and a lot of other things. "Well, hullo," Jean said.

"I met your better half in the street," Elizabeth said, waving to her. "The thing is, Bill Evans and Paul Whet-stone and one or two of the others are going out for a few drinks to-night, and I was wondering whether you'd care to join us. I gather from John that you have a bit of difficulty getting hold of somebody to mind the kids, so I wondered . . ."

"Sorry, just a minute," Jean said to her, then to me: "See to the baby, will you, John? I can't think with all that row."

Quite glad to leave things to the two women, I went up to the baby. Distrust joined the grief in his expression when I knelt down in front of him, but after I'd made a series of noises and faces he fought down his tears, hiccupped and said: "Ah. Ur. Mm. Wor. Ooh." It sounded not at all like baby-talk, but very like an articulate though laconic utterance in some non-Indo-European language, like Yap or Kickapoo. I conversed with him for a time, then got up to find both women looking at me.

"Well, what about it?" I asked.

"You don't honestly think I can come, do you?" Jean asked in return, speaking a little harshly.

"Well no, it doesn't much look like it, does it? Unless . . ."

"Perhaps you could manage it later, when you've put these youngsters to bed," Elizabeth said. "It's early yet. One of us could run back and pick you up. It'd only take a few minutes."

"Where do you imagine we'd get a sitter-in from?" Jean asked me in the same tone as before.

This attempt to class me with the enemy, the damned who will not understand, made me say peevishly: "Go on, I'll sit in. I don't mind. You go. Go and get dressed. I'll put them to bed."

"Come on, Jean, that's a very handsome offer. I told you the old man would come through with it. Aren't you going to take advantage of it?"

Jean had started to say no as Elizabeth began speaking, had politely suspended it, and now completed it. "No," she said. She added: "It's all right, don't worry about me. You go if you're keen, John."

There was, as always, nothing long-suffering about this speech, but there was an edge to it. Discussing the Gruffydd-Williams party with Jean, I'd gone through a long list of things generally regarded as unpleasant, all of which, I'd said, I'd sooner do or have done to me than have anything more to do with that crowd. Then, as I hesitated, I saw that she was looking, not at me, but at the expression on Elizabeth's face as she looked at me. I couldn't read either look with any certainty, but Jean's was one I thought I recognised, or half-recognised: it was of acquiescence in being caused pain. For a second I felt an odd pang of grief; the next second I thought: Pain? Why? What the hell did she think had happened or was going on? I said violently: "Don't be so silly, Jean. You know you'd love to go. You haven't been out for weeks. It won't take you more than a few minutes to get ready. Go on, now; I can manage these two perfectly well."

Jean's face changed. "No, honest, I don't mind a bit, John. I'd rather you went." She winked furtively at me and handed a nightie to Eira, who began putting it on. "I'll leave something cold for you when you come in."

"I feel a bit of a brute, yanking your spouse off like this," Elizabeth said.

Jean looked at her. "Oh, there's no need to feel like that about it."

"We must fix up another tea date," Elizabeth said. "Good fun last time, wasn't it? Could you give me a ring in a day or two?"

Jean said that she could do that, and Elizabeth and I took our leave. When we went out on to the pavement the sun seemed to be shining more brilliantly than ever, although it was well past six o'clock. The man who lived in the house opposite looked up from fixing a new hinge on his gate to stare at us and at the car. He'd recently covered the whole of his front garden with an unusually white kind of concrete, irregularly furrowed to imitate crazy paving, and was notorious in the district for displaying Conservative election-posters in his windows. For a couple of months the previous autumn there'd hardly been a single evening when a whizz-bang, or perhaps a jumping cracker, hadn't been dropped through his letter-box. I waved to him now and he took a screw out of his mouth.

A thrill of pure adolescent excitement at the thought of the car-ride went through me. I said to Elizabeth: "I'm looking forward to this a lot. Lucky we ran into each other."

Switching on the ignition, she gave me a brief glance round the edge of the sunglasses. She looked a bit like a cat, but no human being can look very much like a cat and she impressed me rather as the most accomplished-looking person I'd ever seen. "Yes, very well timed, I thought," she said. "We should have arranged it better, though, so that Jean could have come. Still, you know me, I'm hopeless, never could plan, completely scatter-brained, I'm afraid. You'll just have to allow for it and make the best of me, won't you?"

SIX

"Well, anyway," Bill Evans said, "when we finally got into this hut affair, there were only a couple of Jerries inside. Jerries, mark you, not Czechs. It was a sort of ritual, you know, for the I.O. to tell us we'd be up against Czechs or Poles or bloody Austrian yodellers instead of Jerries. Funnily enough they always turned out to be Jerries. Anyway, these two were the genuine article all right. One of my corporals took care of them, I got hold of their pay-books—rather a messy job—and that was the end of the party. Not quite, though, actually, because on the way out I stumbled over some bod lying full length on the floor. Someone shone his torch on him, and it was a Jerry officer, Iron Cross and all the bloody regalia. I thought that he'd had his lot from one of our other people, but there wasn't a mark on him and he was breathing away like a steam-engine. Then I noticed he was stinking of drink—bottle still in his hand, empty, I'm sorry to say. Calvados or some such hell-brew. Must have been the real stuff, because there'd been the father and mother of a racket going on outside, shouting and banging away, but there he was, out for the count. Well, anyway, we couldn't take him with us, even if we could have got him on to his feet, so . . ."

I eased my position stealthily and looked round the bar of the Queen's Head, Llansili. Until a couple of years ago or less, as I remembered from a coach trip here with a party of my father's workmates, it had more or less merited Elizabeth's nomenclature of country pub. The counter had been an old-fashioned one, with curious wooden pillars, faced with vine-patterned glass, stretching at irregular intervals to the ceiling. These, and much else, had been removed; round glass-topped tables had replaced the old oblong plain-wood ones; pink and green lino covered the wooden floor; the various notices round the bar, instead of advertising penalties for spitting, stealing glasses and passing betting-slips, or discouraging requests for credit on the ground that a refusal often offends, now advertised kinds of liquor or cigarettes, in every case with a mammose young lady in full colour (one of them, in a bathing-suit and with raised knees, sitting on a mirror) shown drinking or smoking the ware in question and inviting the casual customer to join her. This last change, at any rate, I could honestly welcome, but it had apparently been no more successful than any other in causing a corresponding change in the kind of drinker using the place. Except for the group I was in, the people in the bar were much as they'd been on my last visit, labourers from the nearby farms, presumably, or shopkeepers from the village itself. One of these, an old man with a cap and no collar, caught my eye and made as if to call across to me. I returned my attention to Bill Evans.

"Well, I'd used all mine," he was saying, "but Sam had got one left. So he took out the pin, held on to the lever gadget though, and said, 'Seems a shame to wake him. Pity to wake him,' he said. Then—mad sod, old Sam—he bent down and put the thing next to the chap's head. "'Let's go, boys, shall we?' he said, and let go. We were out of the door and ten yards down the dreaded road before she went up. I remember old Sam shouting out to me, "'Bet he's never had a hangover like that before.'" Laughing slightly, Evans shook his head a few times and drank beer from his glass.

The others laughed too, particularly Paul Whetstone, whose accelerating falsetto seemed to indicate a man who knew his laugh and himself to be a bit queer, but had stopped minding. I envied his whole-heartedness, having done a small coughing-fit myself as a laugh-substitute, and seeing this now as a minute but still cowardly evasion. And yet a scowl, or even an obscene gesture, though much more fun to do, would have seemed unpleasantly pharisaical, a wholly disproportionate protest quite apart from possible repercussions. There'd been one or two other things said earlier on which had put me in the same irritating position, and I didn't know how to cope with it, not even whether I should be worrying about how to cope with it. "You mind my bloody business; I'll look after yours," the old man in the cap bawled in the bullying tone traditional to Welsh humorists.

"Of course, that war was the biggest mistake we ever made in our lives," Evans said thoughtfully. "We picked the wrong enemy for once, never stop regretting it. Well, this won't do; who's for another? Gin and french here, isn't it? . . . brandy . . ."

While I was reflecting that Evans's grenade story would turn Probert (where was he to-night?) green with envy, its author tapped me on the shoulder. I was the outermost of the party and more available than Whetstone, the dentist or the dentist's mistress, hemmed in as they were by table-legs and a large evergreen plant in a brass tub. "Like to do me a favour, old boy?" Evans asked. "Good. Think I forgot to put my lights on. Could you do it while I get the drinks? You're on mild, aren't you?" He gave me his keys. "Knob on the extreme right of the dash, you can't miss it. Just the sidelights, of course."

"I shouldn't worry, Bill," Elizabeth called across. "I don't think any traffic goes up that way. It's only a sort of lane."

"Truly, ducks," Evans said, "but it's a little habit of mine always to be on the safe side about these things." I saw the corner of his mouth tighten. "Have I your permission?"

"Oh, it's accorded, Billy dear," she crooned. "Just this once."

He turned very quickly away and nodded to me. "Thanks."

Outside, the air had cooled, although the front of the pub was still in faint sunshine. Across the road a chestnut pony watched me from the field adjoining the churchyard. Near it was a rotting saloon car and a notice weathered into unintelligibility. These signs of the hand of man gave place, over on the right, to a cluster of small but tubby hills, between which the sea, flat and uniform, was visible. There was no one about, but I could hear a bit of shouting and a lot of laughing coming from the corner of the building, where there was a private room that could be hired for dinners and parties. Just about here Evans had backed his car a few yards up a lane which curved round in front of the ¦pub and ran down to join the main road. Elizabeth and the dentist had parked their cars next to one or two others near the pub entrance.

Evans's car was remarkable for its long bonnet. There were several keys on the ring he'd given me and it took a moment or two to find the right one. When I leant inside I had the sense of penetrating into a private corner of his life, of which fragmentary evidence was lying about: a pair of net gloves on the seat, a paper-backed book, *Beautiful But Dead*, in the dashboard cubby-hole, a nest of fag-ends, some of them stained with lipstick, in the ash-tray, the remains of some rally-ticket or other on the windscreen. There seemed to be four knobs under the dials and I pulled the right-hand one. "The end of civilisation as we know it," a voice said. "Good-night." I returned this farewell and pushed the knob back. There was a fifth knob I hadn't seen and this proved to be the one. After what felt like about half an hour and ten trips to the front of the car and back, I'd succeeded in getting the sidelights on and headlights off at the same time. Then I relocked the door and went away, savouring the nostalgic bloom that had fallen on the air. I stood there with my face tilted towards the evening sky, smiling faintly. John Aneurin Lewis, I thought to myself, poet, visionary and wit. A movement at the corner of my eye made me turn my head. Evans's car was very slowly nosing its way out of the lane on a course which would take it, not to the confluence of lane and road, but to a higher point where these were separated by a four-foot drop. I went back to the car. Laughter came from the dining-room.

The slope was so gentle and the car rolling so slowly that for some time I tried to halt it by pulling, then pushing, at it. This didn't work, so I started looking for the door-key on the ring. The car moved on, averaging perhaps two feet per second, towards the edge of the drop. When it was clear that, even if I could get the door open within the next second, I should have insufficient time to get in and find, let alone apply, the brake, I reverted to my old policy of pushing at it from the front and walking slowly backwards. Whether because of this or of a decrease

72

in the gradient, the pace dropped a good deal, but it was only a short time until one front wheel was half-way over the edge and I was standing, or rather crouching, in the angle subtended by the edge and the bumper, using all my strength to keep the car poised where it was. I began deciding what it would be best to shout.

At this point two small dark men came out of the dining-room in front of me. They were giggling loudly and had their trousers rolled up above their knees. They caught sight of me and stopped giggling. Before I could cry out, one of them had shot back into the dining-room and the other had rushed down the incline to my assistance. "Thanks a lot," I gasped as he began straining at the wing. "No wind for speaking," he said with a continental accent. I noticed a few pieces of confetti clinging to his pomaded head. The next moment three more men ran down from the dining-room and joined in the struggle, and the moment after that Bill Evans came into view from the bar, no doubt to see if anything was delaying me. Throwing up his arms like a bowler appealing for leg-before, he came and joined the little group by his car.

"Well, this is handy, isn't it?" he said to me, narrowing his eyes and mouth.

"Sorry," I said with difficulty, "I don't know what can have gone . . ."

"We'll have a little chat about it later," he said. "Come out of there a minute, do you mind?"

He helped me to do this by pulling at my arm, then applied his own strength to the car. Calling out to one another in an unfamiliar tongue, the dark men redoubled their efforts. I now saw that all four of them had their trousers rolled up. The car began moving backwards from the brink.

"Right, thanks, lads, that'll do," Evans called after a few moments. "If you could just hold her there for a bit"

73

—he turned to me—"we'll see what putting the brake back on will do for us, all right?"

"I didn't put the brake off," I said, while one of the dark men was evidently translating Evans's speech to one of his comrades. "I'm sorry about all this, but I'm quite sure I didn't put the brake off."

"Can I have the keys?" he said.

After a minute or two I found these on the ground further up the slope. Evans got into the car and started the motor, then glanced down. An expression of puzzlement came on to his small face and he glanced at me. Next, there was a prolonged crunching while, with bared teeth, he pushed and pulled at the conductor's baton attached to the steering-column. The gear went in at last and, calling "Okay", he revved up the engine. The dark men, no doubt anticipating some slight forward movement, came away from the car. This was fortunate in view of what happened next.

Within perhaps a second and a half the car had moved briskly down the three or four feet of slope, the offside front wheel had gone over the edge, a clanging thud had filled the air and the car had come to rest leaning over slightly. The silence was broken by an outburst of foreign talk ratified by gesture.

Evans got out, rubbing his chin. "That's funny," he said. "I'm dead certain those brakes were all right on the way here. And then of course it's quite easy to get into second instead of reverse with these column-changes. I don't think the makers have ironed out all the snags with them yet. Mind you, there's a lot of shoddy workmanship about these days. Mm. Funny, that. Queer, really. Well, I think you'd better go and get the others, old boy, if you would."

When I returned with the others, four dark women had joined the dark men and a lot of what I now recognised as Italian was being talked. Two labourers had halted and were watching the affair from a distance. So was an un-healthy-looking corgi. A confabulation started, mainly in English.

After a time a group reformed round the front of the car and I made to join it. Elizabeth put her hand on my shoulder. "Go on, leave them to it," she said. "You've done your share of pushing and shoving. You need a drink."

"Oh, I must give them a hand."

"Rubbish," she said, watching two of the Italians jump lightly into the road and reach up towards the over-hanging wheel. "It's all Bill's fault; he ought to have had his brakes seen to. You leave him to it." She turned away towards the bar entrance.

"But those other chaps," I said, beginning to follow her. The dentist's mistress, standing there like some beautiful attendant nymph, looked on for a moment with wide-open, opaque eyes, then walked away to where her lover, with a wealth of gesture that rivalled the Italians', was urging some course of action on Evans. Her white linen blouse recalled in more than one feature the shirt worn by the better of the two tennis-players I'd seen, and indeed made me feel quite glad to see her go.

Elizabeth, having outlined what those other chaps could go and do to themselves, now moved off, adding that she at any rate wanted a drink and I could please myself whether I joined her.

Inside the bar again, I stood at the counter to buy her her drink (a brandy), and stopped myself thinking about what it would cost by marvelling afresh at the way the room was kitted out. The low ceiling, I saw, had had beams added to it of greater regularity and smoothness than is normally associated with wood. Above the till was a calendar with stage-coach, apoplectic-looking innkeeper and posthorns, these last echoing in their texture the various instruments hung round the walls of the pub:

warming-pans, soup-ladles, candle-snuffers—but the place was lit by electricity—and a thing that would have come in handy for getting fried ostrich eggs off a frying-pan. Perhaps in allusion to the name of the house, the grey-tiled fireplace was surmounted by a shoulder-length portrait of the reigning monarch. Here the resources of colour and line were eked out by sequins inlaid in coronet, necklace and order.

Ducking my head to avoid a farmhouse lamp with no flame, I leaned forward over the unattended counter. The old man in the cap called out loudly: "Madame Rachel, a moment of your valuable time, if you would be so kind. Your presence is being solicited by a young gentleman in need of refreshment, so get your bloody skates on, thanks frightfully much, old bean." Then he and his mates laughed.

Eventually I got the drinks and took them over to Elizabeth, who was looking at her face in a pocket-mirror though not doing anything to it. "Still on that awful stuff?" she asked, grimacing at my half-pint of mild. "Why the hell don't you let yourself go and have a decent drink?"

"I've got a lousy head for spirits and things."

"Mm, that's worth knowing, eh?" She stared at me and began grinning.

"What's the joke?"

"What? I was thinking of poor old Bill. He always seems to get the rough end of the stick, doesn't he?"

"I don't know, does he?"

"I'm afraid I do exploit him rather. But it serves him right, always hanging round me with that frightful doggy-devotion look. He just asks for it. He's got the sweetest little wife, too, and a dear little boy, oh, he's an absolute pet. I don't know why he has to keep on pestering me the whole time. I tell him he ought to be at home." She drank half her brandy and pressed her lips together. "Of course, you're not exactly one of his pin-up boys at the moment."

Some sort of apprehension tweaked at my stomach. "Oh? Why's that?"

She shrugged jerkily and muttered something that sounded like "Obvious", then went on in her usual firm clear tone: "Oh, now we've got the chance, I meant to tell you I've had a word with Vernon about this job you're in for at the Library. I promised to tell you what sort of interview they have and so on, didn't I?"

"Yes, you did mention it," I said, still a little shaken.

"Well, I gather there are going to be four people up for the interview. Don't repeat this except to Jean, will you? though I should imagine half Aberdarcy knows about it by now. Anyway, they'll be calling your friend Jenkins, then there's a fellow from Oxford . . . Cigarette?" They were black ones with gold tips in a leather case.

"No thanks, I don't," I said for the fourth time that evening.

"Wise man." She snapped her lighter, inhaled and blew out smoke. "Well, this is more or less the position . . ."

I listened while she talked quietly for some minutes about the interview and other things connected with the job. I gathered that the short list had been provisionally decided on, would be finally fixed at a meeting next week, and at the moment consisted of Ieuan Jenkins, an assistant librarian at an Oxford college, a sub-librarian at Newport who wanted to move, and myself. After a little while I realised that this was all the concrete information Elizabeth had; the rest was speculation and generalised advice. Still, I had something to tell Jean, and my spirits went up as I imagined discussing it with her. At the same time the lack of anything more confidential was letting my conscience tick over gently at

77

something like normal running speed; I should be able to look Ieuan in the face to-morrow, which, although not very rewarding perhaps, was an activity I wanted to continue.

"I think that's just about all for the moment," Elizabeth said. "There may be more after next week's meeting. Well . . ." She stretched, taking her time over it and looking worth looking at. ". . . I suppose we'd better go and see if Bill's got anywhere with that car of his. It's just on ten, anyway."

As we approached the door, the old man in the cap was saying to a friend: "The more I look at your intelligent bloody face . . ." He looked up at me and went on: ". . . the more I'm bloody convinced that Crippen was innocent." I coughed and hurried after Elizabeth.

It was getting dark outside. Evans's car was now in a position where it could be driven on to the road and I could see his figure stooped at its front and peering at something. The crowd seemed to have dispersed, but the little dark man who'd first run to my help was standing with his arm round one of the women in the light from a window. He'd rolled his trouser-legs down by this time. I went up to him and said: "Thanks a lot for helping me out. I don't know what I'd have done without you."

"Oh, that's all right, a pleasure," he said. "Pleased to be of help. It made some excitement for us. But to-day we are already quite enough excited. You must say hullo to Angela." He glanced at his girl and smiled affectionately. "To-day is our marriage day, to-day we are married."

"Congratulations," I said. "All the best to you both."

"You lucky things," Elizabeth, who'd joined the group, added with great emphasis. "I hope you'll be terrifically happy."

It wasn't well done and the man nodded to her coldly, then turned to me and smiled. "Thank you. Thank you very much. To-day my uncle who run Dalessio's Restaurant—perhaps you know it?—he say we have enough of cooking, we'll beat it out to Queen's Head and they'll do all the cooking, we'll get a little pissed-up for after the marriage."

"Aw, Pino, shocking you are, man," Angela said in the native accent of Aberdarcy. "I've told you I don't know how many times not to say that word."

"See how well she speak English," Pino said to me admiringly. "I am only over in England since the war, you know, and I need improvement. But in my uncle's house we're chattering away always in Italian. Now I live with Angela, I shall get on fine with English." He glanced over to where Elizabeth was standing apart with the dentist and his manner changed. "I'm sorry, I'm keeping you away from your friends."

"No you're not, honestly."

"We must go in anyhow. It isn't too warm. Goodnight."

"Good-night, and thanks again."

The dentist glanced up as I approached. His face, in the failing light, looked bewildered and a little hurt. "It took much longer than I expected," he said. "We had to dig half that bank away in the end. Miserable bloody business." He shivered slightly and bit at a fingernail. "Well, may as well push off, I suppose, no use hanging about. Past ten. Have you got a tow-rope, Elizabeth? Bill'll have to give me a tow."

"Christ, don't tell me your buggy's up the creek as well?"

"No, it's on the top line, actually. But, you see, Bill not having any brakes, he's got to have someone towed behind or he won't be able to pull up. I mean he'll have to use my brakes, because . . . ."

"Because he hasn't any of his own, yes, I see that. I don't know whether I've got a rope or not. There's some tools and stuff in the boot, I think. I suppose I'd better have a look."

They walked off, their footsteps crunching hollowly on the gravel. I saw Whetstone, hunched and with hands in pockets, swing over to them stiff-legged. I went to the Gents, which was outside the pub at the back. There was enough light for me to see that all surfaces on which visitors could possibly write or draw had been covered with pebble-dash. It was a fine night and as I came away I heard with sympathetic melancholy the Italian party singing away like mad to a piano in the dining-room. The tune wasn't *Santa Lucia*, nor even *Pappa Piccolino*, but *I'm Getting Sentimental Over You*. So much the better. As I rounded the corner the light went off over the entrance and I heard the voice of the old man in the cap diminishing up the road: "All right, I'll say it again: he was a bloody fine man and as innocent as you or I. Just because he went and cut up his bloody wife doesn't mean . . ."

Evans's car had moved down towards the road and the dentist's was now a yard or two behind it. Between them three figures were doing something with a rope. Before I'd approached them Elizabeth had strolled up to me. "They'll be ages yet. My God, they can talk about female inefficiency. . . . This sort of thing's always happening to Bill. He over-drives that car to death." We turned and sauntered away from the cars towards the far end of the building. "Frightful nuisance, this. I suppose we'd better hang on and follow them in, in case Bill gets a wheel off or catches fire or something. Well, I hope you've had a reasonable sort of evening. Afraid it's been rather broken up in one way and another."

"No, it's been fine."

We halted somewhere near Evans's original parking-place and stood for a moment in silence. Elizabeth's white seersucker dress glimmered in the darkness a yard or so away and the sounds of her movements, the scuff of her shoe and the click of bracelets or something, were amplified. I sensed her as a warm bundle of flesh and clothes and hair occupying a space I couldn't fully determine and so seeming vaguer and larger than life. A faint wind rustled the branches of nearby trees and swung her skirt to and fro. I heard her sigh and swallow, then she said: "I'm afraid we shall have to take that fool Paul back with us. Bill usually drops him but he won't want to to-night. Still, I can drop him first, before I run you home."

I scarcely heeded this. I felt suddenly apprehensive, as if the Aberdarcy Libraries Committee were even now filing out of the Queen's Head and preparing to question me searchingly about my qualifications and experience. The distance between myself and Elizabeth had somehow shrunk to about a foot. All of a sudden it declined even further, and almost irreducibly.

It was quite a long kiss, noteworthy for cordiality and lack of tension. I hugged her affectionately and she put her arms round my neck. She felt smaller than I'd expected, but warmer too, and was altogether direct and genial, breathing evenly and not pushing forward much. It was like a rather lengthy kiss under the mistletoe. When we drew apart, she gave me a little subsidiary kiss on the chin, and I could tell she was smiling when she said: "Well, that really was nice."

"Yes, it was, wasn't it? I thoroughly enjoyed it."

"Whacko. We'd better be getting back to the others, I think. You're not tired, are you? I thought we might go on somewhere else afterwards. I don't want to finish the evening just yet."

" That'll be splendid."

SEVEN

THE PLYWOOD SHIELD on the flimsy blue easel said
MODERN DANCING TONIGHT. The notice over
the kiosk said 2/6 ADMISSION 2/6, and a footnote
read *No Passouts after* 10 *p.m.* Elizabeth went ahead of
me and paid at the kiosk. For the moment there was
little noise, only a deep bass throbbing that could be
felt rather than heard. There was noise all right the
moment we opened the swing doors. My ears were filled
to capacity with an uproar of voices and movement,
behind which a band could be heard quite plainly. A
choking gust of hot perfume blew down the carpeted
passage. In the distance, under an orange light, was a
corner of the dance-floor, where a thick crowd of spectators blocked any view into the room. As I followed
Elizabeth, who seemed to be in a hurry, I read the
posters on the walls of the corridor. DANCE TIME
announces its GREAT NEW 1954 TOP TWENTY
COMPETITION. *Simply select the* 20 *tunes you prefer
from those in* . . . DANCING *Mon* TEENAGER'S NIGHT
Tues OLDE TYME *Wed* MODERN . . . and, more
shortly, *No Loitering in This Passage.*

A huge bewilderment settled upon me as we arrived
in the main hall, where the phalanx of spectators—if
that was the right name for them—was revealed as even
denser and deeper than it had seemed from the passage.
Above the heads of its shortest members the heads of
the tallest dancers were fleetingly to be seen. The noise
was increasing just now in salutation of a solo trombone
passage being played: I could just make out the rocking

head and shoulders of the executant, who was wearing a chocolate-brown coat, above the invisible bandstand at the far end of the room. Three young men broke off from dipping and straightening at the knees, clapping their hands and saying "Yeah" to turn round and stare at us, or rather at Elizabeth. Each of the three appeared to nudge the two others. "Hey, fellows, look what just dropped in," one of them said.

She gave them a short but effective glare, said to me: "I'm off to powder my nose. Hang on here for me, will you?" and pushed unhesitatingly and energetically through the crowd. In a second she was lost to view. She's done this before, I thought.

The three young men looked me up and down at their leisure. They all wore gabardine trousers and navy-blue blazers with large and elaborate crests on the top pocket. The designs differed, but the rigmarole underneath ended in every case with the initials *A.F.C.* All wore white shirts, but, again, their ties differed: one had vertical stripes, another, apparently knitted or crocheted, had alternating strips of green and cream with a green initial *B* on the most prominent cream bit, the third had a knot contrasting in colour with the main body. (How did they manage that?) Each tie was secured with a thick tiepin and gold chain. After a time their three owners turned slowly away, though the one who'd spoken kept rising on tiptoe and peering in the direction Elizabeth had gone. A wave of heat enveloped me. I wished there was somewhere to sit down, then realised that I must soon pay a prolonged visit to a lavatory. A good time would have been now, except that on her return Elizabeth wouldn't know where I'd gone and for some reason I was reluctant to leave her unattended to the three young men.

"Hallo, Mr. Lewis," a voice said over to my right. It was Ken Davies.

:"Hallo," I said with unforced joviality. "So this is where you come on your nights off." Two or three other men were standing with him and now nodded to me unsmilingly.

"That's right, yeah. You come here often?"

"No, haven't been here for years. Not since I was at school." Of course, I thought, Probert used to come here with one of his bus-conductresses and get asked to leave.

"See a change, then, I reckon?"

"Yes, I do. More flash than it was."

"You don't tell me? Gone down a lot recently; they get the wrong kind here now. Dead common, you know? and too ready to make with the fists. Now I don't go for that, speaking personally."

"Nor me. Still, I suppose you get all sorts here."

"You can say that again. On your own?"

"No, I'm waiting . . . for somebody."

He caught my hesitation and grinned. His teeth were long and pointed, like a shark's. "That the doll I seen you with coming into the house?"

"That's the one."

"Some looker, eh, friend? You want to watch out she don't get snatched off you. This is the night the boys come up from the Albany, you know?"

The Albany, a pub on the edge of the dock area, was known to be the headquarters and stamping-ground of an ex-boxer named Joe Leyshon, who headed a notable group of alleged warehouse-robbers, pimps and protection-racketeers. "That's great news," I told Ken. "Thanks for the tip."

"Pleasure," he said. "Well, here's your date, Mr. Lewis. See you again."

"Sorry to keep you waiting," Elizabeth said, glancing from side to side. "There was a bit of a scrum in there. Well, let's get going, shall we?"

"Do you really want to dance?"

"Of course I want to dance. What do you think I came here for? Why, are you finding the place a bit too much for you?" Her hair shone under the light, which had changed to a bright yellow, and her eyes looked wide open. She was moving impatiently from one foot to the other.

"No, I'm loving it. Off we go, then."

Going off was delayed by wriggling slowly through the mass of spectators, who, although quite unco-operative, were surprisingly unresentful of our passage.

We danced perhaps four dances. I knew what kind they were because their titles—Quickstep, Foxtrot, Samba—were displayed by an illuminated sign placed on high at one side of the bandstand. The samba, in particular, made me feel hot. Each member of the band had what was perhaps his Christian name painted in brown on his silver-grey music-stand: Eddie, Pete, Benny, Ray, Louie (short for Llewelyn?). Some of the time I took note of the male patrons' hair-styles. Crew-cuts seemed to be on the wane, superseded by elaborately-waved styles like the Tony Curtis and the D.A., or one I didn't know the official designation of, an affair with the sides left very long and swept back above the ears and the centre strip done in tight curls like carved ebony. One very small man had a Seminole, consisting of a band of hair, perhaps four inches wide and of crew-cut length, running from forehead to nape and the rest of the head shaved to the pate. He looked a bit like a collaborationist branded by the mob, but it was impressive to see on the hoof, so to speak, something I'd never encountered except in the special set of photographs displayed at the local barber's. The Seminole man, who wore no jacket, was dancing with great abandon and vehemence, flinging his girl, who had a red off-the-shoulder blouse and a good deal of hair on her upper lip, about a lot and frequently crying out in an unintelligible accent. Near them a sign said NO BOPPING.

Elizabeth turned out to be a good dancer and I soon began enjoying myself. There was too much noise to speak much, but the bodily contact with her had its own appeal. I could see that there was a lot to be said for dancing as a way of getting one's arms round girls and so on. Like all attractive women, Elizabeth was somehow more attractive close to than at a distance. This was brought home to me with extra force when, after a few minutes, she laid her cheek on mine. She continued, however, to dance with accuracy, not sacrificing her freedom of movement by pressing or leaning against me. Her agility made her seem slimmer and harder than I'd made her out to be during the brief scuffle outside the Queen's Head. When she moved her face away I saw that she had a very good jaw-line, smoothly fleshed but firm and straight. Behind her I saw Dilys Jones from the Library wheel into view with a man of seafaring appearance, and instinctively waved and nodded.

"Who's that?" Elizabeth asked, trying to see.

"Just a girl from the Library."

"Friend of yours?"

"No, not really. She's the one you . . ." For the first time it occurred to me to wonder just what Elizabeth had said to Dilys that afternoon. Well, whatever it was, Dilys had probably deserved it.

"She's what?" Elizabeth went on, raising her voice. "Who?"

"Just one of the juniors."

The dance ended at this point. During the roaring and whistling that followed, Elizabeth looked round for Dilys. "Where is she now?"

"I don't know."

"The next dance," a huge voice announced through a creaking oscillation, "will be a Ladies' Excuse-me."

86

There was an outburst of crashing, rattling and thundering, as if the drummer was trying to kill a wasp with his sticks, and then the whole business started up again. *Quickstep*, the illuminated sign said.

After a minute or so someone tapped me on the shoulder. It was a tall, broad man in an electric-blue suit. His shirt was a gleaming turquoise colour and had the largest collar I'd ever seen. His tie, on the other hand, a bow with extravagant loops and ends, was little thicker than the average bootlace, calling to mind the neckwear of corrupt sheriffs in Western films. He looked and smelt fairly drunk. "Move over," he said.

My chest went tight. "No, you move over."

"Come on, fellow, move over. This is an excuse-me, see?"

"A ladies' excuse-me. You're a gentleman, aren't you?"

"Take no notice, John," Elizabeth said. "He'll go away."

We danced a few more steps while the man lumbered after us. A couple of yards away I could see a similar man having a similar argument with another couple. After a time our man caught us up and this time rested his hand on my shoulder heavily enough to draw us to a halt. His face, broad and high-cheeked, came nearer. "I told you to move over," he said, chewing something. "Move over."

"I'm not moving over," I said. "You move over."

"Go on, clear off," a man near me shouted angrily. Other men joined in with cognate recommendations, some of them varying the second verb.

The big man took his hand off my shoulder. His voice went up into a yelp. "All right; all right," he said. "All right."

We circled away while he looked slowly about him.

"Always making a bloody nuisance of theirselves," the man who'd shouted shouted. "Oughtn't to let 'em in."

"You got a point there, friend," I shouted back.

"Good fun, that," Elizabeth said. She was grinning, her cheeks were slightly flushed and she seemed to be dancing more springily than ever.

"Oh, tremendous," I said. "Wouldn't have missed it for anything." Perhaps as a result of the late encounter, fresh admonitions circled my guts, less resistibly than before, so at the end of the quickstep I took Elizabeth over to the soft-drinks bar, told her to wait for me, and departed.

The lavatory was principally occupied by six youths combing their hair in front of six full-length mirrors. A seventh person, arm pressed on wall and forehead resting on arm, was vomiting sluggishly at the urinal. Both cubicles were occupied. Feeling tired and hungry—I'd had nothing to eat since lunch apart from some sandwiches and crisps at the Queen's Head—I leant against the wall and idly watched the hair-combers. I realised that it wasn't exactly vanity which caused all this sedulousness, but rather that constant checking and adjustment were inevitably involved with hair-dos like these.

One of the combers sheathed his comb in a little leather case which also contained a nail-file and came over to me. "Know me again," he said. He was about eighteen and had side-whiskers.

"I beg your pardon?" I said, feeling a bit like Ieuan Jenkins pretending not to understand a cant term. I could see I'd violated the unspoken code which prohibits the eye from resting on a stranger for more than two seconds.

"Who you staring at, I said."

"I didn't think I was staring at anyone, I'm sorry."

"Yes you was."

"All right then, if you must know, I was staring at you, and no wonder. What of it?" I felt peevish and uncomfortable and perhaps a little light-headed, and furthermore I wanted to try out a routine I'd thought up one afternoon while cataloguing a prize-fighter's memoirs in Jenkins's absence.

"Want to make something of it?"

"Yes, I can't wait. Where do you want it, here or outside? I should warn you I got into the final in the University of Wales boxing tournament the year before last. Disqualified for hitting low, I was. But you won't mind that, will you?"

The other youths were either edging away or leaving. A loud retch came from the man at the urinal.

"Yeah, expect me to believe that?"

"You can please yourself; I'm just warning you, that's all." I got my feet into what I hoped was a professional position on the tiled floor. "Well, what do you say? Here or outside? I haven't got all night." I clenched my teeth and rolled my lips back away from them.

He blinked several times and sniffed. "Don't know what you want to be like that about it for."

"No? Run along, son, before you get hurt."

He stared at me for a moment longer, then went out. Just then a man emerged from one of the cubicles.

When, a few minutes afterwards, I arrived back at the soft-drinks bar, the only people there were a very tall man, probably a bouncer, and a fat man who was leaning over the counter and calling loudly for whisky. "I know you've got some there, you big blue-eyed darling," he bawled. "Come on, turn it in or get outside," the bouncer said. "Well, send out for some, then," the fat man told him.

For a long time I couldn't see Elizabeth anywhere and began wondering if, tired of waiting, she might have gone back to her car. Then I saw her briefly, dancing with a big man in an electric-blue suit and a thin bow-tie. All at once I felt much more tired and bought a cup of

89

tea from the bar. Well, I thought, I've only got to hang on here. She'll come over when this dance is finished.

She didn't. I got another glimpse of her, this time being led by the hand towards the far corner. Yes, we know you won't like doing this, Lewis, I said to myself, but it happens to be your duty. And that's good enough for you, isn't it, Lewis? All right then.

I arrived at the corner to find Elizabeth still being held by the hand. The man in the blue suit had taken her a little way apart from the crowd. He and the man who'd been with him earlier were leaning against the wall talking. I didn't see whether she was talking as well. "Feel like going home?" I asked her. Behind me the dancing began again in a vast shuffling of feet.

She looked up quickly. "Yes. I'm sorry but I couldn't do anything. Let me go, will you?" she said to her captor.

"What, let you go? Not likely, baby. I'm just beginning to enjoy myself. Ah, here's boy friend. Ted, tell boy friend to shove off, will you?"

The other man, who was wearing a bright green corduroy jacket, stepped up to me. "You heard what he said," he said. "Shove off."

I saw Elizabeth struggling to free herself. "Look, don't be silly," I said. "They'll throw you out."

He seized me by the lapels. He was no taller than me but much heavier. "You shove off before you get hurt," he said. "You're liable to get duffed up."

"Let's drop all this, shall we? You won't do yourself any good."

He struck me a covert blow in the side. "Get going, Jack."

I pushed him hard and he fell back, then came forward again.

"Having trouble, Mr. Lewis?" Ken Davies's voice asked. "All right, boys. Come on, Haydn."

Two men crossed in front of me and simultaneously hit the green-jacketed man in the stomach. Ken himself and another man went over to the man in the blue suit. With intense emotion I saw Ken reach up and undo the man's bow-tie (I found out later that this type of haberdashery is called a Slim Jim) while Ken's friend kicked him hard on the shins. Ken now went behind the man and began pulling the Slim Jim very tight round its wearer's neck. "Come on, make with the feet," Ken said. "Beat the bricks."

Before I could sort things out much Elizabeth had joined me, the manager and two bouncers had arrived, another trombone solo had started, and about eleven people, including several members of the public not previously involved, were conveying the two offenders towards the exit through a knot of spectators. I was amazed to see a faint smile on Elizabeth's face, but then Ken Davies reappeared and I forgot about it.

"Sorry you had that trouble, Mr. Lewis."

"My God, you and your boys were wonderful. I didn't know what the hell to do. You were wonderful."

"I'll get my bag," Elizabeth said and slipped away.

"Get away, it was a treat," Ken said to me.

"Were they two of the Albany boys?"

"Christ no, just a couple of drunks from up the Royal. If it had've been Joe's lot we'd have had to leave you to it. I got no inclination to get slashed."

"No, well, thanks a lot. I don't know what I'd have done without you."

"Ah, let it ride. You'll do the same for me some day. By the way, I should blow pretty quick if I was you, before those characters come round."

"Yes, we're going to."

"So long now."

Elizabeth came back and we left. I noticed that since our arrival somebody had added after OLDE TYME the present participle of a verb occupying another semantic area than that of 'dancing'.

While we walked in silence to the side-street where the car was parked, I thought of Elizabeth's behaviour with the two drunks. Surely she could have got away from them without provoking that or any scene. Nobody can be abducted who doesn't want to be abducted, even at a place like that, and if I couldn't think off-hand of a way of avoiding it, she, with her obvious female resourcefulness, could hardly not have known one. Well, what had been going on, then?

Before I could ask her this she'd pulled me into a shadow in the side-street, put her arms around my neck and begun kissing me. It was all quite different from the good-fellowship kind of thing that had happened by the Queen's Head: this time she was tense and trembling, even writhing slightly, and kept pressing herself hard against me. When I responded she opened her mouth, then caught my hand and laid it on her breast. Her heart was going quickly. She bit my tongue a little too hard. "Oh darling," she said in a shaky voice, "that was terrible. I'm so sorry. I was so terrified I couldn't think of anything to do. Thank God you found me. I was absolutely petrified . . . No, darling, we'd better be getting back. It's terribly late."

Feeling as if I'd actually taken part in several fights, and probably looking it too, I got into the car beside her. As we drove I told myself that it all made good sense, and it was very plausible that she should have got too rattled to think. I added to myself that her behaviour of a moment ago was plainly the concomitant of relief and not, as it had perhaps seemed at the time, that of sexual excitement at being fought over. It would all look much clearer to-morrow.

"When shall I see you again?" she asked after a bit.

"I don't really know. What were you thinking of?"

"Can I give you a ring at the Library?"

"Yes, do."

"There's that meeting next week. I'll have to tell you about that, won't I?"

"Yes, I suppose so."

"Why, don't you want me to?"

"Yes, of course I do."

She yawned. "God, I'm tired."

"It's been a long evening."

"Do you mind if I just drop you here on the corner?"

"No, this'll do fine."

"Good-night, then, John. See you soon."

I'd got myself all geared up not to kiss her and it was slightly deflating to find she made no move towards me. I watched her tail-lights pass smoothly and rapidly out of sight and started on the two- or three-hundred-yard stretch to the house. I hurried rather, because I dislike being out alone at night.

Feeling a tremendous rakehell, and not liking myself much for it, and feeling rather a good chap for not liking myself much for it, and not liking myself at all for feeling rather a good chap, I got indoors, vigorously rubbing lipstick off my mouth with my handkerchief. This would form the sole item in a little private wash-day some time to-morrow; Jean used a different shade. I tiptoed along the totally dark passage, which was filled by a long droning snore (probably the dog's) from the downstairs back room, and climbed the stairs.

In the kitchen I found a plateful of food waiting for me and ate the wafers of tongue and the slightly wizened tomatoes. The slice of cheese I restored to its greaseproof wrapper in the food-cupboard; the bread-and-butter I wrapped in an old newspaper and would smuggle out of the house and into the rubbish-bin the next morning.

I could visualise very clearly Jean buttering the top of the loaf and then, rather clumsily, with splayed elbows cutting off the slice and putting it on the plate. That small effort had been wasted. I thought of this while I drank some water, and then of other things which it suggested to me. As well as the private wash-day, to-morrow was inevitably going to be the time for holding a little private levee for guilt and anxiety and the rest of the old bunch. It wasn't so much doing what you wanted to do that was important, I ruminated, as wanting to do what you did. What about writing that down?

I fished in my pocket for paper and drew up a Library card designed for those wanting to join. There were spaces for the applicant's name, etc., and for the name, etc., of the ratepayer agreeing to act as guarantor. During the last week an old shag (a successful greengrocer, as a matter of fact, as well as a Lewis-infuriant and old shag) whose wife wanted to join had handed in three of these cards, variously filled in. The first one had said that his wife wanted to join and that his wife agreed to act as guarantor. After a fresh explanation from me and two days' interval, he'd brought in another one saying that he wanted to join and that he agreed to act as guarantor. The one I now held in my hand said that he wanted to join and that his wife agreed to act as guarantor. I decided to forget about my aphorism and skimmed the card out of the window. I enjoyed seeing it vanish into the night.

EIGHT

"Have you got to go?" I asked irritably.

"No, John, I haven't got to, course I haven't." Jean pulled a cardigan round her shoulders. I suspected she'd lost a bit more weight that month. "I just told her I'd be popping in sometime during the evening, that's all. Why, were you planning something special?"

"Of course not. I was only thinking we could have had an evening in together." I turned away from the window, my hands in my pockets. "And I keep telling you you're letting that woman depend on you too much. How the hell does she manage to stick it, anyway? You're always telling me she drives you up the wall."

"Don't start on that, John. I know she's awful, but a lot of it isn't her fault, and I'm about the only one she sees apart from Ieuan, you know that. Still, if you really don't want me to . . ."

"I can't understand what you find to talk about all the time. How you manage to talk at all, come to that. You've got nothing in common."

"She only wants someone to chat to."

"Still, you're both women. I suppose that's something to have in common."

"Don't be bloody insulting, now."

"I'm not. And I want someone to chat to as well, have you thought of that? And I'm better at it than she is."

"I'll chat to you till you're black in the face when I've come back and you've made me a smashing cup of cocoa."

"Uh. Fine treat that'll be." I stared at her and she gave me one of her big-mouth grins. Unwillingly at first, I joined in. "All right then, mike off. Don't get drunk or anything."

She came over and kissed me. "I'll only be an hour, honest."

"See it's no more, mind. Are they asleep?"

"The little one is; I looked in just now."

"Mm. What about the big one?"

"She'll be off soon, I'm sure."

"It's nice to be sure. What shall I do if he wakes up?"

"If he cries for more than ten minutes warm some milk for him. I've put it in the saucepan."

"Nappy?"

"On the chest of drawers. And if you do change him mind you put his rubber knickers back on. You remember what happened last time when you forgot."

"Yes, I remember. Off you go then, darling."

I went to the window again and saw her come out on to the pavement, glance quickly to and fro as if fearful of snipers, and hurry off across the road, every now and then breaking into a trot for a few paces. I grinned to myself: why could she never walk anywhere? There could be nobody in the world with less dignity than my wife, and few people in less need of that attribute.

Summer was well under way, as was clear this evening from such imponderables as the height of the sky, the thickness of the air and the redness of the sunlight. To me, however, the recent change of season was marked by far more definite changes in my person. The warmer weather meant that I could leave off my pullover, which meant in turn that I was thin enough to wear the re-markable dog-tooth check jacket belonging to the ape-suit's predecessor; the lack of rain permitted the wearing of the badly-holed tan shoes, which I was disinclined to pay for getting repaired; the rough skin on my fingers was no longer impregnated, nor the back of my tongue stained, with the coal-dust kicked up by my long ardours under the stairs. Here, in total darkness, it was my daily task to break off a supply of burnable pieces from one of the half-dozen megaliths that comprised an average fuel delivery. I used to get through it by pretending I was a wicked giant who'd knocked down the Library wall and was dashing certain borrowers on to the stone floor. At each booming concussion a cloud of dust would rise into my eyes and hair, Mrs. Davies's dog would raise a long yelling bark, and a piece of coal about the size of a pencil-eraser would fly from the main lump and tinkle delicately against the wall of the cupboard. This would go on until, at an impact in no way distinguishable from the previous ones, the lump would shatter into small pieces that turned to dust, like jewels in a fairy-tale, as I tried to pick them up. I used to groan then. But that was all over now, for the next five months at least.

This reflexion failed to mollify me. The name of Mrs. Jenkins still dinned in my mind's ear. The belief that words have a sound-value apart from their meaning, though of course untenable, received illusory support from this name. Was it one of the names of Antichrist? It was just the sort of vocable foreign seamen shout at one another while they're getting out their razors. No Comanche, Mohawk, Assiniboine or Seneca but would bare his teeth, fit an arrow to his bowstring and start riding round and round you if you said "Mrs. Jenkins" to him. That was the correct reaction; anything less definite was an eloquent example of the taxes on natural instinct, the levelling-down process, the business of making everyone the same, which an age of advertising and mass-communication will inevitably impose.

Yawning and stretching, feeling languor flood downwards through my muscles, I sat down in one of the ripped and peeling leather armchairs by the empty fireplace and looked round the room in search of something to engage my attention. There wasn't much which could do that. My eyes moved without stopping over the sort of matchwood shrine painted black which discharged some of the less important functions of a sideboard with its tiny square shelves, tinier inch-deep drawers with what looked like old-fashioned pendant earrings attached in the middle, and mirror mounted on bamboo scaffoldings; the gate-leg table whose gate-leg, like any gate, was liable to swing to without warning; the unlicensed, crackle-ridden wireless, surmounted by a cereal-bowl full of nasturtiums stolen from the front garden; the tall box-like couch, said to turn into a bed when the proper forces were applied, and stained with the activities of children. These formed a job lot which was oddly unreal and unconvincing, like a murderer's sitting-room reproduced in the Chamber of Horrors.

Was I to start reading something? A handyman skilled and sometimes energetic enough to arouse even Jean's admiration, I'd recently knocked up and bracketed to the wall a double book-shelf which now held most of my books. I gave them a quick look-over. Some were philosophical works, bought during my College career and still in my possession because the only second-hand bookseller in the town had declined them. Others were the nucleus of a collection, begun a few years previously, of modern books agreed by week-end reviewers to be significant; this project had now lapsed. Others again were novels from the Library awaiting return, and, in many cases, reading as well. The remainder had no nameable reason for being there, or at any rate still there: a few Penguins, an Everyman Jane Austen (a College set-book, I should explain), a guide to Monmouthshire, *The Letters of John Keats*, *The Future of Swearing*. No, it was no good; one book would tell me what I knew already, another what I couldn't understand, a third what I knew to be untrue, a fourth what I didn't want to be told about—especially that. And the next number of *Astounding Science Fiction* wouldn't be out till the 20th.

How, then, was I going to spend the next hour, or rather, adding Jean's usual surcharge, hour and a half? In defending myself, presumably, against a certain feeling. Such defence was never easy, because of its habit of confusing itself with the feeling. How to define this feeling? Depression? Not a bad shot. Boredom? Oh yes. A slight tinge, too, eh, of uneasiness and inert, generalised lust? Yes indeed. The centre of it might be called boredom, but not the same sort as the boredom which was fond of attacking me in slack periods at the Library. That sort was bemused, trance-like, even vaguely pleasurable, like the drowsiness it so often merged into; this, to-night, was restless. It had already stopped me from starting to read, it would shortly drive me to the window again as if I expected someone to call (though I didn't and no one would), it would, later on, make me want to go out to the pub, at the same time informing me that it wouldn't be worth it, that I shouldn't like it there and would at once start wanting to come home.

Yes, it was all very difficult. Curious, too, was the way something so efficient should be so hard to define. But having for once tried to define it instead of letting it sneak up and jump on my back, I felt a little cheered. Yes, and wait a moment, now: I'd got something to do which would entertain me for a good five minutes. Under the seat-cushion of the other armchair was a pile of newspapers, and under them was a copy of an illustrated weekly paper. With animation I drew this out, unfolded it, and began gazing devoutly at the photograph which, under a banner saying SADISTIC TERROR AT A GIRLS' SCHOOL: *See page* 15, occupied most of the front page.

It represented a full-figured girl wearing a curious yachting costume consisting mainly of a peaked cap, a pair of seaman's boots, and a small, inefficient-looking telescope. Apart from these, she wore two pieces of cloth with a nautical stripe, one covering a good deal of the lower half of her breasts, the other an almost irreducible minimum at the crotch. An expression of guarded joviality was on her face. *This jolly skipper*, I read in a panel near her right boot, *is curvesome Marietta DuForgue, now vacationing at Las Palmas. The dimensions of this trim craft are* 38″ *for'ard,* 23″ *amidships, and* 36″ *aft. What wouldn't you give for a chance of getting her to heave to.* Shaking my head over these vulgarities, in particular the maladroit change of image from 'skipper' to 'craft', I went on looking at the photograph. After a moment I settled myself more comfortably in my chair. This, I told myself with conviction, was the sort of thing that was wanted. If only this paper and its two competitors came out once an hour instead of once or twice a week, without impairing the rigour of their standards, solitary evenings, and many other things, would be quite endurable. You're supposed to get fed up with this kind of entertainment after a time, aren't you? but I'd long ago steeled myself to take that risk. Just as I was beginning to wonder whether it was true that, as I suspected, I'd been taking this kind of risk more frequently in the last year or so, a voice, thin in tone but of surprising volume, began to call out: "Dadd-ee. Dadd-eeeeeee. Dadd-*y*."

With a sigh of mingled annoyance, wistfulness and relief I refolded the paper and thrust it back under the cushion. I stood up and stretched again, then sauntered across to the door. I had my hand on the handle when I heard a door open on the floor below. I stayed still and listened. My daughter Eira (for it was she) went on calling me (for it was me) persistently, but without urgency; it was her habit to call me in like this when Jean was out, just for a chat and perhaps a short read.

In another half-minute what I was waiting for happened. A low growling voice, like that of a grizzly bear gifted by an enchanter with near-human speech, called up the stairs: "Mr. Lewis. Mr. Lewis."

"Daddee."

I waited a little longer.

"Mr. Lewis. Are you there, Mr. Lewis?"

I went out on to the landing. "Is there someone calling?" I asked in my special cultured accent, which I retained for the whole of the subsequent dialogue.

"Is that you, Mr. Lewis?"

"That's Mrs. Davies, isn't it? Well, and how are you, Mrs. Davies? Long time no see, as they say."

"Your baby's crying, Mr. Lewis. Crying a long time she've been, poor little soul."

"I think you must be making a mistake, Mrs. Davies: our baby's a little boy. And he's fast asleep now, you know."

"The little girl crying then, is it? Don't make no difference, do it, Mr. Lewis?"

I could see her in the gloom of the passage, bent forward with her arms across her waist, her fuzzy cap of greying red hair, like an anticipatory parody of Jean's, dimly illuminated by the fanlight over the front door. She looked like a front-row member of a street-accident crowd. "Well, I don't really know about that, Mrs. Davies," I said judicially. "Some people might say it made a lot of difference, one way and another."

"Silly to talk like that you are, Mr. Lewis. Why don't you go in to her, now, and find out what she crying for?"

"I might, later on, if I can find the time, Mrs. Davies. I'll be responsible for her, thanks very much all the same."

The woman's voice showed no anger when she said in her querulous guttural rumble: "You're not fit to have charge of little children, the way you go on, Mr. Lewis. Break my heart it do, hearing them crying away, and you doing your reading and never mind the little ones. I don't know what things are coming to, honest I don't."

I wondered what made her impute to me the activity of reading, since our field of discussion had never included the world of letters. "Oh come now, Mrs. Davies," I said, solicitously this time, "you really mustn't let yourself worry. Everything'll turn out all right in the end, just you wait and see. There's no need to take such a gloomy view of things."

"Daddee."

"There she go again—just listen to the poor little mite. Call yourself a father, do you, Mr. Lewis?"

"I not only call myself one, Mrs. Davies; I am one. At least, so my wife tells me."

A man's voice called from the front room: "Edna. Come on in here, pet."

Mrs. Davies began to move away, but still kept her face turned towards the foe. "I'll get the R.S.V.P. Inspector in here to you one day, Mr. Lewis, it's too much for me, when I sees the way you goes on."

"I shall be glad to see him, Mrs. Davies," I said politely. "Tell him I'll send him an invitation card."

"Inhuman, that's what you are, Mr. Lewis. Inhuman."

"Daddee."

"Aw, for Christ's sake, Edna, come in here now like I told you, girl."

"Well, I'm afraid I must get back to my reading, Mrs. Davies. I've enjoyed our chat."

"I'd chat to you all right if I had my way, Mr. Lewis."

"It's very nice of you to say so, Mrs. Davies, but I really must be off now. Good-night."

I went upstairs and into Eira's bedroom. She was sitting up in bed doing some kind of stretching exercise with her arms, and smiled when she saw me.

"Are you all right?" I asked.

"Yas," she said. This lowering of the *e*-phoneme is widespread, I've noticed, in childish dialect.

"What do you want, then?"

"Want a chat. And read me a story."

"You ought to be asleep. You don't really want a chat."

"I . . . *do*."

We had our chat, characterised on her part by rapid and far-ranging changes of subject, and on mine by a tendency to keep saying "Who told you that?" After she'd disclosed to me that a pirate always carried a knife as well as a pistol, that the smoke from the chimneys helped to keep aeroplanes up in the sky, that the milkman was going to buy a car and that tigers didn't lay eggs because they were like whales, she went on to claim that Roger Harries at school had three stories a night. I then read her a short account of the defeat of a car-stealing organisation manned, rather implausibly, by goblins. When this was over, and when Eira had asked for and been given a glass of water, I tucked her up again and returned to my chair. Doing these paternal tasks, plus the encounter with Mrs. Davies, had cheered me up as well as getting me through half an hour.

The Davies incident this evening had been no more than patrol activity, successful from my point of view, but limited. The war had been begun, of course, by Mrs. Davies, not so much out of nastiness as out of a feminine, or middle-aged, or uneducated, or human, inability to see that life involves some inconvenience. Accordingly, she'd succeeded last winter in denying Jean passage through her basement-kitchen—the only route that didn't mean a half-mile detour and a climb over two seven-foot walls with broken glass along the tops—to the back garden of the house, the only place where washing could be hung. By a long and resolute campaign, admirably conducted in its way since it must have been only half-intentional, and consisting only of tones of voice, grimaces, hints, long delays—never overt reluctance—in answering Jean's knocks and in declaring the way to be clear, she'd converted her kitchen door into an obstacle as impassable as an anti-tank ditch.

So the struggle had begun. After a time the combatants had narrowed down to Mrs. Davies on one side and me on the other. Jean's timidity soon ruled her out; Mr. Davies, a dour bus-conductor, silently but unmistakably declared himself neutral; Ken had plenty of other things to think of. I'd struck back at Mrs. Davies where possible by being bad at answering the door when they were all out: not taking a loaf, sending their laundry back, refusing to admit a plumber who'd called to unblock their drain, fixing appointments up for them with door-to-door religious fanatics. Not that I had it all my own way: some months previously circumstances had planted me on the doorstep with no top-coat or latchkey or money. Jean had been out with the children, Mrs. Davies indisputably in. By not answering my knocks she'd kept me walking about in the open for two hours of what the paper said next day had been the coldest night since 1916.

All at once, as I again took up my post at the window, I felt upon me the thought I'd been managing, without fully realising it, to keep out of my head ever since Jean had left the house. My familiar state of not wanting to do or not do anything at all, of not wanting to go out or stay in or read or not read or go to bed or stay up or sit down or stand up, had been invaded by wanting to do something, or at least by wanting something to happen. From where I stood I could visualise exactly the look of the long amphisboenic car drawing up at the kerb below (what wouldn't you give for a chance of getting her to heave to?), of the outward swing of a door, of the foreshortened, dark-haired figure of dear old Elizabeth Gruffydd-Williams hesitantly crossing the pavement and passing out of view towards the front door. And then: "Are you sure this is what you really want?" And then? Something, perhaps, about this thing being bigger than either of us, darling. Yes, that's right: darling.

Full of anger, I walked out into the kitchen and started preparing to wash up the crockery. There was no proper sink, only a washhand-basin too small to allow the kettle to be brought squarely under the single tap. I filled the kettle as far as possible, then topped it up with a jug set aside for the purpose. I began stacking the dishes while the water boiled. From this window I could see the backs of the houses in the next street, with two sets of short back gardens intervening. To the left lay a piece of waste ground conventionally furnished with rusty tins, scraps of discarded clothing and footwear, large stones thrown over the walls by tillers of the adjoining gardens, even what looked like a decomposing stove or oven. Just outside the pane was the home end of the pulley arrangement I'd fixed up, at what cost in fatigue and horror it can be imagined, so that Jean could put out and take in washing without 'troubling' Mrs. Davies. A couple of Eira's frocks and some nappies swayed on the line, catching the last of the evening sun. A man wearing a bright ginger-coloured cap was planting something, or digging it up, in a garden opposite.

My mind found little to fasten on in this scene and, willingly enough now, went back to the Queen's Head and dance-hall session the previous week. At this distance I found it hard to believe that anything very much had happened or was implied between Elizabeth and myself. This was somehow confirmed by her failure, so far, to ring me up as she'd promised. Perhaps it was the thing in her circle to give one's escort a nice little hug occasionally, it being understood that nothing more serious was to follow; I wouldn't have known about that. It would be a bit of luck if that was the right answer: an affair with Elizabeth would be a bad bet, I felt, in the abstract, in the absence of any marital complications. It was luck, again, not self-restraint, that had stopped similar interests of mine from coming to anything during my five and a bit years of marriage. My desire that they should go on not coming to anything was only approached, not yet matched, by my desire that they should come to something, and something big, and something soon. Well, it wasn't going to happen this time. A pity, really, because I could recall quite well what kissing her had been like.

One shouldn't catch sight of a woman, I thought, unless one intended to marry her. That was the only way to fix things up properly.

The kettle boiled at last. Finding the thought of washing up too nasty for steady contemplation, I decided instead to make myself a cup of tea, my favourite drink. I rinsed out a cup, removing the caked sugar with my finger-nail, then picked up the teapot. This proved to weigh more than it should, more than an empty teapot could. Patiently, I rinsed this out as well. I couldn't remember ever, since getting married, going to make a cup of tea without encountering, at the very outset, a heavy teapot. At last, when I'd spooned out a grain of puffed wheat that must have been buried in the sugar, a cup was ready to drink. I drank it, then refilled my cup.

In the most extraordinary way, I found myself thinking about Elizabeth again, having only a moment before dismissed her from my mind. How reprehensible and pleasant it would have been to make a pass at her, a real one. That I'm not one of those to whom the reprehensible automatically becomes pleasant is one of my firmest beliefs about myself. There was no getting away from it, though: here was a bad thing that I had nevertheless tended to like the thought of. The thought of it now, I said to myself, made Jean seem not to exist, never to have existed, sort of; all that was real was the image of Elizabeth, sturdy, supremely determined, smiling with subtle offensiveness. I lifted my cup to my mouth and drank in what I'd better admit was a slow, reverent, nostril-dilating way, wishing Elizabeth was clairvoyant, or had a science-fiction spy cell mounted on the gas cooker, so that she could see the expression on my face.

Immediately I brought out a loud gargling cry. I began giving an incredible imitation of a man whose mouth has been invaded by a swarm of small flies or midges and who now wants to expel them. Spitting, choking, kecking, retching, making a noise at the back of my mouth like one saying "Aagh" to a doctor, I stumbled misty-eyed to the washbasin and began ridding myself of the thousands of tea-leaves I'd taken in with the draught of tea. Each one of them was horrible. Life, that resourceful technician, had administered a typical rebuke.

I decided to wash up after all and started to. Starting to was nasty, and so was continuing to. Both processes had a way of concentrating round me the various imperfections of residence in this house. Perhaps that was really what was bothering me. Wasn't I fussing too much, where in any case was the harm in a spot of the old adultery as long as you didn't take it too seriously, where was the sense of humour I was so keen on vaunting to myself, where was the Lewis who was superior to things like sex, wasn't I letting the ancestral Welsh nonconformist puritanism make a crafty comeback in me after all these years of discredit? It would be nice to lay one's troubles at the door of John Calvin, the noted French reformer and theologian. But it wouldn't really stand up, none of it would. Others might find my problem no more than a trigger for uncontrollable laughter but, nonconformism or no nonconformism, not me, not just laughter. And there was another thing. Wasn't this mood, this depression plus what-have-you, this unsettled feeling, starting to invade the time I spent with Jean as well as occupying my absences from her? This thought was the most unpalatable I'd had that evening, and so when, a moment later, I heard her step on the stairs I hurried out of the kitchen and put my arms round her.

"Christ, here's lover-boy pitched up all of a sudden," she said, smiling.

"Just glad to see you back, that's all. You haven't been more than twice as long as you said. How was Mrs. J.?"

Jean peered into the kitchen. "Been washing up too,

have you? Well done. Oh, she wasn't too good. Apparently Ieuan's managed to convince himself he's not going to get the job."

I backed away from her, striking my bottom on the corner of the table. "The bloody fool," I said, so angrily that she stared at me.

NINE

"When in time's double morning, meaning death,
Denial's four-eyed bird, that Petrine cock,
Crew junction down the sleepers of the breath,
Iron bled that dry tree at the place of rock,
The son of dog snarled at the rat of love,
Holy-in-corner of the tottered sky,
Where angel tiered on angle swung above,
Into each crack and crick and creek of eye,
Angels on horseback wept with vinegar . . ."

The speaker was a small man with the largest head I'd seen for many a long year. The programme said he was representing a character called The Monk, and he wore a kind of brown dressing-gown with cape or hood which reminded me of the outer garment worn by the members of the *Gorsedd*, or bardic council, at *Eisteddfodau*. I hoped for Elizabeth's sake that his costume was as authentic as possible. Standing there now on the corner of the stage under a yellow spotlight, he went on much as before.

The performance of *The Martyr*, verse drama in two acts by Gareth Probert, was getting into something I didn't want it to get into: its stride. Enough material had been presented for me to have a shot at working out what was supposed to be going on. A few moments of whimsical prose at the beginning had hinted that the protagonist, The Martyr himself, had done something, that other people intended to do something to him because of what he'd done, and that The Monk didn't want them to do it. Apart from this there were various linguistic clues, and I felt myself on safe ground in inferring that the whole business was rather on the symbolical side. Words like 'death' and 'life' and 'love' and 'man' cropped up every few lines, but were never attached to anything concrete or specific. 'Death', for example, wasn't my death or your death or his death or her death or our death or their death or my Aunt Fanny's death, but just death, and in the same way 'love' wasn't my, etc., love and wasn't love of one person for another or love of God or love of blackcurrant purée either, but just love. There were also bits from the Bible turned back to front ("In the word was the beginning" and so on), and bits of daring jargon ("No hawkers, circulars or saints", "Dai Christ"). Dear, dear, the thing was symbolical all right.

I thought next of how horrible it was that the play would be such a success, or, which was the same thing, would be called a success by all who might hear of it. Jean, if she hadn't done so already, would no doubt refer to it as 'old-fashioned' (her term for any setting earlier than about 1930, the year of her birth), and plenty of other people would be ready to condemn it in some such fashion, but not out loud, because it was in verse, and if anyone didn't mind condemning verse plays out loud their tongue would stick to the roof of their mouth when they remembered that it was a play by a Welshman about Wales and performed by Welshmen in Wales and therefore redolent of the spirit of Wales. What a disgrace it was, what a reproach to all Welshmen, that so many of the articulate parts of their culture should be invalidated by awful sentimental lying. All those phony novels and stories about the wry rhetorical wisdom of poetical miners, all those boring myths about the wonder and the glory and the terror of life in the valley towns, all those canonisations of literary dead-beats, charlatans and flops—all this in a part of the world where there was enough material to keep a hundred honest poets and novelists chained to the typewriter. And then, as if Goebbels were to have lamented the decay of personal truthfulness in the Third Reich, you got chaps with the emetic impertinence to complain that Welsh culture was declining. If stuff like *The Martyr* represented Welsh culture, then the sooner it shut up the better.

I looked round the audience, laudably silent and immobile on the hard chairs of the Glendower Hall, and wondered how many of them would or could give a correct account of why they were here. Could I, incidentally, give a correct account of why I was here? Any such account would have to start, and perhaps end as well, with a consideration of the person sitting next to me: dear old Elizabeth Gruffydd-Williams.

I moved a little closer to her. She was a very nice sort of person to be sitting next to, even in the Glendower Hall, though without having to strain my imagination perceptibly I found I could quite easily think up alternative and still more rewarding postures we might perhaps get into some time. More than once already I'd found my arm, as if demoniacally possessed all on its own, getting ready to move round her shoulders. I made it go back, but I could tell it didn't want to. There were plenty of reasons, some of them perfectly harmless, why she and I should console ourselves for the thinness of the entertainment in the traditional way, but I knew they wouldn't appeal to her, or, being a woman, she'd pretend they didn't. Of course, there were one or two reasons on the other side as well, like the presence nearby of so many people who must know who she was. And then there was the old one about her being another fellow's wife and me being another young lady's husband—but that wouldn't apply, would it, to a little cuddle during a play? Only be like an evening in the back row of the two-and-threes, wouldn't it? I pressed my knee firmly against hers. After a fitting interval, and as if quite independently of my action, she shifted in her seat and moved her knee away. It wasn't, I said to myself, that she didn't like my knee— that wasn't it at all. It was just that she wanted to give her full attention to the show, see?

Right from the time yesterday morning when she'd made one of her top-speed phone-calls to me at the Library, and reminded me of my 'promise' to come and see this play with her, I'd suspected it would be a waste of time to come; I'd heard and seen nothing at all of her for the previous ten days. It had been arranged, exactly how I was no longer sure, that since the baby-minding problem was unchanged Jean was to come here to-morrow night, together with Whetstone, the dentist and the dentist's mistress, and that Elizabeth and I were to turn up to-night, together with nobody at all. Perhaps it was this last fact which had made me agree to the proposal with some eagerness after all. Well, she couldn't be seen in public without a man, all the others were in the play or other-wise booked, so here I was just watching the play, a punishment deserved in all manner of ways. That ought to teach me.

I watched the play. Action had been introduced into it: The Monk had finished speaking and, supporting a woman (known for the purposes of the play as The Woman) who sounded as if she was crying, left the scene. A very long pause followed, no doubt in the interests of theatrical effectiveness; then one of the two people left on the stage slowly turned his head to stare at his companion. After a sufficient display of equanimity on both sides, the first man began a long speech (how could he remember it all?) about a red-eyed wolf-priest, a bone-house, a grave truth and unable Abel. The high-pitched Welsh histrionic monotone resounded from the low ceiling and the poster-covered walls, multiplied itself under the boarded-up balcony, and fell silent as the second man, with the steadiness and stealth of one on whose wrist a wasp has settled, raised one arm above his head. Some other men, all dressed alike, came hurrying in. They seemed unprepared for finding themselves on the stage.

"All finished and done with, then, is it?" one of them asked.

"Yes. It is finished."

"Glad I am to hear that, captain."

"But who are you?"

"What, don't you know me?"

"What, don't you know him?"

"Little Bowen Thomas?"

"But, Bowen *bach*, they buried you at batlight in a dead winter. Deep, deep they buried you under the woman's hair of grass, you and your wound, the night Menna Pugh's fancy man from Tenby gave her four rum-and-peps and a packet of twenty and showed her the seaman's way, and never a thought for you, poor little Bowen."

"But where was I?"

"Where was he?"

"I was Bowen Thomas, tailor of Llados."

"Who was I?"

"Who was he?"

"I was talking a mouthful of grass under the still hornbeam."

"Amen, is it? R.I.P., right?"

"Aren't you getting a bit fed up with all this?"

The last speaker was Elizabeth. Her utterance, than which none in the whole semantic field could have incited me to a more profound assent, was delivered in a whisper so close to my ear that I felt her warm breath. How nice she really is, I thought, how good and wise and brave and true. "Yes," I said.

"Come on, then."

I found myself following her from our place in the middle of a row between the line of knees and feet and the line of backs of heads. I knocked against a lot of the knees, trod on several of the feet, and without consciously willing it managed to deal almost every head a sharp cuff with my arm. There were sounds of protest, some from afar. "Ssshh," Elizabeth said. A thunderous clank of iron pealed through the hall as she opened a side door. We got outside.

"We need a drink," Elizabeth said when we were in her car, then began disparaging *The Martyr*. Her remarks lacked cohesion or any basis in what those Cambridge chaps used to call critical awareness, but they more than offset this by their violence and, here and there, picturesqueness. I hardly found it necessary to add a word. After a time I said:

"If that's what you think about it, why did you ever get mixed up in it?"

"How do you mean?"

"Well, you had quite a bit to do with the production, didn't you, the costumes and so on? You must have seen some rehearsals."

"Yes, what about it?"

"Well . . . I can't see why you got mixed up in it."

"You've got to support these things, you know."

"I can't see why. And wait a minute: weren't you the one who was telling me what a great poet old Gareth was at that party?"

"Oh, I just did that to cheer him up. The poor sod needs encouraging, after all."

I was silent for a moment, thinking that a stiff dose of discouraging could do nothing but good to that ranting alcoholic grenadier. Then I said: "Walking out of his play won't encourage him much, will it?"

"That's quite different. You must see that."

"By what compulsion must I?"

"What? Stop arguing, can't you?"

We'd now arrived somewhere. I was still under mild sedation from seeing and hearing *The Martyr*, and had barely noticed that our route was taking us to the outskirts of Aberdarcy. Now I saw we were on the strip of gravel between the gates and the façade of the Gruffydd-Williams residence. "What have we come here for?" I asked, getting out of the car.

She gave a quick yap of laughter. "Well, for a drink, I suppose, in the first instance. I thought you'd sooner here than in a pub."

"Yes, I would."

Much of the garden was thickly planted with trees and shrubs, like a mimic jungle for infantry training. I followed Elizabeth past a small copse of rhododendrons and across the paved walk that ran along the front of the house. Here there were plaster urns full of green stuff and at one corner three dolphins linking their tails over a raised ornamental pond. Beyond all question there was a sundial somewhere. The porch light was a lantern of historical design, and there were things that might have been torch-snuffers. All this, instead of hinting that the shade of the poet Pope, strolling back from an inspection of the grotto, might conceivably appear, only made one look nervously round to avoid tripping over any stone rabbits or bearded gnomes with red stocking-caps sitting on toadstools.

Inside the house, which seemed to be deserted, we went up to the first floor and entered what was evidently a small lounge. While Elizabeth got going at a cocktail cabinet mainly constructed of glass and chromium, I thought of all the money that must have been spent on the things in here. The dropsical cheese-like face of a miner stared at me from a large painting, the fellow of the infernal-colliery one downstairs; there was a television set with a gigantic magnifying lens at hand; there was a radiogram obviously capable of dispensing recorded music for several days without attention; there was a curious mirror with cherub-like creatures crawling out of the frame—one, post-horn in hand, seemed to be looked at his reflection (who had chosen *that*?); there were not a few layers of carpet and rug on the floor; there was a marble bust of a nineteenth-century poet whose best-known mistress had cut her throat in a hotel near Aberdarcy station (High Street). I gazed for some moments at these indoor equivalents of the dolphins and torch-snuffers, then felt my role of proletarian spy slip away a little as Elizabeth handed me a drink. It slipped a little further when she took me by the hand and sat me down beside her on an opulent sofa.

We had several drinks and some talk. She was looking very fine, and was improved still further by the air of conscious dignity, co-existing with a slight threat of ludicrousness, which I've noticed before in good-looking women past their first youth. She seemed to be enjoying herself, swigging away at the pink gins, puffing like mad at one gold-tipped black fag after another, doing a fair amount of laughing and wriggling about a bit in her corner of the sofa. I sat there in an easy posture, my arm along the back of the thing some inches from her shoulders, my head lolling comfortably. I was now being the man used to the company of attractive women, the man who accepts without dramatics whatever experience may come his way, but who never strives for anything beyond the bounds of expediency or of self-possession. This being so, it was odd that I had just started to tremble a little bit and to feel, on the whole, like a new boy at a large and prosperous school. "I think I'd better be going," I said.

"Oh, don't be ridiculous, it's only just gone nine, the play won't be over yet. What have you got to get back for?"

"Well . . . nothing special. I just felt I ought to be getting back to Jean, that's all."

"What nonsense. You can stay away from her for a couple of hours, can't you, without giving in to the homing instinct?"

"She's on her own such a lot."

"Oh, come now, don't lay it on. You told me yourself you hardly ever go out."

"I know, but . . . the trouble is I don't seem to see much of her. She's never there. She's up before I am, with the baby, and getting Eira off to school. I usually just have time to have my breakfast and get the bus into town. If I come home for lunch she's usually had hers early and gone to have a rest. She gets very tired, you see. And in the evenings—well, I'm on duty till seven-thirty twice a week, and she's got the washing and things to do. I help her sometimes, but washing isn't a very sociable activity. And she's usually in bed by about half-past nine ready for the next morning. There are the week-ends, but . . ."

"Yes, I see. You must get a bit lonely."

"No, she's the one that's a bit lonely."

"Well, anyway, even if you go now you won't be back before she goes to bed, according to you. Stay and have another, there's plenty of time."

"Yes, thanks, I might as well."

She made no move to get up, but instead put down her glass and began staring at me. I felt as if I'd just been told I'd eaten carrion for tea. Perhaps I had: the pies and ham rolls served at the little café opposite the Library sometimes had a dreadful grey aspect. Anyway, I was queasy. At last she said: "What's eating you?"

I tried not to think of the minute carnivores that might have been living in that last ham roll. "How do you mean?"

"You look like a man with a secret sorrow. What's the matter with you? I've noticed, you often go off like that."

"What? Go off like what?"

"In the middle of a conversation you'll suddenly go quiet, as if you're thinking about something."

"Yes, I sometimes do think."

"You know what I mean. What are you so gloomy about?"

"You've got me all wrong, dear. I'm always full of fun. What you think's me being gloomy's just the sensitivity of my face, see?"

"Oh quite, quite. But I think you ought to . . . you know, have a bash occasionally, let go and enjoy yourself."

"Now you're talking," I said, throwing her cigarette away and getting hold of her. I kissed her energetically for a minute or two, an exercise marked by those frequent rustling changes of position gone in for by people who have the place to themselves. I pushed my hand in between us at chest-level, and that was fine, but then she took her face away from mine and gave me a stare of disturbing intensity, disturbing because it made me afraid that, without really meaning to, and for all my loss of strong-man self-possession, I might laugh. Luckily she soon put her face back where it had come from. When she showed signs of wanting us to stop sitting and to do some lying down instead, and when I was starting to suffer from oxygen-deficiency, I let go of her and stood up. "Well, now I really must be going," I said, though the moment the words were out the prospect rapidly declined in appeal.

She looked up at me from the sofa, shaking her hair back. The eyebrows, no less black than usual, were arched as if in inquiry; the china-like teeth, as usual, showed clenched between the lips; the shoulders and breasts, in a high-necked white blouse, were, though heaving rather, as usual. I examined all this in an attempt to read there whether I should or should not go. It was little use; I might as well have scrutinised a cream bun for moral imperatives or prohibitions. "Don't go, John. Please. Vernon won't be back till late."

The ham roll seemed to fall into the pit of my stomach. "No, I must go." My voice sounded oddly near at hand, as if I was muttering directly into my own ear.

She got up and put her arms round my neck. Wriggling a little, she leaned against me and tried kissing me, as a motorist on a cold morning might abandon the starter button and get going with the handle. I fired on the first swing and very soon we were swaying about, as if a gaucho had got us round the ankles with his lasso or bolas. Then, as I now realised had been fairly probable all along, we went and lay down on the sofa. She put her tongue in my ear, which was noisy and disconcerting and new to me, but which I thought I could learn, given time, to accommodate within my standard practice. Her clothes started getting seriously disarranged. After a little while I said: "Wouldn't this be more fun in the bedroom?"

"I desire you utterly," she said. "I want all your desire."

I smiled mindlessly at her. Her avowal stuck in my mind, and when I was thinking things over afterwards I decided that its embarrassing quality was confined to its stylistics. There was nothing at all wrong with its paraphrasable content; indeed, it was just there that her attraction for me lay, just there that she triumphed utterly over the fairly numerous things about her that repelled me. She was the only girl ever to 'desire' me, whether utterly or not, without a long prelude on my part of arduous and even undignified badgering and pursuit. Nor could I see any prospect, with her, of my having to lay out indefinite reserves of tact and ingratiation in order to stay 'desired'. It was all made easy for me, in other words, and while I agree that a lot of valuable things can't be made easy in that way, one still gets a certain kick out of things that can. Anyway, none of this somehow occurred to me at the time, and all I did was to say, with what might have seemed a rather goatish persistence: "Yes, but wouldn't this be more fun in the bedroom?"

The sound of an approaching car became audible, coming up the drive. I felt as if I'd been suddenly deprived of some salient bodily organ, like heart or lungs. Elizabeth said "Christ" and got up from the sofa. I'd been looking forward to an overall view of her nearly naked, but as things stood I noticed little beyond the general fact. She ran to the window. "Yes, it's him all right. This is going to be bloody marvellous if we're not fairly nippy."

She began dressing with great dexterity and speed while I watched her inattentively, the growing sound of the car in my ears. "Come on," she said, "pull yourself together. You don't look exactly respectable."

Panting a little, unable to hold my mouth closed, I made myself more respectable. The car arrived under the window and had its engine switched off. "What does he want?" I inquired.

"I expect he wants to sell you some oil shares." She was now whipping lipstick on to her mouth. Looking up sharply from her compact-mirror, she said: "For God's sake don't look as if you're going to be shot, and stop that awful panting. Here." She picked up a massively embossed cigarette-box and scattered its contents, twenty or thirty cigarettes, on the floor. "The moment anyone comes up here start picking these up. You can pant as much as you like after that." She snapped the compact shut and hurried out.

One part of my mind listened intently to the sounds from below: footsteps on the stone walk, the front door opening, voices in the hall, Elizabeth's laugh, silence. The other part wanted to find a place, perhaps one of the outer planets of Vega, where life at all levels was transmitted by asexual reproduction. Feet began mounting the stairs; my apathy was pierced; I grovelled on the floor among the cigarettes. Feet approached the door of the lounge; my mouth went drier; I picked up three cigarettes before finding that the box was still on the table. Like a Springbok full-back famed for his deadly tackling, I launched myself at the box from a stooping position and bore it down with me to the ground, crushing the three fags between my fingers. I was burying them in the box under sound ones when the door opened. I looked up to the sound of female laughter.

Elizabeth was alone. She said: "You look wonderful."

"Yes, it's good fun down here."

She gave another laugh, standing with her feet apart and looking full of energy. "The panic's over, old boy. The master of the house has retired to his study."

I put the last cigarettes in the box and stood up. "Ah, that makes everything all right."

"He knows you're here, by the way. He's just got a couple of phone calls to make and then he'll be joining us for a drink and a chat."

"I thought he wasn't supposed to be back till late."

Her high spirits changed a little. "Well actually I was talking a bit at random when I said that. I was so set on making you stay, you see."

"Taking a bit of a risk, weren't you? We'd have looked pretty silly if he'd turned up in ten minutes' time."

"No we shouldn't. We'd already gone as far as we were going when he arrived."

"I don't quite get that."

"I wasn't going to let you take me to bed. Not this time. That would have been too risky."

"What on earth were you up to, then?"

"I just wanted to get you started. It was then or never. I knew if you'd gone when you said, we'd never have got to the point."

I began laughing. "My God, you are the most extra-ordinary . . ."

She moved up to me and stood so that we were nearly

touching. She said quietly, not looking at me: "I wanted to get you to commit yourself. And you've done that now, haven't you?"

I stopped laughing. "Yes, I suppose I have, in a way."

"Give me a kiss, darling."

"Do you mind very much if I don't, just for the time being?"

"Come on, don't be so stuffy. You can't go on behaving like a deacon now."

" Do I ever behave like a deacon? Anyway, your old man's just across the landing."

"We can hear him coming. He's got a tread like a rhinoceros."

"You don't see what I mean. I wouldn't feel too happy about it with him actually in the house."

"But it's all right when he's a couple of miles off, eh?"

"Well no, but it seems sort of worse . . ."

"Now you're being feeble as well as stuffy. What about that kiss?" She stood against me.

A cream-bun addict may resist his darling while it lies in a shop-window, but will rarely refrain from clashing his teeth in it once it is past his lips. I kissed Elizabeth with relish, then said: "I'm going now. Thanks for a nice evening."

"You can't now, it'll look so . . ."

"You can deal with all that, you resourceful little thing. It's getting late. Cheero."

"Give my regards to your wife," she said before I closed the door behind me.

With this parting shaft between my shoulder-blades I hurried down the stairs. Before I reached the bottom I heard footsteps, adequately rhinoceros-like, somewhere close at hand and descending towards me. It was a good few yards to the front door. Without doing much in the way of conscious volition, and uttering a whinnying cry,

I shot through a doorway at the foot of the stairs, slipped on some tiles and came down hard. My whirling arm dislodged innumerable hats belonging to Gruffydd-Williams. An Anthony Eden rebounded from my head; a corduroy cap, a cloth cap, a waterproof cap, a fishing-hat, a beret, a Panama (where did he wear *that*?), a hat made of white mackintosh with large ventilation holes, a velours fell over my arms and back. A bowler, rotating on its brim, sprang away under a washhand-basin. On my knees I turned the key in the lock. Why hadn't the fellow, master of the house or no master of the house, the elementary good taste to stay in his study once there, instead of prowling about the staircase and—as he was now audibly doing—the ground floor? And how long did he think he was going to go on do-ing it?

I replaced the hats, dropping most of them at the first try, then looked round my refuge, which turned out to be a medium-sized closet or cloakroom. It was an acceptable alternative to the Vegan hermitage I'd felt the need of some minutes earlier. I could quite happily pass the remainder of my days in here: meals passed through the window, sanitation at hand, and plenty of coats to make up a snug little pallet-bed. And the door walled up.

TEN

IT WASN'T NEARLY so wonderful in this lavatory, I decided after a few minutes, as it had been in the upstairs one on the night of that party. For one thing, no pictorial embodiment of Gallic wit adorned the wall, only a mirror and the calendar of a steamship line which bore a picture of an unmatronly girl with a matron's bust-measurement. She was grinning. It was terrible to find her here and I told her so, adding that it was all right for her. In my present mood a closer inspection of both her and the mirror was unthinkable. For another thing, somebody with a heavy tread had just tried the handle of the door and gone away again.

A little while later there was the vague noise of a car. With great caution I opened the door and listened. The house was quiet. Right, Lewis, here we go. My hand was an inch or two from the handle of the front door when a fearful buzzing clangour broke out. Someone, having arrived, not departed, by car, was petitioning to be let in. And punctually there sounded, from round a corner of the passage, the tread of a rhinoceros coming to answer the petition.

My hermitage was too far away, on the other side of the hall. I turned rather quickly and hared through another doorway, shutting its door behind me as quickly. Outside I heard a great cry of greeting and welcome, footsteps entering the hall, and a falsetto laugh mingling with Gruffydd-Williams's ergh-ergh-ergh-ergh: Paul Whetstone was unmistakably of the company. I waited for the uproar to recede up the stairs, but it didn't do that; it moved nearer the door I'd just come through. Beginning to wish I'd had that drink with Elizabeth and waited for that chat with Gruffydd-Williams, I crossed the room, which was the one where the recent party had been held, and lay down behind an old but comfortable-looking leather sofa.

The door opened and several persons came in, all talking at once. Whetstone's laugh was raised again, but this time, for a change, it swooped precariously into the bass register.

"Well, yes, an excellent suggestion, Paulie, but I rather doubt whether . . ." (Gruffydd-Williams.)

"Hope you don't mind, but we certainly needed one, so we just thought we'd see whether . . ." (An unidentified man.)

"One or two minor criticisms, but on the whole the main intentions came over better than I'd . . ." (Probert.)

"Barging in on you like this. We're not interrupting anything, I hope?" (A woman.)

"Well, that librarian fellow of Elizabeth's was here just now, but I rather fancy he's cleared off." (Gruffydd-Williams.)

Whetstone laughed again while the unidentified man said: "Oh, that chap."

There was a pause during which Whetstone's laugh trailed off, then Gruffydd-Williams said: "Yes. That chap."

After a short silence, they all began talking at once again. I heard Gruffydd-Williams say something about if it was a drink they were after, and then something about joining Elizabeth. They trooped out.

When all was quiet I got up, wincing as a smart report came from each of my knee-caps. I had much food for reflexion, but thought I should defer this. There was a door on the far side of the room which must lead, directly or indirectly, to the kitchen and back door—a far more attractive escape-route than the one at the front.

In a moment I found myself in what in fact was the kitchen. In it I met a man I'd never seen before and who must have come in by way of the passage. He looked interrogatively at me.

"Good-evening, then," I said in my deepest Cwmhyfryd accent, and, limping to the sink, turned on both taps. Water came out of each. "Ah, running nicely now, see? You shouldn't have any more trouble. Just let us know, like, if you get any more stoppages, is it? An airlock it was."

"Oh, right you are," he said. He was taking some

glasses out of a compartment of the dresser, but still paying a good deal of attention to me. He looked like a bust of Caligula I'd once seen.

I observed the flow from the taps for some time, experimentally turning them off and on and muttering to myself, waiting for the other to go so that I could check in solitude which of three possible doors led directly to God's good air. He opened several other cupboards and peered inside, but kept glancing at me, each time for a longer period. I'd have to make a move.

"Seems okay now," I said briskly, shuffling across to the middle of the three doors and cursing the lack of windows hereabouts which deprived me of a clue. "*Nos-da.*" I opened the door and was confronted by brooms, dust-pans and the great iron phallus of a hot-water tank. I put my hand on this. "Warming up lovely," I said, shut the door, opened the one on the left and found myself at the foot of some stairs. This would have to do for now; he'd be out of the kitchen in a moment. I shut myself in and waited.

It was in fact only a moment before I heard him go out to the passage and give a great bawl of "Elizabeth".

About this time, I suppose, I must have begun gradually relinquishing any rational grasp of the situation. There was really nothing to stop me from re-emerging into the view of the chap who looked like the bust of Caligula and, with another cheery "*Nos-da*", going out through the only remaining possible door. But I could no longer believe that that door really was possible. Why shouldn't it lead to a lift or a menagerie? How could I be sure it didn't? I couldn't, and so I waited while the man bawled that he couldn't find any lime juice anywhere and until Elizabeth's high heels came tapping over the tiles. "If you want anything done, do it your bloody self," I heard her say, then: "Didn't occur to you to look in here, I suppose?"

"I say, I'm terribly sorry I've made a nonsense and got you down for nothing, Lizzie dear."

"Let it go. Well, that's all, isn't it?"

"I say, Lizzie, there was the most peculiar plumber laddie in here a moment ago. Looked rather a sinister type to me, I must say. He said he'd finished and everything was warming up lovely, or some such locution. I hope I did right to let him go."

After a short silence, Elizabeth said: "Oh yes, that's right. He's gone now, you say?"

"Well, so I rather assumed. He went out of that door, I seem to recall."

"That door? Oh yes. He must have gone up to have a look at the . . . tank thing up there."

"But, Lizzie dear, I saw him look at a tank thing down here."

"There's more than one tank in a house, you know, Theo."

"Well, not being a householder, dear, I wouldn't know, but of course you would. Shall we go?"

"You go on up, Theo. I want to have a word with him before he packs up."

"As you say."

In a moment or two Elizabeth opened my door. "Hallo," I said.

She started violently. "I thought it was you, you bloody fool. What the hell do you think you're playing at?"

"Nothing, I got sort of caught before I could get away."

"How do you mean, sort of caught? Eh?"

Slowly doubling up, I began to laugh. "I got behind the sofa when they—owch, owch, owch. They said they—owch, owch, owch."

"Shut up for God's sake." Some distance away there was a small tinkling crash and a cry. "You'd better get out of here."

"Owch, owch, owch."

"Lizzie dear, I'm terribly sorry but I'm afraid I've made another nonsense." The Caligula man's voice approached down the passage. "Have you got a dustpan? I think I remember seeing one somewhere."

I don't know what it was that possessed me to say, when the man appeared, "All right, missis, I'll see to it right away now," and to retreat up the stairs. Anyway, I did it, and in another second or two I was racing from the back regions of the first floor towards the front stairs. Nothing would stop me now, I thought, until I saw the door of the lounge beginning to open. I turned in my stride like a man stepping on a high-tension cable and sped on tiptoe through a convenient open doorway.

I hid behind the door for what must have been five minutes or so until all was quiet again, or rather until all the noise was concentrated in the lounge. I trembled slightly, yawned a great deal and felt hungry and light-headed. I could think of no valid reason for doing or for not doing anything. The room, I discovered, had traces only of feminine occupation and, to judge by articles of clothing lying about and open pots of cosmetics on the dressing-table, was in current use. Did that mean that Elizabeth wasn't sleeping with Gruffydd-Williams these days? The query meant little to me. I opened a cupboard or two. Elizabeth seemed to have a lot of clothes. I found the black costume she'd been wearing the first time I met her, and smiled at it. Another cupboard had things in it that no sane woman would wear in public. I realised after a while that these were theatrical costumes. One of them was the complete outfit of traditional Welshwoman's dress (antique English really, but taken up and stylised by the Welsh): red jacket kind of effort, long black skirt, witch bonnet and the rest of it. Giggling slightly to myself, I began putting it on over my clothes.

The effect, when I looked at myself in the long mirror, wasn't at all bad. I'm pretty slim and by leaving one or two things undone I made a quite plausible picture, especially with a blonde wig with pigtails on my head. The shoes were impossible, but the skirt was very long and almost hid my trouser-legs. This was the guise in which to leave the house. A fluted "*Dim Saesneg*" ("No English") would answer all questions. I giggled again and began to feel much better, regretting only that I couldn't very well walk into the lounge like this and confront them all. Elizabeth, and perhaps some of the others, would have a fit. What instinct had led me to the only therapy which would make me feel ready to face the outside world again? Well, joke over; I'd soon have these farcical garments off and be downstairs and out in half a minute. It must be quite late and I mustn't miss the last bus to Cwmhyfryd.

A clamour abruptly broke out in the room next door, consisting of thumping, trampling, affected yells of pain and Whetstone's laugh. Somebody snatched at the handle of the lounge door and burst on to the landing. Somebody else followed immediately and there was a panting, squealing struggle that seemed to be moving slowly towards the threshold of the room where I was. I got on to the window-seat and drew the curtains across to hide myself. "You will, you know," Whetstone's voice whinnied, tremulous with excitement. "I'll bloody well make you, I promise you." The door flew open and, through a chink in the curtains, I saw Whetstone and Theo, the Caligula man, spin into view and stagger, wrestling fiercely, towards the bed. Shouts of applause and encouragement came from the doorway. I heard Elizabeth laughing. A heave from Theo, who seemed stronger than he'd looked, brought the pair of them thumping and bouncing along the wall towards the window.

I acted quickly. At any moment they might collapse against the curtains and reveal me. I didn't want that. The window was open and I took a brief look down. It was pretty dark but I could see grass or earth below, not so very far below either. Climbing out was unexpectedly easy; any noises I made were well smothered by Theo, who was squealing again. Should I perhaps hang here until things were back to normal? No. I let myself go and landed almost without jolt or sound on soft earth. Liberty at last and, by God, Lewis, you've earned it.

I rested for a little while, then crept round to the front of the house. The mimic jungle would make a splendid place to take off my costume. My bonnet had fallen off in my descent but I'd retrieved it and put it under my arm; it would be a pity to spoil the *ensemble*.

I'd just found a good shrub when the front door opened and Theo came rushing out, pursued by Whetstone. They seemed to be coming straight for me. What lay beyond me was too thickly overgrown to penetrate, even without a skirt on, and the drive was at my side. In a few seconds I was out of the gates and pounding off down the hill, still clutching the bonnet.

Those who've never run far in a long skirt and a wig, especially one with pigtails, can take it from me that you get hot doing it. And I was bothered too, but I kept running until I'd covered perhaps half the mile between the house and my nearest bus-stop. I saw nobody, which was welcome enough in one way, but suggested that the pubs had been shut long enough to give local drinkers time to walk home. This in turn meant that my last bus might go at any moment, if indeed it hadn't gone already. But I must get my disguise off before I got to the more populous areas round the bus-stop. I trotted on for a bit, looking for a likely spot, but none seemed directly inviting. The street-lamps were bright and most houses had some lights on. At last, just before the last block that curved round to the Cwmhyfryd road, I got to a small patch of waste ground that seemed just the job. It was in front of the gates of a timber-yard that lay back from the road and there was a good depth of shadow. I moved in.

I was at one corner of the gates, quite well hidden, and fumbling with the fastenings of my skirt when a policeman came round the other corner and shone his torch on the fastening of the gates. Some of the light shone on me. I closed the press-stud I'd pulled open and walked, with what I hoped was a feminine gait, back on to the footpath. The torch swung round after me, and then without hurry, only in a checking-up spirit most likely, its owner started following me.

I had a few seconds' grace just round the curve of the houses and used it to fold up my trouser-cuffs a couple of turns. Feeling rather frightened, I walked on. Was it my fancy that the policeman had sharpened his pace? I had an idea that female impersonation was sourly regarded in police-courts. I could see the report already in the *News of the World*: 'LIBRARIAN SENTENCED'— then 'John Aneurin Lewis, 26, said to be a librarian, was sentenced . . . when charged, Lewis said: "Oh, can't you overlook it this once?" . . . stated that Lewis had been under strain . . . had thrown away the advantages of a good education . . . wife had promised to stick by him . . . very sorry for what he had done . . . had learned his lesson, but . . . six months' imprisonment, as stated.'

These fancies brought me to the bus-stop at last. There was a fair crowd there, all of whom turned to stare at me. Almost at once a bus appeared. The policeman was still there in the background. I got on the bus. Holding my skirts aloft with what at another time I'd have considered impressive skill, I went upstairs. None of the double seats had both places vacant. I sat down at the back next to a man in rough clothes who seemed to be asleep, and put my bonnet on. It would help to hide the wig, which under a good light was unlikely to be very convincing, and would establish quite certainly what I was, or rather what I was supposed to be. An old woman with glasses in the seat in front turned round, smiled rather charmingly at me, and addressed me in the language of my forefathers.

Pretending to be deaf would probably have been my best bet at this point, but I didn't think of that. Aware that some slight paradox was inherent in my doing so, I told the woman, in the tongue of the Saxon invader and exploiter, that I couldn't speak any Welsh. The voice I adopted for getting this across, however, did me great credit: I had the forethought to pitch my ordinary voice well up instead of relying on piping away in falsetto, where control's likely to be poor. I was so pleased at having thought of this that I started feeling more cheerful than at any time since jumping out of the window. A few stares had come my way since I'd boarded the bus, but these were dying down now. And in a quarter of an hour or so I'd be off, making like a whippet for a lovely field full of bushes that lay just fifty yards from my stop in Cwmhyfryd.

The old woman's smile had faded and she remained silent. She was probably a farmer's wife from Denbighshire and thus isolated from the great English-speaking community of the free world. In a moment, having determined that I'd indeed been speaking in English, she'd say "*Dim Saesneg*" and that would be that. What she did say was: "You're an impostor."

"How do you make that out?" I said, unguardedly letting my voice drop in pitch and at the same time crossing my arms in front of me as I remembered that my chest was unpadded.

"Wearing those clothes. You're nothing but an impostor."

"I'm not, honestly. I know my hair looks funny—it's these soapless shampoos."

"Of course you are," she said, raising her voice alarmingly. "Pretending to be what you're not, isn't that being an impostor? I'd like to know what being an impostor is if it isn't that."

"Madam, you're mistaken. I resent your insinuations very much."

"Great impertinence you have to dress like that in the national dress of your country and not being able to speak its language."

"Oh, that. Oh yes. I'm sorry."

"It's not enough to be sorry. Ashamed you should be. And may I ask where you've been, dressed up like that?"

"I've only been to a party."

"A party, is it? Treating your national costume as a fancy dress. It's a disgrace indeed." With a violent movement she turned her head and shoulders away from me.

"But I played my harp there," I chirped, anxious for some reason to restore good-will.

"And a bloody good job you made of it too, sweetheart, I bet," the man in rough clothes, roused by these exchanges, said as he laid a blue-scarred hand on my knee.

"Would you kindly not do that?" I said, feeling all at once very terrible.

"Aw, up-bloody-stage, eh? Well, I'll tell you this," he said, smacking my knee for emphasis, "it's a bloody poor look-out when a man pays a lady a civil compliment and she turns round on him like a bloody pickpocket. I've been a labouring man all my life and I've seen a good many bloody changes in one way and another. But you're mistaken if you think I'm going to be put off by . . . always know where I'm not wanted." He took his hand off my knee and seemed to fall asleep again instantaneously.

This change of heart was perhaps traceable to the

132

arrival of the conductor, who now stood at my side to demand fares. He was a tall, round-shouldered young man with a faint moustache, regularly on the route and well known to me; at slack periods we'd sometimes exchanged comment on the inability of Aberdarcy Town to find a decent pair of full-backs. My chance of passing myself off to him as a female harpist was something less than good, especially since he was neither drunk, like the life-long labouring man probably was, nor shortsighted, like the bespectacled cultural nationalist probably was. More especially still, he could hardly fail to appreciate my next action, which was fated to be the rolling-up of my skirt and the extraction of money from my trousers pocket. Keeping my head well down I performed this action, twitching my shoulders about and making my arms tremble to suggest eccentricity. There was no reason why an old woman should refrain from wearing a pair of man's trousers under her skirt if she felt like it. Without raising my head I tried to make it catch the light, so that my wig should be recognised as such and deemed a further proof of slight mental imbalance. I gave the conductor the money without looking at him.

After a long pause I heard him turn his handle and tear off my ticket. This he pressed into my hand, closing my fingers over it and saying: "Thanks, mate. I'll look out for you on the telly."

While the labouring man was being roused and canvassed for his fare, I was feeling full of gratitude for the conductor's forbearance. The next time I chatted to him I'd defer to all his views, assent to all his proposed reforms and even praise his sagacity in suggesting what I usually disparaged as impracticable and doctrinaire: the use of the stopper centre-half.

The labouring man, perhaps exhausted by his farepaying efforts, which had been prolonged and spectacular, molested me no more; he even seemed to fall asleep again. The Welsh-speaking lady gave us a disgusted glare as she got out, unfairly suggesting that he and I were in some important respect two of a kind, and she didn't mean that we were both men. My stop soon approached; I got downstairs without giving noticeable offence. While I waited on the platform the conductor discussed me with a colleague being run home. The colleague proved to be Mr. Davies, whom I often saw on the last bus and sometimes walked to our house with. That wouldn't happen to-night.

I let Mr. Davies get off before me and strolled towards the field I'd marked down for a changing-room. Before shinning over the wall I looked round to see that nobody was watching. Somebody was: a man who, though moving irregularly, was making quite a fair speed in my direction. He waved to me and called: "Hallo there, sweetheart. Want some company?" He now broke into a run.

I tossed my bonnet over the wall and made the best speed I could after it. This wasn't nearly such a good speed as I'd hoped and was easily beaten by the labouring man, who despite his allegedly lengthy experience of life made a creditable vault and landed beside me before I could even snatch off my wig. He caught me by the arm, then round the waist, saying: "Ah, you don't get away from me as easy as that, sweetheart."

I gave him quite a hefty punch in the chin and he staggered, tripped up and sat down hard. I ran a stride or two, then, in the grip of some imbecile impulse of loyalty, returned and gathered my bonnet. By the time I was off again the man was getting to his feet. Needing both hands free I jammed the bonnet hard down over the crown of my wig and sprinted with lifted skirts for a place where the wall had lost its top few rows of bricks. I was over in a bound and pelted off down the road. A voice behind me called: "You're no bloody woman, you aren't. I'll show you, I'll bloody fix you." The man was no more than ten yards behind.

The pair of us ran down the main street of Cwmhyfryd where the shops are, a matter of two or three hundred yards. The corner of my street lay just ahead. I glanced over my shoulder and saw that the man hadn't lost an inch. That settled it: I must get indoors at all costs. Another half-minute should do it.

Rounding the corner I immediately caught sight of Mr. Davies just approaching the house. I managed to find my key and passed him at the gate. He gave a shout of what may well have been surprise and alarm. I lost my balance and dropped the key. The labouring man arrived and darted towards me.

"Here, here, what's going on?" Mr. Davies bawled, grabbing the other by the arm.

"I'll knock his bloody block off," the man yelled pantingly.

"It's me, Mr. Davies, me, John Lewis from upstairs."

"Now get away, you, till we sort this out."

"Let me get at him, I'll break his bloody . . ."

Mr. Davies, dependable as his son, kicked the man hard on the shins and said: "But Mr. Lewis, what are you doing all dressed up like that, for Christ's sake?"

I gulped for breath. "Been to a fancy-dress party, hadn't time to change, bus . . ."

"Now you just clear off, whoever you are, unless you want both of us on to you," Mr. Davies said to the man. "I know your sort."

The man walked waveringly across the road and sat down with his back against the wall while Mr. Davies said to me: "Nasty customer that, know him by sight. What happened?"

I explained briefly and Mr. Davies nodded at salient points: "Mm . . . yes . . . I know . . . bloody awkward, of course. Well, we'd better get in before the women come out and fetch us." Several lights had come on in the house since the shouting began. "Don't want a confabulation on the doorstep, do we? You'll want to get that clobber off, too." He seemed to be repressing a laugh.

"Thanks very much for what you did just now, Mr. Davies."

"Pleasure, man."

We looked across the road, but the labouring man had gone. "Nasty customer, that," Mr. Davies said, handing me my key.

Opening the front door I nearly knocked Mrs. Davies down. I had the pleasure of saying good evening to her and getting, for once, no reply. As I went upstairs, it occurred to me that, despite her, I owed a sizeable debt of gratitude to the Davies family. One of these days I would try to repay it.

ELEVEN

"WHAT SHALL I do with this, Mr. Lewis?" Dilys Jones asked.

It was a large book on the history of costume, the property, as I saw from the slip inside, of the people of Wandsworth. After a moment I recognised it as the one Elizabeth had borrowed in order to authenticate the costumes of *The Martyr*. My recognition was delayed by the absence of the dust-jacket. "Where did you find this, Dilys?"

"That lady give it to me. You know, the one who was rude to me before."

"I know. Was she rude this time?"

"Nothing to shout about. She just came into Reference and give it to me. I asked her about the ticket and she said to throw it away, thank you, and then she stalked out, like."

"Mm. She didn't leave any message, I suppose?"

"No, nothing at all, Mr. Lewis. Should she have, then?"

"No, I just wondered, that's all. Okay, Dilys, I'll see to it."

Not knowing that seeing to this involved nothing more arduous than walking a few yards and literally dropping it into Ieuan Jenkins's lap, Dilys gave me a grateful and possibly admiring smile. I felt I could do with everything in that line that came my way these days, and as I got up from my table I pursed my lips and knotted my brow and so on to suggest the complexity of my task. Mucking about like this, though, wasn't as much fun as it had been in the old days. As I hurried out of the Lending Department and round an old bitch stuck becalmed at the top of the main steps and off down the echoing corridor I was feeling just a wee bit fed up, you know, about Elizabeth's failure to come and see ME on her visit to the Library, which seemed to follow up rather nastily her typical failure to ring me up here since the transvestist incident last week. Was I being dropped? Had my refusal to stay for that drink and chat, or my plumber-impersonation, alienated her? Well, I ought to feel relieved if this was so, but somehow I just felt just a wee bit fed up, you know.

Jenkins was in the cataloguing-room, to all appearance asleep, and leaning back in his chair to expose a lap clad in dark-grey multiple-store trousering. I dealt with the book as foreshadowed above. He opened his eyes and smiled lethargically, then plucked up the book as if it was burning him. "What's this? What's this?" When I explained, he nodded several times and said: "There's a fine on it, I see. And what has happened to the jacket, do you suppose?"

"It's all right, I'll pay the fine," I said. "And . . . I don't remember there being any jacket."

"Indeed there was a jacket, John, pardon me. I recall it most distinctly, boy. What's to be done about it, that's the question. It would be quite irregular, of course, for you to pay the fine. Not that I mind that exactly, you understand, but I think that woman ought to . . ." He seemed to have been attending less and less to what he was saying, and now his voice trailed off, his thick dark lips drooped, his hand smoothed convulsively at his grey crop as he turned away. "But then she's a friend of yours, isn't she? so I suppose that doesn't apply."

"I'm afraid I don't quite follow you," I said, turning against him one of his best-loved idioms.

His eyes flicked to my face and away again. They looked fairly unhappy. "Mind you, this is no business of mine," he muttered, "but I had heard, from a source I should prefer not to name, that you were seeing a good deal of the Gruffydd-Williamses."

This use of the plural was less bad. "Well, a little, you know. I don't think I'd say a good deal. What about it, anyway?"

Jenkins hesitated; he was going through one of his token struggles with reticence and caution. "I hope you don't resent my mentioning this, John."

"No, of course not. You go ahead."

"Things have been rather on my mind."

"Quite understandable."

Suddenly abandoning these vamp-till-ready gestures (which I thought sounded much more like me than him) Jenkins plunged into the refrain: "You know, John, that I'm in fairly close touch with the Council?"

"Yes." This fairly close touch, publicised by Jenkins almost daily, was a hyperbole, or perhaps a euphemism, for his relations with a chicaning and tattling old alderman who enjoyed beating him hollow at snooker at the Labour Club and then filling up the void with usually quite fribbling morsels of local-government gossip. Jenkins in his turn enjoyed disgorging these in front of me. Somewhere in him there was a man who admired and wanted power, the one aspect of him I had anything less than affection for.

"Well, I gather from a very reputable source that our friend Gruffydd-Williams has been taking an interest in your career. Going by what I heard, it wouldn't surprise me in the least if he decided to throw his influence behind you in the matter of the forthcoming election."

While Jenkins paused, perhaps to review the propriety of an *influence* being said to be *thrown behind* a person, I exulted for a moment. Then I glimpsed the factors making against exultation. I said: "I see."

Jenkins had turned his lustrous gaze full upon me. "Now I'm not reproaching you, John boy, but doesn't that seem to you to savour of . . . well, of log-rolling, shall I term it?"

"You're way off the beam, Ieuan," I said. Somehow phrases like this always, and only, occurred to me when with Jenkins.

"I beg your pardon?"

"I mean you've got quite the wrong idea." I was going to add that Gruffydd-Williams and I had never even discussed the business, but remembered our conversation at that party. "I've hardly ever spoken to the man. You surely don't think I've been trying to push . . ."

"No no, you mistake my meaning, boy. I know you too well to entertain the slightest suspicion of your integrity; that's not my implication at all, no indeed. I was merely remarking that it was unfortunate that some people in high places, so to call them, may throw . . . may use their influence to benefit their friends in such matters. They . . ."

"But look here, Ieuan, I'm not a friend of this chap, he doesn't know me, he just about knows of me. I've only met him once."

"Then how do you account for my information?"

"Your mate must be bloody well dreaming, I should imagine," I said without much conviction.

"I think not," Jenkins said, sniffing. "I think not. Isn't it all of a piece with what we know about the practices of municipal politicians? We've discussed this many a time, John. How often have the two of us agreed with the truth of Lord Acton's dictum that power corrupts? We can see it happening all around us to-day on a national scale, in the Trade Unions and elsewhere. A bad example's being set at the top. And followed very readily lower down. Our system, in this country as well as in England, is chronically corrupt. That's agreed between us."

I could see all manner of logical flaws, especially that of irrelevance, in Jenkins's oration, and yet he was managing to make me feel voluntarily implicated in this chronically-corrupt business of his. I also felt responsible for the growing agitation of his manner. So what was the point of asking him what I ought to do, whether I ought to plead with Gruffydd-Williams to queer my chances, how I could help people in high places knowing my name? All I wanted to say was: "Yes, you're quite right." I said it.

Jenkins nodded, abstractedly flipping over the pages of the book on costume. He gazed for some time at a picture of an evil-looking jester capering idiotically about, then said slowly: "To tell you the truth, John, I'm rather surprised that you have any acquaintance of any sort with people like that."

"You disapprove, do you?"

"I have no right either to approve or disapprove, as you know. It merely seems to me that they are not your sort, or you are not their sort, whichever you prefer." He slammed the book shut and threw it down on his table, where it capsized a packet of paper-clips, and his agitation returned. He lifted his fist. "Who can be relied upon? Where is there any loyalty left, any . . . any trust?" His voice trembled. "What's happened to common decency?" His fist crashed down. "Finished. All finished."

Next Sunday at 6.30 p.m., I thought to myself, MR. I. A. JENKINS, B.A., will speak on MAN WITHOUT GOD. All are welcome. Thinking this disposed of Jenkins's stylistics, but, just as with Elizabeth's desire-you-utterly avowal, the general drift retained much of its effect. I roused myself and spoke quickly: "Now listen, Ieuan, you're worrying unnecessarily, see? My father's known your alderman pal for years and he's got his number, I mean he understands him perfectly. The old boy's just trying to take a rise out of you, that's all. Probably these fellows have been chatting it over and Gruffydd-Williams happened to say he'd met me. No more to it than that. You know how these things get exaggerated."

"Yes yes." Sighing, Jenkins screwed up his eyes and pinched at the bridge of his nose. "I'm seeing things all out of proportion these days. Don't know what's the matter with me."

"Oh, we're all of us neurotics here, and bloody good luck to us, I say."

"I'm sorry, John. I shouldn't have said what I did."

"Rubbish, it's got it off your chest." And on to mine, I said to myself. Ah, Lewis, what a crazy old moralist you are, loading your chest up with this and all the time you're carrying the sins of the world on those stock-size shoulders of yours. Now you're all set for bags of fun deciding just how you can distil the tastiest guilt from this situation. God go with you, my boy.

"I owe you an apology," Jenkins was chuntering on.

"You will if you get that job instead of me, *wus.* Now how much is that fine? I'll get the money off her if that'll put the books straight. And I'll ask about the jacket next time I get together with them to do a bit of log-rolling."

As I was leaving, Jenkins, cheerful again, suddenly handed me a piece of paper which he described as my pigeon. I walked back along the corridor trying to puzzle out whether this description was accurate. What he'd actually given me was a sheet hastily torn from a pad bearing a few ill-written lines in green ink. Without formality the writer announced that he was thinking of emigrating to the Argentine, would like the recipient of his note to look out some books about that region and would call in to fetch them 'in due course'. He'd be writing again 'before very long' and signed himself 'L. S. Caton'.

I crumpled all this up and threw it down the main steps into the street. Next, I showed a man of seafaring appearance, who said he'd like to look up something in a medical dictionary, the door into the Reference Department. This good office discharged, I went back to the Lending Department and told Webster, the Sub-Librarian, that since it was four minutes after the end of my statutory spell of duty I was going home now.

Home, however, was just where I wasn't going, at least not at once. I was beginning to get into the habit of dropping in at a pub on my way to the bus-stop and throwing down a couple of beers before I got on my way.

It was a nice evening, and the rush-hour crowds gave everything a look of pleasant animation. I reflected briefly and to little effect on Jenkins's report about Gruffydd-Williams and his alleged readiness to roll logs on my behalf. If there was, as theoretically there ought to be, comfort in the thought that I couldn't myself influence the outcome of whatever was going on there, why did

I feel that I'd done Jenkins a bad turn and was shortly about to do him another? This feeling remained undispelled when I ordered myself to believe that Jenkins's chicaning tattler really was tattling through his hat. It was almost as if I didn't want Webster's job after all, wasn't it?

I entered the pub. For me, its virtue lay in its position, at the corner of the square which formed the turning-round point for the Cwmhyfryd bus-route. Seeing a bus pass the windows from left to right gave nice time to drink up, stroll outside and catch it as it completed its tour past the chain stores, the Hubert Barrington Huws Art Gallery and Concert Rooms and the seven mass-production high-class tailoring establishments, and finally moved from right to left up to the queue-shelter in front of the Electricity Showrooms. The convenience of this outweighed the slight disadvantage afforded by visual and aural contact with the pub's other patrons, who in any case tended to be rather thin on the ground at this early hour. You might get, it was true, an occasional grocer or butcher in his Yacht Club blazer and lavender trousers, a publican or two in subfusc accompanied by an ignorant doctor or two in sportive checks, the odd golfing-jacketed cinema-manager, café-owner or fish-shop proprietor, and you might even hear a couple of such people lamenting the fact that there wasn't the money about these days before ordering two double *cordon bleu* brandies and forty cigarettes, but there was often something strangely inspiriting, even uplifting, in the sight of such well-equipped pursuit of the good life. And if it all made you reflect that these chaps represented the new privileged classes in 'our society', you could console yourself with the thought that there was a lot to be said for them compared with the old privileged classes. At least this crowd had enough bad taste to drink brandy before 'dinner'. Such at any rate were my musings as I bought myself a half of mild, ate a huge potato crisp and went and sat in a sort of static rocking-chair by the window, which was curtained with a reproduction of some rotten old tapestry: HAROLDVS INTERFECTVS EST, I read.

Normally I was keen enough to get home after duty to see something of my family, but this prospect, since the day after my initiation as a female impersonator, had ceased to attract me much. Jean was given in the ordinary way to long periods of silence that, as far as I'd been able to discover, had no particular significance. But any fool could have read some significance into her recent disinclination to talk to me or have me talk to her. When I'd finally nerved myself to begin a long, lying, but circumstantial account of what had happened that evening and of how the near-brawl on the doorstep had developed, she'd walked out of the sitting-room into the kitchen. When, still spouting, I joined her in the kitchen, she went back into the sitting-room. When I asked her, as I continued to do at intervals for the next couple of days, what was the matter, she said nothing was the matter, that she was tired and/or that she didn't feel in the mood for talking. She spent as much time as possible in bed or working in the kitchen or visiting Mrs. Jenkins or going out for a shandy with a friend of her college days, a young married woman living nearby whose husband worked late. When I joined Jean in bed, she was firmly asleep; when I started helping her in the kitchen, she at once moved off to one of her three other zones. She knew, or thought she knew, something; but just what, and how, it would be hard to say and disagreeable to find out.

A bus entered the square. I went and ordered another mild from the landlord, who'd just come in rubbing his hands hard together. He was a very well-dressed man with a carnation in his buttonhole and long, carefully-brushed grey hair. I thought it would be nice to exchange the pleasures of meditation for those of communion with my fellow-creatures, and addressed him. After a brisk left-right-left of platitude ("Good-evening"—"Lovely drop of weather, what?"—"Marvellous, isn't it?") I at once went on to rehearse the nice-room-this gambit, the it-must-be-a-tie-running-a-pub gambit, the but-I-suppose-it's-an-interesting-job gambit, the tax-on-beer gambit, and finally silence. The landlord offered the what-do-you-do gambit, the I-drew-up-the-plan-for-this-place-myself gambit, the of-course-television's-ruining-this-business gambit, the still-I-always-say-with-customers-you-can't-have-quantity-and-quality gambit, the how-do-you-like-these-titchy-bottles-I-only-got-them-just-for-silly gambit, and finally silence. His smiles, however, grew more and more intimate as the talk petered out. Before he could ask me if I'd like a ride in his car some time when he wasn't so busy, I returned to my seat, thinking how much it stood to my credit that my interest in Elizabeth was at any rate directed towards the right sex. On the other hand, being one of the landlord's sort undoubtedly gave you an edge over my sort when it came to dealing with Elizabeth's sort.

All right then, what about a nice quick phone-call to dear Lizzie just to brighten up the evening? I could dun her for the fourpence I'd paid on her behalf to Ieuan Jenkins, demand the return of the book-jacket, or inquire whether the Welshwoman's costume, sent to her by post (without covering letter) the day after its brief loan to me, had reached her in good order. No, she might easily guess what I really wanted. And she wouldn't give it to me, either, as her recent silence proved. And Gruffydd-Williams might answer the phone, and I might hear him calling "It's that librarian fellow of yours, Elizabeth", or, more shortly, "It's that chap". If that was how he viewed me, by the way, how come he was alleged to be ready to log-roll for me? He couldn't really be, then. What a pity I couldn't explain all this to Jenkins and quiet his suspicions. I raised my glass and drank to Elizabeth and the beer fizzed up through the back of my nose as she entered the bar, closely followed by Bill Evans wearing an azure bow-tie.

She saw me and looked startled. Then she called: "Hallo, Johnny boy," and laughed rather. "Well, well, long time no see. What brings you to these parts?" She came jauntily over and stood by me, turning to call: "Gin and french, please, Bill."

"I just popped in for a drink on my way home."

"Well, you don't look as if you're enjoying it much, I must say. And no wonder; why do you always stick to that awful horse-pee, eh? Let old Bill get you something stronger. He'd love to."

"No, thank you, I've got to be off in a minute."

"Have you really, now? Tell me, why so pale and wan, fond lover? Here, this is a bit of luck; I want to have a chat with you. Just hang on a minute, will you?"

She went back to the counter and talked briefly to old Probert's fellow-grenadier, whose face seemed to melt fleetingly above the azure bow and at once set again as it might look in twenty years' time; then, carrying a small glass, she returned and sat down with animation opposite me. The cigarette-case was produced and held out.

"I don't smoke, thanks."

"Oh no, so you don't." One of the black affairs was lit and had smoke puffed from it. "Now, first of all, Mr. Lewis, sir"—she gave one of her yaps of laugher—"what was the meaning of that extraordinary scene in my kitchen the other day?"

"Well, I was trying to get away without being seen."

"I can't imagine why. Fine job you made of it, too, didn't you? I had a devil of a time convincing Vernon that Theo James really had seen a plumber. How did you get into the kitchen on your way out, may I ask?"

I caught Evans's eye and he turned away like an alcoholic sighting a pink rat. "Oh, it just happened like that."

"Oh, don't worry about Bill, he'll just adore discussing the Boy Scout movement with Gloriana."

"With who?"

"Thought you wouldn't get that. Gloriana—the Faerie Queene, get it? Spenser called . . ."

"All right, I catch the allusion," I said coldly. "I bet you didn't make it up, anyway."

"Ah, now that's more like your usual form. Lewis is himself again. No, as a matter of fact I got it from Theo James."

"Well, just you give it back to Theo James, see?"

"I say, do you mind if I use that? They've asked me to write a comedy for the Darcy Players."

"Of course, go ahead. I heard it in a film."

"That reminds me. The B.B.C. are going to put on *The Martyr.*"

I screamed shrilly. "Not on the London?"

"No, just the Welsh."

"Oh, that's not so bad."

She grinned and licked her upper lip. "I thought you'd be interested in hearing that. Right; back to the agenda, please, Mr. Lewis, sir. How did you get out of the house in the end? I was waiting for you to come rushing in and yelling that you'd come to read the gas-meter."

"I disguised myself as a Welshwoman and jumped out of the bedroom window."

"You jumped . . . Do you know, I believe you did? So you're the one . . . I thought I must have lent that stuff to someone in the Players and forgotten who. But why? Whatever possessed you?"

"I don't know why," I said.

"But it seemed a good idea at the time, is that it? How did you get home?"

I gave her an outline, compressing the labouring-man incident a good deal. She began laughing and I found myself joining in. At last, after informing me that I was completely mad, that she mustn't let herself get carried away, and that she really did want to see me about something, she said:

"I've had a chat with Vernon and he's going to back you for this job you're in for."

"Oh God, why did you have to tell me that?"

"What do you mean? Aren't you bucked?"

"Look . . . I want to get the job all right, but I don't want to get it like that."

"Like what?"

"You know what I mean . . . just because he knows me . . ."

"But he doesn't know you, does he?"

"Well, because you know me, then."

She looked at me with her tortoiseshell-coloured eyes. They were the sort sometimes loosely referred to as bloody great lamps. She said: "It's got nothing to do with that, you sap. This isn't Chicago. Not that it would matter anyway, as far as I can see. But Vernon's only backing you because if you're appointed, then old Rowlands will . . ." She hesitated in a way that I was later to remember, continuing: "He'll have the best man for the job, you see. They've been going through the applications. You're the best on paper and all you have to do is to see you don't let yourself down at the interview. No reason why you should. Just answer up straightforwardly without saying anything and you can't miss. Have you been notified about the interview yet?"

"No, not yet."

"You'll hear to-morrow, I expect." She smiled with her head on one side. "There, now what do I get for giving you that piece of good news?" She was wearing a rather low-cut summer dress; there was a gentle tan on her cheeks and brow; her lips were parted and slightly everted; her knee touched mine under the table. She was making it all very difficult, and for some reason I found it hard to concentrate on the piece of good news to the exclusion of her proposed honorarium.

I scratched my head violently, trying to work some sense into it. The trouble was I felt too full of fun for any sense to get beyond the epidermis. Should I avow a passionate admiration for Gloriana, confess that all I really liked was being harnessed to a little chariot and driven round the drawing-room, describe an unfortunate childhood accident concerned with climbing over some sharp railings? I could, easily, but she wouldn't believe me. I sighed. "You get my sincere thanks," I said.

"What, nothing more than that?"

"Elizabeth, you know what I'd really like to give you." Less sincerely, I went on: "But . . . things are in rather a mess at the moment. Let's wait till they sort themselves out . . ."

"Waiting never did this kind of thing any good, you know."

"Don't say that, there's a good girl. It's just that things aren't too bright at home."

"I'm sorry to hear that, but you'll just have to wear it, won't you? Don't forget you've committed yourself. Or are you proposing to go back on that?"

I got to my feet and looked down with a sort of theoretical pain at the chalk-white parting in her hair. "I don't want to, darling. I wish I wasn't like this about it. It'll be all right. I'll have to go now."

"Okay, Johnny boy," she said, also getting up as I left. "Bye-bye, then."

At the entrance I met a man who said: "What's the Test score?"

"I'm afraid I don't know," I said. Usually I like

149

knowing Test and other scores, but this field of knowledge was pretty well closed to me round about that time.

He flexed his knees in an odd way and breathed hard through his nose. He seemed to be an Englishman. "It's after six-thirty, isn't it?" he asked furiously, and made off past me into the bar.

I looked in the window as I went by and saw Elizabeth in her yellow summer dress, her hand on Evans's shoulder, swaying about with laughter and showing me exactly how waiting could be said never to do this kind of thing any good. But she was behind the game there. There wasn't going to be any waiting, see? Because there wasn't now going to be any of that kind of thing as far as she and I were concerned. Her news, the full meaning of which was now falling about me like a warm shower, meant that I could swap her for Jean: Jean would come round when she'd heard what I'd got to say about the job, and at the same time I was under no obligation to Elizabeth. As she said, this wasn't Chicago.

Further proof of this hypothesis was now furnished by the white-painted legend on the black leather jerkin of a motor-cyclist who was rattling by at about 50 m.p.h. and was one of my favourite chaps. 'WHAT THINK YE OF CHRIST?' he mutely demanded. This question, which was repeated on several large hoardings round the town, was one to which I'd never propounded a satisfactory answer, but on this evening's showing a favourable view seemed to be called for. Yes, what Elizabeth had just heard me say was my farewell. Well done, Lewis, this time you really have unfixed it. Stay under cover, Lewis, and you won't get hurt.

A fresh external phenomenon was now manifested. A lot of men in blue suits were passing me in groups of three or four. I saw with emotion that each wore in his lapel a little notice giving what was presumably his name and his place of origin or home parish. 'NOAH

SIMS', I read, '—*Brynbwrla*'. Then there was 'DAFYDD B. RHYS—*Haverfordnorth*'. Who were they all, I wondered to myself, and thought how much more fun it was to wonder that than to wonder about Elizabeth, or even about such peripheral, almost purely ornamental, enigmas as Elizabeth's relations with Bill Evans. He must have been with her when she handed the costume book in at the Library, not that it mattered now. Perhaps it was only in inessentials that life had cast him for the role of poor sod.

That still didn't solve the problem of who the labelled men were, and perhaps it would now have to be abandoned. I took a sixpence from my pocket and offered it to Evan Popkin Havard of Harrieston, who declined it.

Two small dark men stopped in front of me. They were carrying the kind of large toffee-tins in which lascars are prone to stow their personal effects. I'd once encountered six such men, each with his toffee-tin, in the parlour of a house on the Cwmhyfryd road which, out for a walk one Sunday afternoon, I'd taken for a café. The rhythmic creaking of a bed upstairs had been clearly audible. One of this present pair of men seemed to ask me: "Where is pain and bitter laugh?"

This was just the question for me, but before I could strike my breast and cry "In here, friend" the other little man had said: "My cousin say, we are new in these town and we wish to know where is piano and bit of life, please?"

"Ah yes, I know the very place for you boys. See where I'm pointing? That pub on the corner of the square there, just where that bus is now. They'll see you right, take it from me. Just walk straight in and ask for Lizzie."

"Thanks, mister. You very good."

"Yes, I'm very good all right."

TWELVE

"Good-evening, john," Mrs. Jenkins said, looking sidelong at me as if she wondered whether, or how heavily, I was armed.

"Hallo, Mrs. Jenkins," I said to her. "Hallo, ducks," I said to Jean, who hadn't turned round when I came in and now made no reply. "Can I have some of that tea?"

"I'm going in a minute," Mrs. Jenkins said in obvious alarm. "I just happened to pop in, that's all. Just happened . . ."

Jean had got her hair tied at the nape of the neck, which made her look younger and more severe at the same time. Still not looking at me, she said: "You can get yourself a cup from the kitchen if you really want some."

"I'll get you a cup, Daddy," Eira offered. She was sitting on the arm of Jean's chair in her nightdress. Her glance showed that she expected me to mention the time and send her to bed, and that she hoped and believed a display of courtesy would postpone this or even wash it out altogether.

"No, it's all right, thank you, dear; I'll go."

I wanted a moment alone to swear and dance about in connexion with Mrs. Jenkins. I'd been getting ready to plunge straight into the story about the job and Gruffydd-Williams's support, and I couldn't do that in her presence. I couldn't have mentioned any matter of any importance in her presence, come to that, because of her aspects as domestic version of the Medusa and female version of Generalissimo Chiang Kai-shek (there was a physical resemblance too). Rinsing at the wash-basin a cup that had recently held rose-hip syrup, dancing about a little as anticipated, and imputing to Mrs. Jenkins sexual behaviour of a fantastic or unlikely character, I let my eyes wander over the scene outside the window, where rain had begun to fall. Jean had hauled in her own washing with my pulley, but that of Mrs. Davies was for some reason still out, lots of it, all getting very wet. That was good.

Mrs. Jenkins watched me carefully when I returned with my cup of tea. I think she knew that I only returned so as to bring pressure on her to leave. Where she went just a wee bit wrong was in assuming, as she gave every sign of doing, that if she stayed another few minutes I might suddenly spring at her with a hatchet, or possibly not bother to fetch the hatchet and just sink my canines into her jugular. I sometimes had a go at feeling sorry for her when she wasn't there, and at no time wished her irrecoverable harm, but I did wish she wouldn't use every vocal inflexion and every bodily and facial movement to show that she detected some cunning threat to her welfare in everything she saw and heard. And yet, looking back, I suppose she had reason enough to regard things in general as potentially hostile. Catching her eye now I bared my fangs in a smile, trying to look as lupine as I could. She got up at once, but Jean made her sit down. This was going to be a fine dilemma for her.

As I moved towards them I saw, on the black match-wood shrine, a letter addressed to me in my father's hand-writing. I removed from a chair a pile of ironing sur-mounted by the head and torso of a golliwog, sat down and opened the envelope. Involuntarily, before it focused on the handwriting, my gaze fell upon the nearmost quadrant of the floor, which was scattered with the usual archipelago of clothing, toys, foodstuffs and crockery. The sight somehow made me aware that this room contrasted with Gloriana's saloon bar, and that it was also different from the upstairs lounge at the Gruffydd-Williamses'. I began reading.

I was born when my parents were middle-aged and my father, a widower now for seven years, would shortly be retiring from his job in the check office of the small colliery near our home. He lived alone and I was the only one of his children who saw him at all often. My eldest brother had died of wounds in North Africa; the middle brother had joined a firm of industrial consultants in Lancashire; my sister married an Englishman and now lived at Bristol—a fairly easy journey from South Wales, admittedly, but not worth their while considering how much she and my father disliked each other. Like everyone else who knows them both, except my brother-in-law, and the last time I saw him he didn't seem too clear in his mind about it, I'm on my father's side and always will be. Anyway, such are his relations with his children. He's got no brothers or sisters living, and though he sometimes sees a bit of a widowed younger sister of my mother's, who's amiable enough, she's a drinker as well as being amiable, and my father doesn't really like that.

It was to me alone, then, I imagine, that my father started to write letters when retirement started to seem imminent to him, six months or more before this. Their motive was obvious enough, but not from their text, which was regularly divided into news of doings at the colliery and of neighbours, reasoned abuse of the Conservative Government and of the leadership of the Labour Party, and inquiries about our welfare. I have a great affection for my father and I admired him for never making any appeal to that affection. As I read this latest letter I reflected, as I always did, that nobody else I knew would face the coming addition of idleness to solitude without voicing self-pity in some form.

Well that crowd are certainly demonstrating their traditional tolerance and impartiality over Cyprus, I read. *Even your pal Gaynor Harries let two men go by without noticing when we discussed it in the street last Saturday. No radical change in the situation there by the way. That fellow from the Insurance seems to have flown the district. Can't say I blame him even although it's hard on poor old Gaynor. She'd be well advised not to peer into their faces like she does, it alarms them and no wonder.*

I am carrying on here about the same and am pretty well. I expect the better weather will mean that you and the rest of the Quartette can get out more when you're free from the Library. Which reminds me, any news yet of the better job you're going for, be sure to let me know. Warmest regards to you all, John and my dear Jean and my little Eira and Baby.

I refolded the letter and put it back in the envelope. The last sentence, in particular, seemed a cogent enough adverse commentary on my last few remarks to Elizabeth that evening. It also made me recall what it had felt like to hear the door of Gruffydd-Williams's car slam shut beneath the lounge window some time ago. I almost began wanting Mrs. Jenkins to stay.

She at once got up with a fair show of decision and began a careful flanking approach to the door, securing her rear by sidling with her back to the tall box-like couch described earlier.

"Well, it's been very nice to see you, Mrs. Jenkins," Jean said. Neither she nor I had ever been able to call her by her Christian name, though often instructed to do so.

I too stood up, trying to express in the movement my keen self-reproach at having spent so much of her visit reading a letter. "Yes, it has indeed," I said vehemently.

After briefly running over in her mind some of my possible motives for this obvious deception, she said:

"Ieuan's worrying himself sick about the interview, John. And it's next week, you know." She was trying to blame me for the date of the interview as well as for her husband's condition.

"The week after next," I corrected her.

"The Tuesday," she countered.

"Well, I really don't see he's got anything to worry about," I said, and Jean said she didn't think so either. It heartened me to have her agreement, even on an issue like this, and I went on more confidently: "Everybody thinks he's got an excellent chance, take it from me."

"It means a lot to us, see, that extra money," Mrs. Jenkins said.

"Yes, naturally."

"Well, I mustn't keep you," she muttered, then said distinctly and with something of the air of a headmistress at a prizegiving: "I've never seen him like this before in nearly twenty years. It means everything in the world to him, everything in the world, you know."

"Cheerio," Eira suddenly shouted at the top of her voice, dancing up to me and grabbing hold of my hands. "Cheerio, cheerio, Mrs. Jankies."

"Be quiet, Eira," and "Don't be so rude," Jean and I said at the same time. "Take no notice of her, Mrs. Jenkins," I added with a shocked expression.

Eira flung herself backwards; I had to hold on to her hands to stop her falling. In a hoarse, mannish voice she roared: "Cheerio and off you go; cheerio and off you go; cheerio . . ."

I pulled her upright and aimed a token cuff at her head; unfortunately it caught her heavily on the ear. For a moment her enormous eyes looked into mine; then she ran across the room and lowered her top half into the seat-cushion of one of the arm-chairs. "I'm sorry, Mrs. Jenkins," I said; "I don't know where she picks up these . . ."

"Ah, she's going to be difficult to control, I can see that. Well, now I really must be going." She directed a movement at me that was half nod, half valedictory start of alarm, and went out, pursued by Jean.

It was something, I thought, to be relieved of having to hear Mrs. Jenkins address Eira as her handsome girl, as her blossom, or as Queen of England—habitual leave-taking formulas. She was usually rather nice to Eira, or tried to be, and the 'cheerio' outburst, purely incantatory though it was, must have hurt her a little. Well, there was nothing to be done about that.

Eira looked up. "Has she gone, Daddy?"

"Yes, and you're a very naughty girl. How dare you say things like that to Mrs. Jenkins?"

She turned her head away and plumped herself down on to the cushion again. After a quarter of a minute or so she uttered a loud mooing wail.

I went over to her. "Here, there's no need for that. All finished now, monkey."

"You're cross," she bawled.

"I'm not now."

"You . . . *are*."

"No, I'm not. Here." I took her hand, flattened the palm, and ran my index finger round it in circles, reciting the following:

> " Round and round the racing-track
> Runs a teddy-bear;
> One step, two steps . . ."

Just as she began to laugh, Jean came in. Frowning, she said: "Don't make her laugh, John. You ought to send her to bed instead of fooling around. I had a hell of a job pacifying the old . . ."—she glanced at Eira—"pacifying her."

"Yes, I know. I'm sorry, dear. Eira, it's time you

157

were in bed anyway. Off you go, now. I'll come and say good-night when you're in if you get a move on."

"Want some cornflakes."

"Well, you don't get any, my girl," Jean said. "No more nonsense or I'll tell Daddy what you did to the baby this morning."

Eira usually took as long as possible to do what we wanted, but this time she made for the door as if it led to a sweet-shop. In a moment I heard her bedroom door slam.

"What did she do to the baby, Jean?"

Without replying, Jean began collecting the used teacups.

"Listen, dear, I've got something to tell you."

"Not interested, sorry."

"You will be in this. It's about the job."

"What about it?"

"I think I'm going to get it." Here I had to pause and follow her out into the kitchen. "Gruffydd-Williams is going to back me, apparently. I don't see how I can miss."

She turned and faced me by the washbasin, a cup in each hand. "Quite sure of this, are you?"

"Well, it's what Elizabeth told me this evening."

"You've been round there again, I suppose; that's why you're so late."

"No, we just met by chance. Honestly."

"I bet she was glad to see you like that."

"Like what?"

"You've got a bogey on your nose. Improves your looks no end."

I was near the mirror I used for shaving and which hung above the washbasin. I peeped in and saw the bogey. It was large and vermiform and clung to the wing of my right nostril. I removed it, feeling a little downcast. Even the dignity of Charles I on the scaffold, I reasoned, would have been deflated by the executioner telling him what Jean had just told me, and so might that of Demosthenes by similar information after delivering the *De Corona*.

"Aren't you pleased about this?" I asked.

"You believe this story of hers, do you?"

"Yes, of course. Why not? Don't you?"

"I can't really say, can I, not knowing her as well as you do."

I swallowed. "Now look here, darling, let's cut out the cracks for now. I'm quite sure Elizabeth was telling the truth to-night. She's no reason not to, after all. That means I've got a damned good chance of getting this thing. Well, isn't that good news?" I started helping her to wash up.

She said flatly: "Yes, of course it is."

"But . . . you don't seem really pleased."

"Don't worry, I expect I'll be pleased when I get round to it."

"How do you mean? Why aren't you pleased now?" I stared at her and seemed to read in her face an angry and obdurate resistance to me and a sufficient answer to my question. It was almost as if she'd taken physical hurt from my Elizabeth business: her eyes were narrowed, I thought, not in the familiar nervous peering, but in flinching; her neck was thinned by an apparent constriction of the throat. Her mouth tightened and she looked down at her hand, where there was a small recent burn. Then she said, faltering a little:

"I . . . just don't feel like it."

"Darling . . ." I stepped towards her.

She looked up sharply and retreated, her eyes wide open now. "None of that. I don't want any of that."

"I'm sorry. Can't we talk this over, sort of clear the air?"

"No, don't tell me anything, there's nothing I want to hear."

"Jean, you're wrong about this. It isn't like you think, I promise you. I haven't . . ."

"You're not having an affair with her?"

"Well, no, not in the way you mean."

"That's smashing, man. That makes it all okay, does it?"

"Don't be like that about it, Jean. I can see why you feel like you do, but let's have it out now we've started. I must tell you about it."

"I've told you I don't want to hear, it's nothing to do with me. You do as you like, only don't tell me about it, I don't want to know, see?" She passed me Eira's piggy-plate and I began drying it without much attention. "That's about the lot. You can leave me in peace now."

"Oh, please, darling, I only want to apologise, and I want to promise you . . ."

"It's no use talking, John, apologising and promising and Christ knows what. Do what you want to do, but don't keep up this talk, talk, talk. I've got enough to put up with without that. Shut up, do." She scoured a saucepan, bending forward over the basin. I saw that one of her apron-strings was missing and the apron was fastened with one of the baby's blue safety-pins.

"But what can I do? All I can do is tell you . . ."

"And when you've told me you'll feel all right about it until the next time, and then we have this again? That's what you want, isn't it?" She threw the things into the basin and turned and faced me. "Now you listen to me. Perhaps you think I don't know you. I do, though. I know the look you get when you start fancying a woman. You had it that night at the party when you came over to me, thought you'd better not spend any more time talking to her, not with me there, I might spot you. You seem to think I'm bloody blind." She folded her arms and narrowed her eyes. "I don't mind that part now. But I don't want to hear any more from you, understand? You think you can get rid of what you do by coming and telling me about it afterwards. Well, you can't. You know you'll always do what you want to do, why have you got to talk about it? Go off and do her if you want to, as long as you don't tell me. What you do's nothing to do with me. It doesn't interest me, get that? I couldn't care less what you get up to, I never even think about it, see? Just give me my housekeeping every week and stay out of my way and that's all I want out of you. And get that job while you're about it, you might as well."

"Jean, I can understand . . ."

"Great one for understanding you are, aren't you? 'Oh yes, I understand how you feel, I understand you're feeling a bit cheesed just at the moment so let me cheer you up, I' . . ."

"Isn't there anything I can do?"

"Yes, now I think of it, you can go and tell your rich girl-friend to stop bothering me. She's got what she was after so she needn't go on going through the bloody motions with me. She's another one who thinks I'm dead stupid. So you can go and tell her not to bother giving me any more invitations to tea like she did yesterday. I bet she didn't get round to mentioning that when she ran into you by accident."

"She was here, was she? What did you tell her?"

"I told her to keep bloody clear of me if she knew what was good for her. And you can tell her the same. Now don't stand there giving me that little-boy face, you're getting too old for it. Try it on her, she's not so particular. Go on, get out."

Why could you hurt people so much worse in their absence than in their presence? Because it was so much easier in their absence? I went slowly downstairs thinking this, buttoning my raincoat and listening for any movement Jean might make. From the communal bathroom came the terrifying rumble of the old verdigrisy geyser and the irregular plashing of its jet of water on the rustpocked bath. Above the tumult could be heard the voice of Ken Davies, back from the early shift at the Coliseum and no doubt preparing for an evening's dancing at his favourite bull-ring. *"Olé,"* he was singing, "I am a bandit." He and the geyser made it impossible to hear any sound from the kitchen. I hesitated, then went on down; if she was crying she might as well do it in peace, and if she wasn't there could be no point in going back.

As soon as I was outside the door the wind, an old enemy of mine (like vanity), sprang at me, changing the position of every hair on my head (why?) and bringing its crony, the rain, up in support. I really must treat myself to a beret; they looked silly and foreign, but better that than expose my head to the rigours of an Aberdarcy summer, and Eira's red mackintosh hat attracted more attention when guarding my head than, on the whole, I cared to receive. I passed a fried-fish shop where, I saw with approval, there was going to be frying to-night, then, at the corner by the Y.M.C.A., crossed over and turned off. This brought me a view of the sea. It looked like an almost smooth sheet of yellowish rock running from the line of roof-tops hiding the beach to the docks over on the right, to the power-station at Tai-mawr, and, beyond the estuary, to the blast furnace at the Abertwit strip-mill, a fat red cylinder rising, so it seemed at this distance, from the surface of the water. Somewhere in the background were the narrow-waisted tanks of the Cambrio-Sudanese people, full, among other things, of the wherewithal for more dry Martinis, garden statuary and black cigarettes with gold tips. I trod on a loose paving-stone, a hazard in which this district abounded; it tipped up and squirted cold dirty water into my shoe.

What could I do in order to hurt myself? Had Jean really meant that our marriage was off for good, except as a domestic arrangement? Or perhaps she'd only been angry, which of course I could . . . I made up my mind never again, this side of the grave at any rate, to use the word 'understand' or any of its synonyms or any item of its or their conjugations or noun- or adjective-derivatives, even to myself and not out loud. If my character was, as it appeared to be, not so much bad or weak as unworkable, farcically unfitted for its task, like an asbestos fire-lighter, then that was more than merely bad luck on Jean. I wished I could discover, like a galactic-federation physicist in a science-fiction story, some chink or warp in time that would age Jean and me five years in five minutes. The alternative, presumably, was to start liking being the kind of man I evidently was.

I entered a phone-box and picked up the directory. There were no vestigial sandwiches to impede or irk me this time, only a large sheet of wet brown paper which clung affectionately round my ankles. As before, though, I looked through several pages of the house of Williams before realising that these people must file themselves under Gruffydd. Here they were. Holding my breath, I pulled all the change out of my pocket; then awe and bewilderment overcame me at the sight of no fewer than five pennies, all in good condition, lying in my palm. I put three in the thing and began dialling the number.

If Gruffydd-Williams answered, I'd announce myself as that librarian fellow of Elizabeth's or possibly just as that chap. I'd get hold of her anyway somehow. She must be in, she'd have to be. I'd tell her. I could count on ten seconds or so in which to outline my present opinion of her, and even to start going into detail, before she hung up. Should I work out in advance what I was going to say? I paused in my dialling and noticed that I was breathing rather quickly and trembling a little and that my eyes felt bunged up. I soon got going again with the last couple of digits: a condition of rage wasn't perhaps a bad starting point on its own and should rule out the danger of being too indirect.

The distant bell whirred a few times, stopped, and gave place to Elizabeth's voice saying: "Hallo. Mrs. Gruffydd-Williams."

"Hallo," I said. "Mr. Lewis. This is just to tell you that I hate your guts. And your husband's guts. Tell him he can work his Sub-Librarian's job up him. And I hate all your friends' guts too. Tell them that librarian fellow of yours says so. And as for you, you stupid bitch . . ." I stopped, quite out of breath, and leant my forehead on the damp glass.

"Hallo," Elizabeth said in a puzzled tone. "Hallo, who's that? I can't hear you. Speak up, can't you?"

I spoke up all right, even screamed at her a little. Then I suddenly noticed I hadn't pressed Button A, and so although I could hear her she couldn't hear me. I rested my thumb on the button and hesitated. I no longer wanted to say what I'd just been saying, did I? What good would it do? It wouldn't work, anyway; straightforward abuse would leave them all untouched, would somehow bounce off the cherub-encrusted mirror, get soaked up by the picture of the cheese-faced miner, be extinguished by the torch-snuffers before it could even get in the front door. And it wasn't really my line either. The way to get through, or rather round, their defences was to come cartwheeling into the upstairs lounge in front of them all and do a can-can wearing the Welshwoman's outfit, modified in advance by having SOD THE WHOLE LOT OF YOU worked in gamboge across the shoulder-blades. That would be more the sort of thing.

Elizabeth had rung off some time ago. I pressed Button B for the return of my threepence and a whole shower of pennies, eight or nine of them, came clattering out. I silently thanked the unknown provider of this symbolical reward. Well, no, not symbolical; it was real, wasn't it? And there was just enough of it to buy me a half of mild at the General Picton. That was good.

THIRTEEN

"IF YOU'LL JUST wait in here, gentlemen," the clerk said, "the Committee will call you in one by one. Alphabetical order." He was leaving us in the waiting-room when the Oxford man said:

"Excuse me just one moment."

"Yes?" the clerk said rather irritably.

The other raised his eyebrows and, in the space of perhaps four microseconds, whipped off his thick-rimmed spectacles. He looked smaller without them. "Will the Committee announce their appointment to-day, do you suppose?"

"Naturally. Naturally they will." The clerk's eyes glinted with a sort of hilarious cruelty behind the little wire-rimmed glasses which he personally favoured. I wondered how it was that anyone with such short hair had still not shaved to-day. With the manner of a rubber-hose expert about to launch an interrogation, he said: "The result will be announced shortly after the conclusion of the last interview."

"Thank you. That's exactly what I wanted to know."

We all relaxed and looked round at each other as the clerk left. The room was about the size of the Lewis kitchen, though in other respects unlike it, with two pairs of chairs facing one another and an empty green and brown table between them. Ieuan Jenkins and I sat on one side, the Oxford man and O. Killa Beynon (no relation to Probert's fatty Beynon, thank God) on the other. The only remaining object in the room was a miniature version of the picture of Lord Beaconsfield which hung in the Lending Department. In this form he looked compassionate as well as queasy. The sound of typewriters came from not far away and every now and then a distant phone rang.

Beynon, a very broad man of fifty-odd who'd already demonstrated the fact that he was almost the same height standing up as sitting down (a not all that rare type of physique in Wales), put his great hands on his great knees and cleared his throat. "Well, that's a relief," he said. "I shall be in first and get it over."

"Oh, you'd say that was an advantage, would you?" the Oxford man asked.

"In two ways," Beynon said briskly. "First, they'll be fresh. Won't have had time to get sick of the job and want to get home. Secondly, first impressions stick. Nobody's been in before to set the standard."

"That's really most interesting," the Oxford man murmured.

"Of course, you're by way of being a bit of an expert on interviews, aren't you, Killa?" Ieuan Jenkins, who knew him slightly, said.

"Ought to be, Jenkins, ought to be. I deputised for our chief for over a year when he was down with his trouble, you remember. And I've been on the receiving end a few times, of course." He shook slowly with laughter.

The Oxford man looked from face to face. I felt sorry for him; he was probably younger than me and knew nothing of Wales. How could he guess, as I already had, that he was here chiefly to give the members of the Committee a comfortable feeling when they discussed his qualifications and experience in the meeting and told their families about it afterwards? A young fellow we had from Oxford, very nice young fellow he was, and brilliant too, one of the best students of his year his professor said. But of course you can't expect a young fellow like that to fit into the picture down here. Well, I thought, there's something in it.

Beynon and Jenkins were going at him fairly hard

now. "When did you sit your College exam then, Mr. Howard?" Beynon was asking.

"Sit my . . . oh yes, I did Schools in 1953."

"And you got a good result, I've no doubt?" Jenkins asked, smiling encouragingly.

"Well, I got a First," Howard said, half-glancing at me. He'd gone rather red, and was busily rotating his glasses in his hand.

"A First Class Degree," Beynon said with sonority, spacing the words out. "Well, now. That's a very fine achievement, Mr. Howard, a very fine achievement indeed. And, of course, a First Class at Oxford is worth a good deal more than a First Class at Swansea, say, or Aberystwyth, don't you agree, Jenkins?"

"Most certainly I agree. And what have you been doing since then, Mr. Howard?"

"I've been . . . they took me on in the library at my college, actually, and I managed to get my A.L.A. this year."

"Hm," Beynon said consideringly. "What part of England do you come from, Mr. Howard?"

"Manchester."

"Ah, now I know Manchester well. I was there during the war, you know. A fine city, Manchester, but rather too large to my way of thinking. A little bit like London in that respect. Tell me: are you married, Mr. Howard?"

"No." Howard rapidly put his glasses back on and uncrossed and recrossed his legs. "No, I'm not married."

"Not thinking of taking the step if you should pull off this job?"

I tried to stop myself from listening to this by reciting to myself the arguments against each of the four candidates. As I did so, every one seemed more and more overwhelming. Howard was a bit young, too diffident, probably quite intelligent, rather highly qualified academically, too inexperienced, not Welsh; Jenkins was a bit old (why hasn't he got this sort of job already?), much too diffident, of unusual appearance (you can't see him making a good committee man, or getting on with the people who count, can you, now?), a North Walian; Beynon was even older, too confident, the writer of a number of pamphlets on Welsh antiquities (we can't appoint anyone who isn't going to give his whole time and his whole mind and his whole heart to the job), a Monmouthshire man; I was a bit young, both too confident and too diffident, of proven mediocre ability in the very library I had the impertinence to consider myself fit to adorn as vicegerent, probably disagreeable in some way obscure to myself but clear to all others.

Jenkins murmured to me: "How are you feeling, John?"

"Not too bad."

"You're extremely fortunate to have the temperament for these things. I haven't, I must confess."

"You mustn't worry, Ieuan. You've got a better chance than any of us. You're obviously the man."

"I'm afraid they won't think so, though thank you, John, for saying it."

"Why shouldn't they think so? You can bet old Rowlands has pushed you as hard as he can. No doubt about that."

"He's not here to-day, he's had to go to Pontypool to see his sister; she's gravely ill, poor woman. And his opinion doesn't count. If he has, as you say, pushed me, they're as likely to take it against me as for me. More likely. Old Rowlands has never been popular with the Committee, as I happen to know. And that's what counts, I'm afraid."

"Well, you'll get it on merit and experience, then." I said this with some sincerity: Elizabeth's assurance that Gruffydd-Williams was backing me had shown a curious tendency, in the last quarter of an hour, to appear unreliable and irrelevant. Nor did the task of merely 'seeing I didn't let myself down at the interview' seem as light as it once had.

Jenkins had said that he wished he thought so and relapsed into silence. Across the table I heard Howard say to Beynon, with a note of ungovernable eagerness: "You mean they actually have books in this library, printed in Welsh?"

"Thousands of them, I've no doubt."

"Well, that's really most interesting."

"Tell me, Mr. Howard, what's your father's profession?"

Poor dab, I thought, he'll never have had anything like this in his whole life before. He'd begun to look round rather wildly right at the start, when Beynon had given him the two-minute handshake (a traditional Welsh greeting); I began to wonder whether he'd manage to make the interview while still in his right mind. I said to Jenkins: "Don't forget, Ieuan, they like appointing someone who's got first-hand experience of the place. They know you and they know you know the job."

He shook his grey head. "No, they'd be more likely to keep me on as I am to advise the new man, if he comes from outside. And they know you too, don't they?"

"Not as well as they know you."

"It's kind of you to try to encourage me, John, but . . . no."

"And a scholarship you got to Oxford, Mr. Howard, was it? or perhaps your father could send you at his own expense?"

Instead of answering Beynon, Howard leaned forward to me and said: "I say, you don't happen to have a cigarette, do you?"

"I'm sorry, I don't smoke," I said, but Beynon was pulling out a twenty packet and giving it to Howard with "Here you are, boy, help yourself."

"Thanks very much," Howard said, opening it with all speed.

"I suppose you hadn't the chance to buy any on the train, and then when you got down here things moved a bit fast, as it were?" Beynon asked, smiling.

"Aren't you having one yourself?" Howard said.

"No, they'll be calling me any minute now." Beynon struck a match for him. "Won't be worth it. Don't smoke a great deal, anyway, you know."

"Well, thank you very much." He held the packet out to Beynon.

"No, no, keep them, Mr. Howard. You've run out."

"But I can't let you just . . ."

"There's only a few in there. Go on, man, put 'em away."

"But you'll be . . . "

"Mr. Beynon, please," the clerk said at the threshold. Yes, perhaps he was growing a beard. That must be it.

"Well, here we go, boys." Beynon got up, gaining perhaps two inches in stature. "You hold on to those smokes, Mr. Howard, now. See you all later."

Howard wished him good luck in ringing tones, Jenkins and I provided a quieter echo, and he followed the clerk out. Howard smoked away without apparent enjoyment; out of the corner of my eye I saw him sliding the cigarettes guiltily into his pocket. Jenkins glanced at me, but I pretended not to notice. I wasn't so full of calm myself as to have any to lend him. I linked my hands behind my head and closed my eyes. To pass the time, I began devising the ideal interview, which would secure the ideal candidate in the minimum time.

Q. What is your name?
A. *Teifion Llewelyn Glyndwr Talfan ap Rhys Thomas.*
Q. You are Welsh?
A. *Yes.*

Q. Married?

A. *Yes.*

Q. Children?

A. *Yes.*

Q. Religion?

A. *Chapel.*

Q. Politics?

A. *Trade Union.*

Q. What do you consider to be the main duties of a Sub-Librarian?

A. *To see that the date-stamps are correctly set, the corridors swept, the Newspaper Room free from unemployed and undesirables, the Town Clerk promptly informed of all books not returned after three months, the fine-tickets always at hand for borrowers with whom I am unacquainted, a five per cent random sample of fiction regularly catalogued as biography and memoirs and a twenty-five per cent selected sample of essays and belles-lettres catalogued as fiction.*

Q. Have you any other interests?

A. *Welsh History, Welsh manners and customs, Welsh Rugby football, Dylan Thomas, Welsh amateur drama, Welsh arts and culture.*

Q. Have you heard of T. S. Eliot?

A. *Yes.*

Q. Are you interested in films, drinking, American novels, women's breasts, jazz, science fiction?

A. *Give me a good play any day, I like a quiet pint or two at the Club on a Sunday after chapel, I read Mark Twain at school, my wife is a schoolteacher, I'd sooner hear a nice choir, I don't seem to get much time for recreational reading.*

Q. Have you any irritating mannerisms or habits?

A. *I run about shouting in the Lending Department if a book is momentarily mislaid, I borrow newly-arrived books without recording their arrival or my borrowing, I spit when I talk.*

Q. Now, think carefully before you answer this: if you were fat as well as stupid, would you be as proud of being fat as you are of being stupid?

A. *Yes.*

Q. Thank you. Would you mind waiting outside?

"It's a worrying time," Jenkins said.

"Yes, it is."

"My wife feels it, you know, more than I do, I'm quite certain. Extraordinary how women feel things, isn't it? But then she's in poor health, as you know."

"How's she been recently?"

"No better, no worse. That's how it goes from day to day." He sighed and smacked his lips. "Yes, that's how it goes, I'm afraid."

"I'm sorry to hear that, Ieuan."

"You see," he said, dropping his voice still further, "it's her sleep that's been affected, this last year. She complains of a sort of stomach cramp in the early morning very often. And that's something it's difficult to relieve, it seems."

"Has she seen the doctor about it?"

"Times without number, boy. But it seems to do her remarkably little good." His voice had acquired a slight tang of bitterness.

"Well, I suppose it's a case where one has just got to go on persevering."

He removed his glance from mine as if I'd insulted him. "Persevering," he said with great specific bitterness. "Persevering."

Ieuan deserved to get this job. Even I, with my incorruptible self-centredness, could see that. He needed the extra money, in the first place to buy his wife holidays, special food, and expensive treatment, and in the second place to buy himself holidays (with girls), special food (eaten at luxurious restaurants with girls), and expensive treatment (very superior old pale brandies and specially selected real Havana leaf cigars savoured in the company of girls). I wouldn't say no to a bit of some of those things myself, except the cigars, but it was nice to think that, if I did get the job, it would be because I was thought capable of doing it, not because I knew Gruffydd-Williams or his bloody wife.

"They're a long time with Beynon," Jenkins said hoarsely.

"Oh, not ten minutes yet," I said.

Howard glanced at his wrist-watch but said nothing.

The door opened and a spectacled girl came in. "Mr. Lewis?" she said, yawning.

"Yes?" I said.

"Telephone call for you."

"Telephone message?"

"No, telephone call."

I hesitated and looked at Jenkins, who said: "Go on, John, there's Mr. Howard and me to go in before you."

"Are you sure you've got the right person?" I asked the girl. "I'm only here for an interview."

"Yes, I know that. The lady said where to find you."

I went out after the girl, feeling so full of energy that if Probert had appeared at that moment I could have picked him up and thrown him through a glass door with one hand. I really was going to get the job. It was made certain by the fact that Jean had rung me up, and she could only have done that so as to wish me luck. Leaving the house after lunch I'd told her that the interview was at four-thirty, and she hadn't replied. Now she'd thought better of it. That was good.

"You can take it in here," said the girl.

We entered another kitchen-sized room where another girl, an attractive one with shining blonde hair, was turning over a pile of papers and making ticks on a list.

173

She looked up at me, but I avoided her eye and went to the phone. "John Lewis here," I said into it, feeling a bit queer.

"Hallo? John?" Elizabeth's voice said.

I now felt as if a policeman had said to me: "John Aneurin Lewis, I arrest you for the murder of Edna Davies," and wondered for a moment whether, at the same time, one of the girls in the room mightn't have crawled up on all fours and hit me behind the knees with a rolled newspaper. Then other sensations overcame me at the thought that Jean probably never even let herself hear my remark about the interview.

"Hallo, are you there? Who's that?" Elizabeth asked. "Hallo."

"Yes," I said. "I'm here."

"Cheer up, ducky. You haven't been in yet, have you?"

"No, not yet."

"I thought so. Are you all right?"

"Yes, I'm all right. How are you?"

She talked for a time, then asked: "Are you listening?"

"Yes."

"Do pay attention, John, this is important. I've got something for you. Now: when you go in, look round for an old sod wearing a dog-collar. That's . . ."

I pulled from my pocket a small but thick magazine with an extravagant title and a cover showing a man and a robot and a fly about the size of an albatross all having a fight. I got it open at a story that interested me: it was about a man (a different man from the man shown on the cover) who'd managed to transfer to himself the process, hitherto available only to much humbler forms of life, of reproduction by fission. At the moment when I'd had to stop reading, there were 512 personages, all identical, considering the situation likely to arise when they became 1,024 in ten minutes' time. They were travelling in a small space-ship, which by now they filled to the air-locks, between two planetary systems in the constellation Boötes.

While I read on I was aware that Elizabeth had somehow come by some extra information about the interview and was telling it to me. Quite apart from the pleasure and interest I took in what I was reading, I was glad not to be listening to her. Not listening to her had been made fairly easy for me by listening to Jenkins some minutes earlier.

The 512 identical twins in the space-ship had reached the point of agreeing to throw half of each generation out of the air-locks, but not the point of deciding in advance which of each new pair should throw and which be thrown. It was a knotty problem. I realised now that the original man had solved the problem of asexual reproduction that had first consciously presented itself to me the other week in Elizabeth's upstairs lounge—the difference of locale (Vega's in Lyra, not Boötes) was trifling. But this chap, too, had got himself into difficulties. Perhaps budding-off, the method of H. G. Wells's Martians, would have been safer.

"I think that's the lot," I heard Elizabeth say.

"Right. Thanks very much."

"A pleasure."

"Anything else you want to know?"

"No thanks."

"John?"

"Yes?"

"Is anything the matter?"

"I don't think so, why?"

"You sound rather queer."

"I'm all right, really."

"Good. Look, what are you doing to-night?"

"Nothing special."

"There's a party on—would you like to come?"

By this time my self-assurance had drained away. I could almost have drawn a diagram of my special feeling (depression, boredom, *et. al.*) flopping astride my shoulders, like a child being given a 'flying angel', the moment I went into the sitting-room and saw Jean not look up at my entry. "Yes, I would," I said.

In the next few moments I was told some more about the party, made arrangements, and put my magazine back in my pocket. I also studied the blonde girl's arms—she wore a sleeveless pullover. As I did so I felt my nostrils carefully, testing for bogeys. The result was negative. I finally rang off, looked again at the blonde girl, who avoided my eye, and went back to the waiting-room, which now contained all three of my rivals.

"That's a curious nickname," Howard was saying in a thin, parched voice. His legs were tightly crossed, his trousers were covered with cigarette-ash, and his eyeballs were rolling a bit.

"Nickname?" Beynon asked.

"Yes: Killer. Did you get it in the war?"

"It's not a nickname, Mr. Howard," Beynon said loudly and slowly. "It's a name. A very old Welsh name. K, I, L, L, A. Killa. A very old Welsh name, it is. Though, of course, you wouldn't know that, would you, Mr. Howard?"

I'd expected Howard to scream a little, or at least confusedly apologise, but he did neither. His eyelids wavered for a second, as if he were on the point of dropping asleep. "Really? Well, that's most interesting," he said in a monotone. "Really very interesting."

At this point the clerk reappeared, making both Howard and Jenkins start with some violence. The clerk took in the scene with evident enjoyment before asking Mr. Jenkins to come this way.

Jenkins got to his feet, drawing in his breath. "Here we go then," he said, looking at me.

"Good luck, Ieuan," I said.

"All the best," Howard croaked.

FOURTEEN

"SIT DOWN, PLEASE, Mr. Lewis," Gruffydd-Williams said, smiling faintly. I was surprised, and tried not to feel pleased, to find him evidently taking the chair. (I found out afterwards that the regular Chairman was away ill.) Gradually, like a herd of big game scenting man, the members of the Committee began turning their heads in my direction. As each gaze reached my face it became keen and searching, and soon they were all engaged in that activity which Welshmen love and in which, more than most things, they like to think they excel: summing the fellow up. It seems, though I didn't think of this at the time, that my countrymen have long been noted for this idiosyncrasy. I can remember finding, in a pile of coverless books lying about the library, a rotten old play about Welsh humours in which the following occurs:

Ap Hughe: Py Cot, coufin, you think to finde me as Green as a *Leek*. Think you not I ſhall *ſmell out your Knauerie* in ij VVaggs of yr Tong, py Iubider? Know you not a *VVelſhman* can euer look een to the Hart of a man and know her, by what Deception soeer her hope to ſcape knowing. Now *Cots plutter and nailes*, get you gone or as I am a Knights ſon I will peat you to death.

Exeunt, Ap Hughe beating Maggott.

When a dozen Welshmen are looking to the heart of a man, or even thinking they're doing so, the man can't help feeling a little hemmed in. My impression was that nobody loved me.

177

I was sitting at the mid-point of the longer side of a rectangular table, with Gruffydd-Williams opposite me. Throughout the interview I was to be conscious of disquieting mutterings and fidgetings at the two lateral extremities of my vision, and was to wonder all the time just what conundrum or death's-head they might be rigging up for me on the flanks. I tried to show I didn't mind it much when the Committee asked each other my name, went on looking to the heart of me, and turned through their sheaves of papers to find the stuff about me. The stuff about me had been provided solely by me, in association with the younger of the Library's two typewriters (*né c.* 1913). A mere twenty copies of the application had been required, so it definitely hadn't been worth while to go to a printer. All the same, it did strike me occasionally—for example, just after putting 'Assitsant' instead of 'Assistant', rubbing it out on original and all four carbons, and then putting 'Assistnat'—that you could do a lot worse than go to a printer, and even that it wasn't really worth putting in for the job at all. While I pursued this vein of reminiscence I tried to give a bodily and facial impersonation of the thoroughly good, sound, honest, reliable, trustworthy, competent, responsible, steady, sober, level-headed chap, with just that touch of imagination which makes all the difference. I moved my lips forward a couple of millimetres to indicate this last property, but kept my brow trustworthy and my eyes competent.

The interview began. Prompted occasionally by the clerk, Gruffydd-Williams took me through my application, making sure that I wasn't an impostor, or at least wouldn't own up to being one at this stage. An alderman sitting on the other side of Gruffydd-Williams then asked me whether I thought I could do the job, and I said I thought I could. Next he wondered aloud whether I wasn't too young for such a responsible position, and I said I didn't think I was, at the same time trying to show that I found his wonderment both subtle and instructive. He asked me finally why I wanted the job. I'd have liked to match his impertinence by asking him if he was all right with God, but I said only that I wanted the extra money, felt an urge to rise in my profession and would like to have a crack at the problems of organisation which the post involved. This was a pre-selected answer, designed to avoid the pitfalls of mere avarice (too crude), mere ambition (too crude), and mere vanity (too unworldly).

This part clearly went down all right, but it was only a limbering up on both sides, an overture saluted chiefly by yawns but which all the same plays over some of the main themes, a phase corresponding to the mutual circumambulation of two dogs, like the components of a binary sun-system, before they fly at each other. A man in his early thirties with a savage red face now cleared his throat and looked at Gruffydd-Williams from a couple of places along. He was Salter, an interfering Liverpudlian who lectured on constitutional history at the local University College, and who, by patiently going on losing his temper in the Library, had got himself co-opted on to this Committee. "Mr. Salter," Gruffydd-Williams said. This was it.

"Oh, Mr. Lewis," Salter said in his thick, retching voice. "You did History at the College under Professor Furriskey, didn't you? Would you tell the Committee what class you obtained in the degree examination in your final honours year?"

To be fair to him, Salter's prolixity was intended, I could tell, to give the other people on the Committee a chance to follow him along the difficult path of academic technicality. "Yes, sir," I said. "I got a Two A."

"A Two One, yes," Salter said, giving emphasis by variety.

Before he could go on, one of the several Trade Union members present, a big sallow man from the T. & G.W.U., slewed his head towards the middle of the table and said: "What's this Two One A business, please? I'm afraid I didn't just grasp that."

Salter bowed his own head before turning it, so that his eyes and voice were coming upwards into the interrupter. "Class Two, Division One, Mr. Jones," he said, unexpectedly deferential. "A good Honours degree."

"Aw, Honours, is it?"

"That's correct, yes. And . . . Mr. Lewis, you have your A.L.A., I believe?"

"Yes, sir."

"Don't bother with all this Two One A.A.A. business, Mr. Salter," Jones said. "It's not the letters after his name that interests us. If he got his School Cert and went through the College all right, it's enough for me, see?"

Salter looked at me with undiminished hatred, but in a way that suggested I wasn't its only object. His face was a little redder, and when he spoke again it was as if his already over-large tongue had been stung by a wasp. "I'd like to tell the Committee," he said spitefully, "that I've found Mr. Lewis extremely helpful in seeking out the kind of obscure and little-known books that only a scholar like myself would want. I will say that he seems to have an excellent knowledge of what the Library contains in that way."

Wishing that Salter hadn't used the rather double-edged term 'scholar', I bowed my head as if my health had been proposed.

"Now, Mr. Lewis," Salter went on; "do you consider that that kind of knowledge is an important qualification for the post you've applied for?"

"Well, sir, that's not a simple question," I said, meaning it. To minimise the importance of 'that kind of knowledge' would antagonise Salter and possibly others;

to stress it would establish me as an intellectual. "I think I'd say that the first duty of a Sub-Librarian—as of a librarian of any grade—is to the ordinary borrower," ("Hear hear" Jones said robustly) "but anyone with any self-respect would of course regard catering for the expert as an integral part of his duties." Yes, that's right, I thought as I said this: showing the expert where to find the *Encyclopædia Britannica* or the *Cambridge History of English Literature*. But I was pleased with what I'd said.

Salter wasn't; his mouth tightened and his face seemed to grow narrower. "That's all very well, Mr. Lewis, but it doesn't tell us much, does it? Don't you think a Sub-Librarian should have some particular field of study in which he himself is something of an expert, if only so that he can understand the problems of the expert?"

"Yes, I suppose that would help him."

Salter's mouth became asymmetrical; he was smiling. "In that case, Mr. Lewis, what's your special field?"

I paused for a moment; I couldn't say 'constitutional history', because Salter would at once shoot me down on his own subject, and that would look bad even to those who didn't like Salter or constitutional history. On the other hand, it was about the only subject I knew at all well in library terms, except science fiction and the modern American novel, and they wouldn't do. Almost at random, I said: "The drama," thinking of the time I'd helped a man from Brynbwrla Community Centre to confirm the absence from catalogue and shelves of *The Duchess of Malfi*.

"Do you mean to tell me, Mr. Lewis," Salter said with luxurious elaboration, "that you regard that as a specialist field?"

"I do."

"Why? How?"

At this awkward point, the pressure was relieved by another interruption from Jones, who'd been showing more and more plainly by wriggling and fiddling about that he thought this had gone on quite long enough. "The drama is a most important field indeed," he declared. "I agree with the applicant, Mr. Salter."

"I didn't say it wasn't important, Mr. Jones, I was just querying whether the degree of specialisation involved in . . ."

"Perhaps you aren't aware, Mr. Salter, that there are no fewer than sixty-three amateur drama groups in this town and its neighbouring environs?"

"No, but I wasn't trying to . . ."

"And you tell our friend here that drama isn't important? I'd like in that case to know what you do see fit to consider important, Mr. Salter. In this area, as in many others in Great Britain as a whole, though I thank God we've less to contend with here than in some other places I happen to know of, well anyway, we've all got to bear in mind the problem of juvenile delinquency which has arisen as a result of wartime conditions. We have to keep our young people off the streets, and provide them with some leisure activity. Myself, I look upon the recent growth of these amateur dramatic groups as a most hopeful sign. I don't know what other people think . . ."

Several other people thought to say "Hear hear", notably a middle-aged clergyman with a tiny withered face like one of last year's nuts. This man now said: "What Wales needs to-day is an upsurge of the native Welsh culture, and the Welsh drama, I agree with my friend Mr. Jones, with whom I've disagreed so often in the past, and so it gives me particular pleasure to agree with him now, I say the Welsh drama is a fundamental form of Welsh cultural expression, though Mr. Salter, who's only recently come to live among us, may not think so. The Welsh drama . . ."

I was sure for a few moments that this, delivered in the

accents of a film Welshman and accompanied by continuous gesture, would beat Salter into the ground, but he came back strongly with: "That's not my point at all, Mr. Chairman. I wasn't running down anybody . . ."

"I don't think you realise either, Mr. Salter," Jones cut in, "that many plays by local authors have aroused considerable . . ."

The clergyman had taken longer than Jones to work out what Salter had just said, but having done so he saw no reason for delaying his response to it. "It is the point, it is the point. Here we are, seeking to provide the cultural needs of a growing Welsh industrial area, with all these new factories . . ."

Jones took him up: ". . . like the mounted toy soldier factory near Fforestfawr, they're making denture boxes just on the other side of Llantwrch, and then there's the bicycle saddles starting up next month at Cwmpant . . ."

During this, I glanced at Gruffydd-Williams, wondering when he was going to interfere. He sat there, his eyebrows raised, his eyes on the scribbles he was making with a pencil, looking very intelligent and clearly not caring. Why didn't he care? What was the point of him if he didn't care? Was he too important to care?

"But the drama as a specialist field, Mr. Chairman," Salter said desperately.

Gruffydd-Williams gave him an encouraging smile, as if to say he'd be glad to hear Salter on this subject at any time, particularly now.

"I know Mr. Salter won't think we've done much so far," the clergyman was going on, "but we haven't had everything made easy for us in Wales. You must give us time, Mr. Salter. Really, you must be reasonable."

There was an assenting rustle and mutter. When it had quite died away, Gruffydd-Williams said quietly, but moving his mouth a lot: "Have you any more questions to ask the applicant, Mr. Salter? Anything to add?"

Salter let his body sag and flopped it to and fro for a moment, like a cretin; then he said, in a tone of fairly impressive weariness and contempt: "Let it pass, Mr. Chairman. Thank you all the same."

An interlude followed, during which one of the block-headed doctors who abound in Aberdarcy (this one was crazy about collecting antique inkwells so as to be able to boast of his extravagance, and had recently joined the Labour Party in a vain attempt to get on to the Council) asked me a question about redecorating the Library and how important I thought it was. Reflecting that his head was if anything smaller than Bill Evans's and more blockish, and how both heads would roll when the Day came and Ken Davies was appointed Minister of Culture, I said I thought redecoration was pretty important. The interlude was used by the others for the lighting of pipes and cigarettes, nose-blowing, and a brisk rattle of conversation. At the end of it Jones spoke up.

"Perhaps I might ask a few questions, Mr. Chairman?" He said it like a teacher at a meeting of a pupils' society.

"Mr. Jones."

"Now, young man, I shan't keep you long if you answer up and stick to the point. Now, speaking as . . . um," he paused with a frown, "as Secretary of the Fabian Society, as you know, Mr. Lewis, we've for years enjoyed the privilege of using the Reference room at the Library for our meetings—Mr. Rowlands and Mr. Webster have always been very co-operative in that particular. But, er, thinking on what I might describe as a wider front, through the experience I've had the good fortune to acquire as Literature Secretary of the Aberdarcy Labour Party, I know for a fact that many people would welcome opportunities for smaller, more informal discussions than the kind I've just mentioned. I'd like to know your views on this point, Mr. Lewis. I feel myself that we must try to make the Library less of a . . . what shall I say? an institution of the intellect, purely of the intellect, and more in touch with the needs of the people. After all," he looked seriously round at his colleagues, "we are public servants. Now, what would you say to that?"

"I'm quite in agreement there, sir. Our first duty is to the public, after all."

"Quite so." He stared at me with his blunt bus-inspector's face, a face empty of all curiosity, all uneasiness, all spite, all humour. Why had he taken the trouble to speak at all, or even come to the meeting, get on to the Committee in the first place, work his way up in the Union and the Party? He began to speak again; he hadn't finished yet. What hadn't he finished? "You feel we'd do well to widen our field in the way I suggest?"

"I think there's a great danger in proceeding on too narrow a front, sir. No facility ever suffered through being made available to a more extensive cross-section of the community."

"That's very well put indeed. As Class Secretary of the W.E.A., now—as you know, our class on modern political thought is one of the oldest-established classes in the area —well, occasional meetings thrown open to the public would broaden the basis of appeal, and I feel strongly that the Library should play its part in this. Do you agree?"

I said I did. What Jones was really saying was that he intended to go on organising people, organising more and more people, causing complications with the caretaker about locking up, leaving lights on, losing the keys, re-arranging the furniture and not putting it back, holding meetings so as to clash with bookings made by bodies like the Coed-y-Mor Old Age Pensioners' *Eisteddfod* Organising Committee (Vocal Section). Well, in a way I didn't mind him doing it all.

Jones, after informing me that his official capacity at this meeting was as the representative of the Secretary of the Trades and Labour Council, went on talking, but somehow I had to stop listening. Gruffydd-Williams was looking at me with a faint smile, much as at my entry into the room. Was he laughing to himself at what that librarian fellow of his wife's was undergoing? It was nice of him to back me, if he was backing me. For a moment I wished I'd got to know him in some other way, nothing to do with Elizabeth or jobs. In spite of his commanding air he seemed a very nice chap. I wondered what went on behind that bored but appraising expression, what he really thought of Whetstone and Theo James and Evans and the dentist and the dentist's mistress, not forgetting his own wife. It would be difficult to find out. I now heard Jones ask me what I thought the service provided could be improved.

"Well, sir," I said capably, "I feel we have nothing to be ashamed of in our progress up till now in this matter . . ." It was good to see a man who hadn't said anything so far nodding his head vigorously at my tribute to our progress up to now in whatever matter it was. ". . . But as far as the future goes we should give all possible improvements our earnest attention—and I mean that not as a mere piece of vague approval, but as something quite real and urgent."

"Thank you," Jones said. "Now you can imagine that this also affects me in my capacity as the Workers' Educational Trade Union Committee representative. Do you think it desirable that the type of literature I've mentioned should be freely available in the Library?"

This, so late, when Jones seemed to have announced the full muster of his titles, nearly floored me. Was he talking about books containing mention of the sexual act, or did he mean things like those frightful pamphlets on the history of the tin-plate industry and so on with which I was steadily filling up Jenkins's room? "I do, sir," I said loudly, staring fervidly at him.

It was the right answer, but before I could congratulate myself a woman who didn't look like a woman was saying in a rapid monotone and without taking breath: "I think, Mr. Chairman, that the type of literature supplied in our libraries, without seeking to provide propaganda, should nevertheless help the working classes to shoulder their responsibilities in striving for progress and a more equitable distribution of the means of production and exchange—what are the applicant's views?" The restiveness at the flanks of the table grew very marked during this short speech.

I opened my mouth to utter some superlatives of agreement when I saw one of the aldermen glaring at me. I knew this old shag by repute: he was the most prominent of Aberdarcy's outfitters, sat as an Independent (i.e. Tory) Councillor, was President of the local British Legion Branch and completely controlled the Golf Club. Since the imposition of that control, he was known to boast, no Jew, Catholic or non-Britisher had had the impertinence even to put up for membership. I said in a lukewarm tone: "I would maintain at any rate that the Library stands behind every individual in his or her search for the fuller life and in equipping everyone to play his or her part in the community." It would take a Central or South American President (of a Republic, I mean, not a British Legion branch) to object to that.

A pause followed, in which I speculated how much more there could be of this, considered that this Committee had slipped up badly in not co-opting Mrs. Davies, and felt I wouldn't say no to a cup of tea. The nut-faced clergyman was next. As before, he waved his arms about all the time while he talked, which he proceeded to do at length. The first few minutes of his address were devoted to thanking the Committee for letting him know and letting him come and letting him speak, and in saying, with profuse illustrative detail, how good he was. This old shag

I also knew. Like many another minister, he'd brought a bus-load of his congregation to pack the public meeting about Sunday cinemas three or four years previously. Again, like many others, he'd found the hall already bursting with squads from other chapels who'd turned up even earlier to make sure nobody who wanted Sunday cinemas could get in to vote. So he'd set up his pitch outside the hall and led an inflammatory and very loud rendition of *Caersalem* (the noted Congregationalist hymn). It was still one of his chief claims to importance that when, ten years or so ago, a task force of Welsh Nationalists had torn down and burnt the 'English' flag at Treherbert aerodrome, he'd only just not been among them. Each time I met him I was re-convinced, for the first couple of minutes, that he was trying to be funny. But I've often been wrong about that sort of thing.

He now began to include me, by degrees, within the bounds of his discourse, and before many minutes had passed had gone on to seem to be asking me what proportion of books in the Library should, in my opinion, be in Welsh. I said I thought these should be supplied as asked for. Holding out his arms to me as if he wanted me to run round the table and jump on to his lap, he said with emotion: "I wonder if you know that two people out of every five in this part of Wales are Welsh-speaking?"

"Monoglots?" I asked offensively.

"Welsh-speaking, I said," he said.

I shrugged my shoulders. "I very seldom get asked for books in Welsh. People want to read stuff about Everest and the Kon-Tiki expedition and escapes from prison-camps and so on. They might still want to if the stuff was translated into Welsh and the English copies burnt. It's difficult to be sure."

There was a slight but fairly general laugh at this. The clergyman spread his arms out sideways like a conductor allotting to his orchestra their share of applause. "It is our solemn duty to encourage and popularise our local authors," he said, glaring.

"Which authors are you referring to, sir?"

"I'm referring to such poets as Owain, Sion and Wiliam, and . . . to take a different kind of instance, to my own colleague, the Reverend Traherne Williams, his history of the Rhondda Baptists . . ."

"I'm afraid I'm not familiar with . . ."

"Our greatest poets? Him with six bardic chairs?"

"I've never been asked for . . ."

"A scandal, that's what it is. A scandal and a tragedy."

"We have other duties, sir, which I would regard as more . . ."

Nobody who hadn't been interrupting people for years could have interrupted as the woman now did, saying: "I think we agreed, Mr. Chairman, that what we have primarily to consider is the equipping of every person to play his or her part in the community. That and giving our full support to each and everyone in his struggle to attain a fuller life."

There was silence. Gruffydd-Williams drew in his breath. "Well, if there are no more questions . . ."

A little man in a check suit near the end of the table said: "Just one, Mr. Chairman." Every head switched angrily to him, but he held on bravely. "Won't take a minute."

"Mr. Wynn."

"You perhaps are familiar with the cultural habits of normal families in this area, Mr. Lewis?"

Liking 'normal' a lot, I said I was.

"Could you say, in the light of your experience, whether, in your opinion, the rents of council houses should be economic?"

"Yes, they should," I said instantly. "No question about it."

The little man began nodding, slowly at first, then stepping it up. His lips pursed tighter and tighter as he wrung every drop of significance from my answer. His eyes gradually shut. After a time, he said: "Yes," then, galvanically rousing himself, added: "Thank you, Mr. Chairman."

Gruffydd-Williams conferred with the clerk and at last said I could go. As I went out, it seemed to me that I was just on the brink of realising why he'd taken so little notice of what had been going on, but the thought eluded me and I couldn't bring it back. Someone was saying "No" loudly as I shut the door.

FIFTEEN

"HERE YOU ARE," the dentist said, giving me a tumbler of sherry, "this'll buck you up." His mistress, her glance more mediumistic than ever, confirmed this prognosis with an unsteady nod. She was wearing a kind of striped playsuit thing which began below the armpits and finished above the knee. The dentist looked at her every few seconds in amazement. Sometimes he'd shift his look from her to me, as if to say: "Look at this, eh? Bloody marvellous, isn't it? Look at this, then."

I smiled at them and drank some of the sherry, feeling I could do with being bucked up. I'd felt rather hot and tired coming out of Aberdarcy in Elizabeth's car, very hot and tired walking down the cliff path to the beach-hut which was the focus of the party, still hot and tired with my coat off walking across a lot of big stones, and a little bit hotter and more tired sitting on the sandy wooden steps of the hut while the other people milled about drinking and talking in front of me. Elizabeth wasn't among them. In a tone that left it open whether she was revealing a cut-and-dried plan or taking a sudden decision, she'd told me as I got out of the car that she was going to make a quick trip in the Aberdarcy direction to fetch more 'booze' and 'some of the other characters' while I was to go and find the hut. No, I couldn't come back with her, nor was I to mind the fact, just this moment recalled to mind, that Theo James was going to be among the personnel on the beach; it seemed that he had a bad memory, not only for plumbers' faces, but for everything. The guaranteed presence of James shored up my spirits a bit; skilfully managed, conversation with him might prove amusing. He'd given me a long imperatorial stare when I first arrived, but at the moment was near the water's edge chasing Whetstone with a bough of dried seaweed. The others present, apart from the dental couple, were a thin pug-nosed man wearing his shirt outside his trousers and a thin long-nosed woman with goose-pimpled arms and a very short hair-do. This last expedient gave her head and neck a melancholy, denuded appearance, like a tree cut back for the winter.

The dentist, uttering a groan, settled himself at my side. He took each foot from the ground in turn and waggled it fretfully. "Good to get the weight off your feet," he said. "That's the snag about my line: on your feet all flipping day, day in and day out. No end to it. Gets you down, you know."

"I'm sure it does," I said.

He turned abruptly to look at me as if I'd said he was the whitest man I knew. "Yes. It certainly does. Not many people realise that, believe me. Very few. Yes. Really gets you down. Takes all the use out of you." With another sudden change of mood, signalled by a choking laugh, he grabbed his mistress's hand and jerked her towards him. "Not quite all, though, eh? Not quite all.

Eh? Sweetheart? Some use left in the old man when the old surgery door's bolted and barred? Eh?"

Though her smile recalled nothing more literary than lipstick advertisements, the girl's demeanour on being pulled half on to his knee suggested that of some *farouche*, almost dementedly sensitive novelist about to be seduced by the president of a book society. Delicately withdrawing herself a little, she leant against one of the upright spars of the hut in an attitude clearly meant to be unconsciously provocative. I studied for some short time the veins on her feet and the blonde down on her legs, then averted my gaze and met that of the dentist. Having first jerked his head towards his mistress, he went on to shake it slightly, as one confessing an inability to expound or even to apprehend. He did, however, say: "Not bad, is she, eh? My little sweetheart? Not too bad?"

"Not bad at all," I said.

Again an expression of gratitude and affection suddenly manifested itself on his face. "You're dead right," he said, slapping my knee. "Dead right. Come on, more to drink. Knock that back, now. Let's go to town." Sherry clacked and glugged up to the lip of my glass. "No, I think you've got enough there to last you, my sweet. I said you're not having any more." He turned excitedly back to me, offered me a cigarette and took my refusal in very good part. "Wise man. Wish I wasn't such a blessed slave to the beastly things. Just habit, nothing but habit. As soon as my chair's empty, out comes the packet. You don't miss much, believe me. And gives you more money for the old grogging. Good luck to you." He drank several fluid ounces from his glass, which he was refilling from a dark square-shouldered bottle he kept at his side, between his feet or on his lap. He suddenly bawled: "Here, Stan. Come and join the company. Stop skulking over there with your wife. Don't like to see fellows skulking with their wives. Someone here I want you to meet."

The thin couple came over and were introduced to me as Stan and Margot Johns. Both of them shook hands cordially. The dentist asked them how things were going.

Stan Johns said they were going fine, and added: "Just had a good bit of news about my talk. Yes, the one on the state of Welsh music. You remember, on the seventeenth of last month."

"I remember it coming off, Stan," the dentist said. "Afraid I had to miss it, though. Got called in at the hospital on an emergency. A kid, little girl of eight, with two supernumerary . . ."

"Well, this talk," Johns said. "I had a letter from the London people this morning—no, yesterday it was. It appears they want me to revise it a little and give it on the London. Mind you, I'm not surprised."

"Good stuff," the dentist said absently, fondling the neck of his bottle. His animation seemed to have departed.

"I'm not surprised, because it was bloody good. Absolutely first-rate. Margot said it was the best talk she's ever heard on the B.B.C."

"Since the war," Margot amended.

"This London fellow thought I might have said more about some of the other people and less about my own work, but as I told him in my reply that would give a false emphasis. After all," and here Johns laughed slightly, glancing amicably at me, "if you're going to talk about Welsh music at all you've got to give well over half your time to me, if not more. There just isn't much Welsh music worth considering apart from mine, you see. I think you could tell what a gulf there is between me and the rest just from hearing my *Sinfonia Concertante* down here last autumn. Old Arwel Jenkins brought out the jazz rhythms to perfection, I thought. And, of course, this opera I'm doing with Keidrych Rhys is going to be the biggest musical event in Britain since the war. But I really shouldn't talk about myself so much."

This recital helped on the sense of well-being that had started to drive out my slight feeling of dissatisfaction at Elizabeth's absence. Johns had addressed himself to me almost all through, and his manner had been friendly and attentive. He seemed to be implying that if all these lovely things had to happen to someone else instead of him, he'd nominate me if consulted. To be singled out like that by a chap whose grasp on phenomena external to himself was clearly so slight was a bit of a compliment. So was being picked on by the dentist to assist at the vagaries of his fancy. That practitioner again slapped me on the knee at this point and again urged me to drink up. Even Whetstone and James, who'd now come panting up the beach in search of refreshment and talk, were ready to listen and occasionally to laugh when I launched myself gingerly into the conversational flow and mentioned some of the funny things that had gone on at my interview. Johns naturally didn't take any notice of what I had to say, but at least twice he glanced over from where he was explaining to his wife something about his music, and smiled at me approvingly.

Time passed. I'd suspected Whetstone and the dental couple of having harboured certain suspicions and reservations about me, but these had apparently vanished. Well, I was prepared to abandon mine about them. They might not be very bright and they did perhaps fit into my old category of upper-class, but it was getting rather late in the day to bother with things like categories. There weren't so many amiable and light-hearted people about that one could afford to turn sour or sociological on them when they turned up. Theo James siphoned off a little of this feeling of mine when he came nearer to me, peered at my face, and said:

"I say, do forgive me, but don't we know each other?"

"I don't think so, do we?"

"Do excuse me, as I say, but I do have the most extra-ordinary feeling that we've encountered each other in the fairly recent past, don't you?"

"Well, now you come to mention it, I don't, no."

"I thought it might have been under the auspices of the fair Elizabeth on some occasion or other."

"Yes, it might have been, but it can't have been."

"Yes, I take your meaning. You wouldn't be a member of the Aero Club, I take it, nor yet of the Yacht Club?"

I shook my head a lot at this. "No, that's just what I wouldn't be."

"No, I see. Well, do pardon me for this show of vulgar curiosity, but I really could have sworn, as the phrase is." He went on peering covertly at my face.

"It's one of those queer things that happen in life," I said, giving it just a minim or two of the plumber's accent.

Every part of him stopped moving at once, as if I'd given him a beam with a twenty-first-century stun-gun, but Whetstone, suddenly bringing the lip of a wineglass between his teeth and tilting it, revived him into giggling struggles.

Deciding the dentist was a right guy and needling James was all very fine and large, but where was Elizabeth all this time, eh? The light was just starting to go and the party was warming up. The second of these propositions gained impressive support a moment later when the dentist's mistress, calling out: "This is the life" in a staggeringly deep voice, fell across her lover's knees and vomited, deftly and without fuss, on to the sand. The dentist remained quite immobile except for drinking once from his glass with a gourmet's deliberation. He said to me in an undertone: "I warned her, you see. She's got to learn. Well, it's not surprising in a way. Knocking the flipping stuff back as if it was gripe-water. Bound to catch up with you in the end. Okay, you go ahead if you want to."

The last phrase was uttered as I helped the girl to her feet and asked her if she was feeling better. Resting her hand on my shoulder, she said she was, but could do with a little walk. We set off diagonally down the beach with me supporting her.

"I know I get drunk, see," she said. This was only the second sentence I'd ever heard her speak, and her voice had changed to a childish treble which, it transpired, was her norm.

"I shouldn't worry about it," I said.

"No, but it is worrying, you know. Not the getting drunk, but we're getting married in August."

"Well, that'll be fine, won't it?"

"I was hoping his wife'd never divorce him, but now she says she's going to, and he wants to get married straight after."

"Isn't that what you want?"

"Yes, in a way, but I'm worried that I shan't enjoy it when it isn't wrong any more. It's been fine all these years when it's been wrong. I might not like it when we're married and it stops being wrong to do it. Sounds silly, I know."

"Don't let it get you down. You're probably getting steamed up over nothing."

"Think so? Don't you find you like it more when it's wrong?"

I made no reply to this, and just then we arrived at a small clump of rocks at the water's edge. Here she kicked off her shoes and waded in a little way, bending gracefully down and washing her hands and face in the clear water, finally gargling in an attractive musical trill. A movement in the middle distance caught my eye. It was unmistakably Elizabeth, and the tall male figure following with an impeded gait was almost as quickly recognisable. Bill Evans, his arms round some large unidentifiable burden, was just debouching from the cliff path on to the sand.

While I was reviewing my feelings at the sight of him, the dentist's mistress came out of the water and stood in the lee of one of the rocks, flicking water from her hands and shivering slightly.

I went over to her. "How are you feeling now?"

"Ooh, much better, thanks. Cold, though."

When she put her hands on the small of my back and we started kissing each other a certain amount, I reflected that for me to be doing this with Elizabeth only a hundred yards away was to be living for the moment on an altogether more opulent scale, like a garage mechanic or somebody treating himself to a cigar and a glass of port after Christmas dinner. The dentist's bride-to-be felt like a little elongated parcel in my arms, trim and snug, though she was more active than most parcels. After a moment, she said: "You'd be much better off with me, you know, than with that Elizabeth."

"Why, what's the matter with her?"

"I shouldn't say this, I know, but I'd stay away from her if I was you. She's no good to you. We'd better be getting back. What did you want to get mixed up with her for?"

"It just sort of happened. And I'm not really mixed up with her." Side by side, we left the shelter of the clump of rocks.

"No? Well, it'd be easy, then. Why not ditch her?"

Again I didn't answer her, this time because I was watching an interesting scene enacted by the beach-hut. Evans, who'd glimpsed me as soon as I appeared, had stared at me for some seconds and now swung violently round on Elizabeth. Some sort of altercation seemed to follow, with Evans gesturing exhaustively. Many of these gestures were evidently designed to point me out to Elizabeth. A mumble of voices could be heard, though we were still too far away, and making too much noise walking across a patch of shingle, to distinguish any words. As I got nearer I felt more and more like a man going in to bat in his first Test Match with the score at nineteen for three. I realised that Evans had somehow been kept in ignorance of my being at the party until just now, and after advertising his consequent displeasure to Elizabeth was about to notify me in person. Actually this never happened, because at about the time when I was coming into talking range Elizabeth said something to him which made him look at her for a moment and then plunge off effortfully, his shoes kicking up gouts of sand, towards the cliff path he'd come down by so recently. A kind of valediction was provided by the sound of a ship's siren out in the bay, a low-pitched, harsh moan like an ogre breaking wind.

"I feel sorry for that poor bloody fool," the dentist's mistress said to me in a piping undertone. "That's the way they get treated, see, when she's finished with 'em."

Yet again I said nothing. There was a certain coldness in Elizabeth's manner as she held the two of us in her glance. "Had a nice walk?" she asked, opening her cigarette-case.

"What happened to old Bill?" I retorted.

"Oh . . . he had to go back."

"Pity. It's rather a long way, isn't it?"

There was a pause, during which the other people present went on looking at nothing much. Then the dentist said loudly: "Well, better now, sweetheart? Eh? That's the way. Here," and he gave the girl a glass of something yellow, "this'll buck you up. Good as new when you've got that down you. Drink it up." He seemed to have forgotten his recent strictures on her drinking, perhaps because he'd got much drunker himself in the last few minutes. Silenus now to her Artemis, he put his arm round her thighs and drew her towards him. She sipped softly at the yellow stuff, clasping the glass in both hands like a child, and glanced at me over the top of it. Her eyes appeared to have glazed over again, though they'd sparkled merrily enough when she was telling me about Elizabeth. Furtively, she winked one of them at me.

At another corner of the tiny veranda of the hut, Stan Johns had resumed telling Whetstone about his wind quintet. He was saying that it had jazz rhythms in it. Margot Johns was nearby, sitting with James and telling him something too. "Oh, I do agree with you so devoutly," I heard him say. Their features were just beginning to blur in the dusk.

Elizabeth, quite cordial now, asked me to help her with the things. These proved to form the burden that Evans had, rather pathetically, carried all the way from the car, and, apart from several bottles of beer and cider, consisted of some tins of soup and packets of biscuits and groceries. The next half-hour was spent in unpacking them, heating up some of them on a miniature cooker brought out from inside the hut, and eating all of them. Not having felt like eating after the interview I was very hungry, and had a hard time getting enough food for myself without seeming absolutely given up to swinish greed. With the meal I drank some wine, rather cryptically described by the dentist, who was pressing it on me, as *Père et Fils*. He said it would buck me up.

Without my really noticing it, an air of abandon crept over the final stages of supper and its aftermath. The dentist, an unlighted cigarette between his lips and with tousled hair, had yielded up all his abundant store of vivacity and was lying on the sand with his head on Margot Johns's lap. She was stroking his face and yawning a lot. After some minutes of pushing and pulling—made necessary by inertia rather than resistance—Stan Johns had induced the dentist's mistress to accompany him inside the hut. Every now and then I heard a creak or a crash as one or other of them came into contact with some item of furniture. Theo James had taken Whetstone off to show him how to clean a frying-pan with sand and sea-water, but although they'd had time to conduct and witness the cleaning of a dozen frying-pans they hadn't yet come back. The empty tins, bottles and paper bags scattered about the veranda gave it a ravaged and rather forlorn air.

A silence of some duration was broken by Elizabeth leaning over to me and whispering: "Nobody seems to want us very much, do they? Look at those two."

The dentist, reaching up, was trying feebly but persistently to pull Margot Johns's face down towards his own. I could have gone over to him, tapped him on the shoulder and explained to him that anatomical arrangements prohibit, in most cases, the face being brought within inches of the thighs without the knees being lifted, but I only laughed sparingly and agreed with Elizabeth.

She got up and stretched and threw a burning fag-end down the beach. "What about going for a little walk and leaving them to it for a bit?"

I said I thought that was a good idea, and we began strolling across the soft sand towards the more remote corner of the bay. What with the food and the drink I was feeling pretty contented and was enjoying the companionable silence between Elizabeth and myself. She broke it after a minute or two by saying: "Do you feel like a bathe?"

"Well." I hesitated, feeling rather frightened or something. "I haven't got a costume."

"Neither have I. It doesn't matter, does it?"

"No, I suppose it doesn't." I realised that we'd somehow taken the opposite direction from the frying-pan duo.

"Nobody's likely to try and stop us. And it's still very warm."

This, at any rate, was true, although it was already fairly dark. There was still a faint glow above the headland at the opposite arm of the bay, but the sea was almost black. The lights of a car showed for a moment, moving along the coast road towards Aberdarcy. I turned my back on it and began to undress, vainly trying to keep sand away from the inside of my trousers.

Elizabeth, unencumbered by shoelaces and socks, was quicker than I was and soon sauntered away towards the edge of the sea. I could see her quite clearly, a slightly hunched white figure with, I could tell, her arms clasped round her body. Yes, that's right, I thought as I took off my pants, it's not as hot as it was, is it? Perhaps Bill Evans knew what he was doing when he started for home. No explanation, by the way, had yet been given for his departure, nor had I asked for any. To do so would probably have been destructive in some way: I was back on the old footing with Elizabeth and wanted to stay on it. It wasn't a footing I could begin to define, but I felt it was one I liked. The dry sand under the soles of my feet made a curious tickling. I walked up to Elizabeth and put my arm round her waist.

She turned towards me and kissed me jovially. Though she seemed to be shivering, she felt warm enough, as if she'd been rubbed with rough towels. When I tried to infuse something more personal than joviality into our embrace, she surprised me by pulling away and leading me by the hand down the beach. Why? What was there down there? Then I heard the sea. Oh, of course, something had been said about a bathe, hadn't it? Well; my God: she must have been serious about it all the time, then.

After a few yards on terrible shingle I could feel moisture underfoot. The waves were quite loud now and distinctly visible, and one of them darted forward and submerged my feet. Very soon they felt like the feet of a statue dipped in a bath of acid. I hadn't thought there were temperatures like this inside a planetary atmosphere. Elizabeth instructed me to look at the phosphorescence, adding that it was caused by plankton in the water. I was silent, standing still with my hands on my knees; a wave, unmarked by the usual band of white, slopped upwards over my wrists. I closed my eyes. Wading noisily out to sea, Elizabeth pulled me after her, saying: "Come on in, it's wonderful, you'll feel marvellous when you come out."

I tried to get my brain to frame a sentence about its being all right for her with her thicker layer of subcutaneous fat, but it wouldn't. "If I come out," I said instead, to which she answered: "What?"

As a man burning to death will hurl himself blindly through a window-pane or over a stairhead, I hurried after her, slipping and hurting my feet on the large stones, hardly noticing the titanic agony when the water reached my crotch, falling at last with scarcely a cry and going under the surface all over. After some minutes of oxygen-starvation, I found I was standing up to my chest in an element that, rightly considered, wasn't immediately lethal. I looked towards the shore: there was a bit of Aberdarcy with its lights and neon signs and the line of the hill behind it, also lighted, and there was the coast road again, its home stretch marked by a double band of yellow lamps, and there, as somebody struck a match, was the hut, much further away than I'd have thought. Out at sea there was a small reddish gleam. There was something to be happy about in being at the centre of so huge an area in the dark. I waded towards Elizabeth, the water pouring itself against every inch of the submerged part of me, and we kissed again. I ran my hand down her back and her flesh felt hard and marine, not like a person's, and her hair when it brushed my shoulder was like a sheaf of wet grasses.

Quite soon I'd had enough. The pressure of cold on my skin had settled into an overall ache, and the shaved parts of my face, fanatically depilated for the interview, were smarting. I swam about for a bit, noticing that

Elizabeth didn't seem such a good swimmer as she might be thought to look, and emerged into the dry cold of the beach. I rubbed myself with my shirt and, priding myself on having thought of it, with my trouser-legs. Soon I felt less cold and the salt started pricking and itching on my back. Elizabeth began to talk, asking for and being granted the loan of my shirt, comparing the coldness of the water with that encountered at other times, and saying how much she'd enjoyed the bathe. When I was fairly dry, except for my hair, I went over to her. It was darker now. I could see the outlines of her shoulders and hips, the blackness, glimpsed against the tenuous whiteness of the skin, at her loins, and the effect of legginess rather than legs lower down. "Well, I think that's about as much as I can do with the materials available," she said in a chatty voice. "We shan't feel cold once we've got our . . ."

She stopped speaking with an endearing lack of surprise when I took her by the arms and drew her down with me to a kneeling position on the sand. She got hold of what must have been her skirt and blouse and spread them out. Close together, we lay down on them side by side. Although the salt flaked lightly under my fingertips and faint runnels of moisture wandered from her hair, her flesh no longer felt hard or non-human, and although her arms and legs were cool her body was warm again. Her face stayed wet and, in the darkness, couldn't sustain the hard maturity or the self-will I'd seen on it. When her breathing became rapid it took on no strained shallowness. The antagonism that can last so long between two persons in this situation, and can even finally persist, seemed to vanish for good.

There was something I didn't want to mention which I knew I had to mention. I mentioned it.

"It's all right, darling," she said in a blurred voice, "it doesn't matter with me; I can't. It's perfectly safe, honestly."

"Are you sure?"

"Yes, darling, oh yes . . ."

So at last we did it. She moved about in my arms and then, with a sudden deep breath, went taut and still. I could hear her voice mixed up with my own. My first real thought after this was that I did like her a very great deal, more than I'd realised and too much for me to tell her how much without giving up any last remnant of sense I might still retain.

She sighed and shifted her position. "That was good, wasn't it, darling?"

"Yes, it was good all right."

"You're quite a man, aren't you?"

"Oh, I don't know. It's just that you love it."

"Well, don't you love it?"

"Yes, as a rule. I did then, anyway."

"It's not it, that's not what I love. I love you."

"No, you'd better not say that."

"At least, of course I love it, but I love you as well."

"No, darling."

"Listen, John, it does look as if we're going to have a marvellous time together, doesn't it? Fancy it being like that the first time. We must suit each other awfully well for that to have happened. I do love you."

"No, don't."

"It's all right, I'm not trying to make you say you love me. I just like saying I love you. That's all. Of course, I know it must be a lot to do with not having had anything as good as that for a long time, I mean just in the physical way."

"Yes, I know."

"Darling, you're rather heavy, do you mind getting off?"

"Seems a pity, doesn't it?"

"Yes, but I . . . Ah, that's better. I'm awfully glad we've got round to doing it in the end, aren't you? I was afraid we weren't going to, ever."

"So was I, but I think I must have realised all along we were—you know, it was just going to be a matter of time."

"Did you? When did you realise that?"

"About five minutes after I met you, I suppose."

"Oh God, how dreadful, so did I. I didn't think it was as obvious as all that."

I grinned to myself. "It wasn't really obvious. I thought it was just me, all just my idea. I didn't know what you were feeling about it."

"Well, that's what I was feeling." She said nothing for a bit, then: "Don't let's go back yet. It's so lovely, lying here."

"Won't they be wondering where we've got to?"

"I shouldn't think they're capable of wondering anything."

"Here, didn't you say Vernon was coming down later?"

"He won't be here yet. And it won't matter much if he does turn up, actually."

I hesitated. "Why won't it?"

"Vernon knows all about me, don't worry. You must have guessed, haven't you, that there've been other chaps before you?"

"Yes, I think I had."

"You're not to mind it, darling. None of them compared with you. I couldn't know I was going to meet someone like you."

"I've really been the lucky one."

"No, me."

We got up and began dressing. I wondered how it was possible to ache so much and have so much sand on the body and inside the clothing without minding. "God, what sights they'll think we are when we get back."

"It's all right, I'll say we've had a bathe. I quite often do it these summer nights."

"That's a comfort. You're lucky to have a husband

like Vernon. What does he do all the time? Does he have girls?"

"No, he just makes money," she said in a rather far-off tone.

"I can't see much point in that, just that, I mean. But he's a very odd chap, isn't he? I think he's rather interesting, really. Got a lot in him. You ready?"

"Yes, ready," she said, more far-off than ever.

I could see the white of her blouse and sensed that she was standing there a bit stiffly. I went and took her hand. "What's the matter, darling?" I asked, feeling slightly alarmed at the tenderness in my manner.

"We are going to see each other again, aren't we?"

"Of course we are. Why shouldn't we?"

"Well, no, but I just thought . . . it just crossed my mind . . ."

"What did? Come here and tell me." I put my arm round her shoulders; they seemed as broad as ever and I couldn't help grinning again in the darkness.

"I thought perhaps you only wanted to . . . you know. I thought perhaps you didn't really like me much and only wanted to . . . you know."

She said it in a version of the clenched-teeth voice that had seemed to me so much a part of her confidence and self-assurance. Hearing that voice saying what it had now said aroused feelings in me that were hard to restrain. "Darling, of course I didn't only want that. You mustn't be such a silly little thing. You know I like you. I'm going to prove it to you."

"I thought when you said I wasn't to say I loved you, that's what you meant. I thought you meant it didn't mean anything more to you than just, well, thank you very much and that's that." She gave a loud and jerky sniff into my ear.

"That's ridiculous. Ring me up to-morrow morning at the Library and I'll try to slip out for a cup of coffee with you. Special treat, see?" I kissed her and rubbed the small of her back. "I've got a lot of things to say to you, but there isn't time now."

She moved off at my side. "I'm sorry I was such a fool," she said, and sniffed again. "I am a bit of a fool. You'll have to get used to it."

"Don't cry, angel. There's no need to."

"It's all right, I don't want to now."

With our arms round each other's waists we walked back along the shore towards the hut. A light was burning there, probably a candle, and figures wavered to and fro across it. The moon was coming up and making everything look frosty. Twice, unmistakably, I heard Whetstone's laugh from near the hut. Some sort of nervousness was rising out of the pit of my stomach and making me want to shiver a little. At first I thought it was just the prospect of experiencing Whetstone's laugh, plus a knowing look, at close quarters. But that in itself wasn't enough to explain how I felt. Perhaps it was because Gruffydd-Williams might have turned up, was probably even now waiting by the hut, one of the I-know-you smiles on his face, to greet Elizabeth and that librarian fellow of hers. Yes, that must be it.

"I never got a chance to ask you how the interview went off," Elizabeth said, skipping to get in step with me.

"Oh, not too bad. It lasted a tremendous time."

"Oh yes, they like to go through the motions."

"I'll say they do. Every possible motion."

"Was it very harrowing?"

"Not too bad."

"You don't sound too happy about it. Look, we'd better leave go now, in case anyone's peering at us. Thanks for being so sweet to me, darling."

"Oh, it was a pleasure."

She started to say something, but let it go as we came within range of the others. James, Whetstone and Johns were standing in a group with glasses in their hands, displaying animation. "It was like a baby's arm with a boxing glove on the fist," I heard Johns say. Whetstone raised his laugh then. The dentist was sitting on the steps without a glass in his hand and not displaying any animation. His mistress, who was sitting in silence with Margot Johns, looked up as we approached and fixed her dreamy gaze on me. It grew less dreamy for a moment while she tightened her mouth and nodded slowly and slightly a few times before turning abruptly away. Unless couched in ambush inside the hut, Gruffydd-Williams hadn't arrived, but I still felt rather awful, rather more awful on the whole, even after it was clear that nobody was going to do any kind of boggling at Elizabeth's and my reunion with our fellow-revellers.

After a little while, Elizabeth brought me a drink and drew me aside. "Look here, you're not really worrying about that interview, are you?"

"Yes, I think I . . . I am, rather. They're not letting us know till next week, who's been picked, I mean. They told us at the start they'd tell us as soon as the last chap came out, but they forgot about that, of course."

"You do sound down in the mouth, darling. I can tell you, it's absolutely in the bag."

"Here, do you mind if I have one of those? I think I'd like to try one."

"I'm sorry, darling, I'd got out of the way of asking you when you refused every time. I'll light it for you. Now, you just let me give you the low-down on the whole thing. . . . Here."

"Thanks." I drew at the black thing cautiously; its end seemed to crackle like a firework. "Go ahead."

"Cheero, then, Elizabeth," Stan Johns called out. "See you next week. And thanks again. Lovely party."

"Bye-bye, Stan, bye-bye, Margot . . . Now listen, John. It's all fixed for you to get the job. Vernon told me."

"Oh? When did he tell you that?"

"Darling, you don't honestly think the interview's got anything to do with it, do you? Though I'm sure you'd have got it anyway. No, Vernon made up his mind last week that you were to get it. I just rang you up to make an excuse to talk to you. I will say this for my husband, he can always get what he wants. And you needn't thank me for it, either. That's the funny part. No, he just hates old Rowlands's guts. And the thing that would annoy Rowlands most would be having you as his second-in-command. So you're going to be his second-in-command. He's only got a couple of years more to run, anyway. Vernon's got that committee in the palm of his hand, they just can't afford not to do as he says. Well, what do you think of it? Aren't you pleased?"

No wonder Gruffydd-Williams had seemed bored at my interview.

SIXTEEN

"WHAT'S THE MATTER, darling?" Elizabeth asked. "You are pleased, aren't you?" She stood with her back to the hut, her face faintly touched by moonlight. The candle, almost behind her, lighted up the corner of one square jaw.

I swallowed. "Of course I'm pleased. It was rather unexpected, that's all."

"You don't sound very pleased."

"I am, honestly. Is that the only reason Vernon picked me, to spite Rowlands?"

"Well, not entirely, of course. Obviously he couldn't afford to pick a complete bloody fool."

"I'm glad to hear that. But that was the main reason?"

"That's what he told me. But you mustn't be silly about it, darling; you're the best man for the job anyway."

"According to him."

"Whatever's the matter with you? Here." She got hold of my hand and pulled me some yards further away from the hut. We sat down on a hump of earth, sparsely covered with spiny grass, which lay at the edge of the brambled waste running back from the beach. "Now: you still want this job, I take it?"

"Just how much had you got to do with fixing this up?"

"I told you, not much. We talked about you, naturally, and I explained how you were fixed, not much money and so on, and anxious to get a place of your own to live, all that kind of thing. I suppose I shouldn't have done that, is that the line?"

"He'd never have known about me at all if it hadn't been for you, would he?"

"I don't know, perhaps he wouldn't. What's the matter, anyway? You've got the job. What have you got to worry about? Feeling slighted because you didn't get it completely on your merits? That's childish, darling."

I'd started shivering; a bathe causes the body to lose a great deal of heat, I reflected. I drew at my cigarette. It stuck between my lips, and my fingers, sliding down, pulled off the lit end and got slightly burnt. I threw the stub away. "I don't much care for this business."

"Now just you listen to me, John. Get this straight. In your position you can't afford to look a gift horse in the mouth. I can tell you, I've seen a good bit of this sort of thing since I've been married to Vernon. You can take it from me that nobody ever gets any kind of job or position in this world completely on his merits. There's always something else that enters into it. It may be politics, it may be having the right kind of face or education or background or whatever you like to call it, it may be, well, doing someone a personal favour. Now I can quite see how you'd feel happier if you could feel you'd got the job simply by being the best bloke to do it. But you've got to be sensible about it as well."

I'd been thinking about Ieuan Jenkins on and off for the past couple of minutes, but now my attention had wandered from him as well as not remaining entirely with Elizabeth. For what seemed the first time I realised that, behind the clumps of rocks earlier that evening, I'd been quite as prepared, during those few seconds, to lie down on the sand with the dentist's mistress as I'd been to do the same with Elizabeth. I began pulling up blades of grass and winding them round my fingers.

"You've got nothing to be ashamed of at all," Elizabeth was going on. "If you must bring this moral side of yours into it, tell yourself it's the best thing for everyone that you should be Sub-Lieutenant or whatever it is rather than any of the other boys. That's right, isn't it? You haven't had much experience, but in time you'll be doing old Rowlands's job as well as your own—running the place. This isn't just a sort of prize you've won, it's a job, and affects a lot of people, not just the ones who didn't get the job."

"I know all about that," I said. "But it's a fiddle just the same, and I don't like fiddles. One of the things I feel rather strongly about is fiddles. You've no right to feel like that about a thing if you let fiddles go on when they're ones that happen to work in your favour. You can't just let yourself pack it in and not care. You're being a bastard if you do. And I've decided now I don't agree I could do the job better. I don't know, perhaps I could, I just can't tell. But old Beynon looked pretty good to me. So did Howard. It was up to that ragtime bloody committee to sort that one out. Instead of which it was all rigged before they even sat down. Or are you denying that?"

"Christ, who's trying to deny it? But if you think it

matters as much as all that, then you're being stupid and self-centred. There are more people mixed up in this than just you, you and your conscience."

"I don't care about any of that. It's a dirty deal."

"Look here, John, try and grow up. This is the way things are, can't you see that? And talking of dirty deals, you're hardly in a position to go round moaning about them. I suppose adultery isn't a dirty deal according to your way of thinking. You and your conscience are quite happy about that, eh?"

"You know I'm not."

"Yes, I know you're not all right. I'm glad we've got to that, mister chapel deacon. If you want to work your guilty feelings off, wait till I'm out of the way. Your trouble is you don't think, not even for a second. You can't see the most obvious things. That marriage of yours, now. How long do you think it's going to last, even in the state it's in now, unless you can get out of that foul place a bit sharp, and find somewhere decent to live? Can't you see that money's the most important thing; without this spot of extra money you and Jean haven't got a hope?"

I shivered again. "Nice of you to be so considerate about Jean, but you've left it a bit late, haven't you?"

"Ha ha, three cheers." She got up and stared at me, her hands on her hips, looking very tough. "I thought we'd hear something like that eventually. Yes, you struggled like hell, didn't you? All my idea, wasn't it? Well, I apologise for raping you back there. I should keep your mouth shut if I were you, for a bit. Give yourself a chance to let it wear off."

"Yes, I think I will, that's not a bad idea. Well, cheero. You can tell the others I had too much to drink and had to go home."

She caught me by the arm, and I had another impression of how strong she was. "Stop behaving like a bloody fool."

"I'm very sorry," I said, pulling my arm free. "I didn't want any of this to happen."

"If you go now, that's the end of it as far as I'm concerned. It's finished."

"Thanks for making it nice and easy." I walked away.

"You won't get a bus at this time," she called after me. "It'll take you two hours. On foot all the way."

This argument, by far the most telling, was unfortunately not the one I could allow myself to yield to. I walked on towards the hut, where the candle was guttering and the dentist stretched out full length on the veranda. Nobody else was about.

"Give my regards to your wife," I heard her shouting. The dentist groaned loudly.

She's used that one before, I thought, but it's a good one all the same. I couldn't blame her for using it; what I'd done must strike her as perverse, cruel and absurd. It struck me a bit like that too. But the thing now was to get home.

As I neared the place where the cliff path started I heard someone call "Hallo!" It was Whetstone, I found, sitting on a stone and talking to the dentist's mistress. Throughout the short conversation which followed, she stared fixedly past my shoulder.

He peered up at me. "Oh, it's you," he said. There was just enough light for me to note for the first time, and with idle surprise, that his ears were invisible in full-face.

"Hallo, Paul," I said. "How are you getting on?"

"Not as well as you, I don't suppose, old boy."

"Oh? I'm sorry to hear that. Well, I mustn't interrupt you. I'm just on my way home."

"Ah, I suppose you've had all you want out of the party by now. Going to have a long walk, aren't you? Perhaps someone'll give you a lift when you get near Aber. But don't build on it."

"I won't, don't worry."

"Pity Theo's only just left, running the Johnses home. From your point of view, I mean. Personally I'm quite reconciled to it. In fact I think it might do you good to walk. Might limber you up, if you know what I mean."

"I'm awfully sorry, I must be getting dense. Limber me up?"

"Well, Bill had to walk, you remember, and he hadn't spent so long down here as you have, and to much less effect, too."

"I shouldn't worry about old Bill. He'd have got a bus."

"Doesn't really affect my main point. Rather helps it, in a sense. Bill deserved to get a bus. I don't think you do."

"I've been naughty, have I?"

"You know best about that, old boy. No, I don't feel you quite get my drift. I happen to think Bill Evans is rather a good chap, you see. And if you don't mind my saying so, I'm not very much of the same opinion about you. Quite the contrary, in fact. Sorry to have to mention it."

Barking excitedly, I gave him the English snooks (left hand to nose with fingers extended, right hand subjoined with fingers extended), then German snooks as Jean had demonstrated them (left hand as before, but right hand curled up and rotated as if cranking a cine-camera), then the donkey's-ears treatment with raspberry or Bronx cheer *obligato*. This completed, I moved off once more, feeling a little toned up for the moment.

The cliff path was gradual, but of uneven texture; sand, grass, gravel and bare earth. My foot slipped a few times without making me fall. I could hear the waves breaking on the small rocks that ran out from the base of the cliff, and once the whine of a late lorry along the coast road. Near the summit I entered a thin patch of wood, where unexpectedly there seemed to be more light. The moon was behind a thin sheet of cloud but a number of stars were showing between the branches of the trees. I stopped, out of breath, and looked about me. Although Aberdarcy itself was hidden by a lump of cliff, I could see the glare of its lights in the sky. Elsewhere there was little but large, ill-defined masses of cliff and hill running off to both sides and away downwards from under my feet. A gust of wind rustled the boughs and the grasses and I began to feel a slight bewilderment. Then I saw someone hurrying up the way I'd come.

It was Elizabeth, less out of breath than I'd been, and evidently better able to see in the dark. "I thought I might as well drive you back," she said at once. "I don't want to stay at that party any longer."

"There's no need to . . ."

"I told you I don't want to stay. Come on, no use standing about here." She walked past me towards the car, which was now a couple of hundred yards away. Her bearing had all its old energy and decisiveness.

I hurried to keep up with her. Would it be too ridiculous to say nothing for the rest of the way? "What about Vernon?" I asked conversationally. "Won't he wonder where you've gone? Or won't he be showing up now?"

"I'd rather not talk if you don't mind."

My thoughts turned to Whetstone: it must surely be a good thing to be disliked by someone like that. But why was he so annoyed? Was he against immorality, or heterosexuality, or just me? Or, contrary to all appearance, was he, had he once been, keen on Elizabeth? The bloody fool. Yes, it definitely was a good thing to be disliked by someone like that. On the other hand, if he and I had had to fall out, it would have been more satisfactory and praiseworthy to reject him first, before he had the chance of rejecting me. Too late for that now.

Elizabeth unlocked the door of her driving-seat and got into the car, then reached across and unclicked the other door. "Get in," she said. I got in.

Acting as if she wanted to leave the company of a man with a gun, she started the engine, switched on the lights and drove across the grass in low gear, the engine bellowing and me jigging up and down beside her like a tenderfoot on a mustang. We rushed out into the road, turning sharply so that I was bundled against my door, then shot off towards Aberdarcy. As she changed into top gear and the car, with an appalling readiness, flung itself forward again, I saw the glow of headlights round the next bend. I glanced at Elizabeth and saw her profile gradually become outlined against the beam of the oncoming lights. I could read nothing in it.

An outburst of hooting made me lose interest in this enigma and look back to the road. It was at once clear that unless Elizabeth pulled over to our side of the road there was going to be a collision, roughly along the line of the respective offside wheels, within five seconds. Nothing happened for a little while, then there was a loud noise of brakes, the car swerved as Elizabeth wrenched at the wheel, and, without any actual impact, we entered upon a completely new mode of movement, swinging from one side of the road to the other in smooth leaps, rather like, I suppose, a canoe shooting rapids. The amplitude of the swings increased and I began to take an intense interest in a stone wall that advanced and receded on Elizabeth's side of the car. I moved along the seat towards her; there seemed to be tons of time. I knew her lips were drawn back from set teeth as she struggled with the wheel. "I'll take over if you're tired," I said. There was a bang behind us and the car appeared to be trying to turn round. I put my arm across Elizabeth's chest. I forget what happened then.

A car drove down the road towards us. I was sitting

with one hand under Elizabeth's near armpit and the other on her far shoulder; she was bent forward half-over the steering-wheel. I tried to pull her upright and she fell on to my lap. Something about the movement made me wonder whether bad driving alone could account for this business. The door on my side was opened and a torch was flashed into my face. I said to myself that it was very quick-witted of whoever it was to have brought it with him from his car. "Everybody all right here?" Gruffydd-Williams asked. "Oh, it's you, Lewis. Is that Elizabeth?"

"Yes."

"How is she?"

"Don't know."

"Get out of that seat, will you, and let me have a look. That's right. Now . . ." He reached up and clicked a switch. A dim light came on in the roof. I watched him turn her over and smooth her hair away from her face. Her eyes were closed. There was a dark wound of some sort above one eyebrow and some blood somewhere else; it was difficult to see. "Mm," he said.

"How is she?"

"What? Oh, she's all right. Knocked herself on the wheel, I expect. She'll be round in a minute. You were lucky there's this bit of verge on this side. There'd have been a different tale to tell if you'd gone straight into the wall instead of hitting it with the wing. Damn lucky, really. I don't know what she thought she was doing coming round on the crown of the road at that lick. Yes, well, I'll run her back and knock up old Elwyn Price. She might have a bit of concussion. Better be on the safe side. Then the car. That can wait till the morning, I should think; you're well off the road here. Mm. That'll be the best thing."

He was sitting there holding her head and looking into her face. "Yes, I was sure she'd do something like this one day. Good job it's no worse." He looked suddenly up at me. "What about you? You're not hurt, I suppose?"

"No, I'm all right."

"You're all right, yes," he said in a peculiar tone. "Good. There's no need to worry about you, then."

"No."

"Good. We won't worry about you, then. We know how you stand, don't we, Lewis?"

"Yes."

"Yes, we know just how you stand. And we won't worry about it any more, will we?"

"No."

"Just give me a hand with her, into my car, will you?" he asked in a different tone, one that suggested he was cutting through a digression of mine back to the main topic. "I'll lift her this way and you take her legs when I'm clear."

Her legs felt cold without stockings and with her hair over her face again she looked unkempt and undefended. We got her into the back of his car. He stayed in there with her for a minute or two, and I heard him murmuring. I walked over to the other car. From this side it appeared to be quite whole, even new, in the moonlight. I leaned in and switched off the lamp in the roof, noticing as I did so Elizabeth's cigarette-case on the seat. She'll be wanting that, I thought, and slipped it into my pocket.

I sauntered back across the road, noticing that my right hand had begun to throb. There was a long contusion on the back of it, with blood and flakes of skin here and there. I heard Gruffydd-Williams raise his voice: "No, of course I won't, my darling. Whatever do you take me for? No, never, dearest, I promise you. Now just you relax and go to sleep and we'll have you in bed in five minutes." He got out and I saw he'd left his jacket over her.

"She's come round, has she?" I asked.

"You come in front with me," he said, getting into his seat.

"Hadn't I better . . . in case she . . .?"

"You come in front with me, if you want to come at all."

I got in beside him and we drove off. His behaviour to-night was quite different from that of a man who lets his wife go her own way and doesn't care. Nor did he at all resemble any longer the subtle, detached, irresponsible aesthete of power he'd once seemed to be. He drove fast, but with great skill and care. He said nothing until we were on the outskirts of Aberdarcy; then he drew up at the pavement and turned to me.

"I'm dropping you off here, Lewis," he said. "I'm going to take her up to the doctor's now. You'll have to walk the rest of the way." He paused, apparently biting a fingernail. "There's a good deal I could say, but I'm only going to say this. Don't ring up or call in to see how she is, or make any attempt to get in touch with her. Ever. Is that clear?"

"Yes," I said. I got out. "I'm sorry."

"Yes. Good-night." I slammed the door and he drove off.

I ran most of the way home, chiefly because of my dislike of being out alone at night. I didn't see a soul about anywhere and kept trying to work out what time it was. When I got to the house the light was burning in our sitting-room upstairs. It was on in the passage too and Mrs. Davies was standing at the top of the basement stairs. "Is that you, Mr. Lewis?" she said, coming forward. She was wearing a bottle-green dressing-gown, seemingly of taffeta, and had a hairnet on which drew the reddish frizz close to her head. She looked like an ancient boy.

"Yes, it's me, Mrs. Davies."

Barring my path, she said: "Just a minute if you don't mind, Mr. Lewis."

"What's the matter, Mrs. Davies? It's getting rather late."

"I know, that's what I'm so worried about. Don't want to bother you, Mr. Lewis, but Ken haven't come home yet, and I'm a bit worried, like."

"Well, what can I do about it?"

"Didn't happen to see him as you was coming along, did you, Mr. Lewis?"

"No, and I really must be . . ."

"Don't go, please, Mr. Lewis. He've only gone up to the public house in Alton, and now it's after one, see? And he's in with such a bad lot recently, too. That Haydn's no good to him, I keep telling him, but he won't listen. I'm afraid of what might have happened to him, honest I am." She growled it out at me as usual, her voice showing no perturbation.

"Well, honestly, I can't think of anything to do about it. What about your husband? What does he say?"

"Aw, he's in bed and won't wake up. Calls me daft for bothering, he do. Won't you help me, Mr. Lewis?"

"But he might be anywhere. He's probably gone along to somebody's house for a . . . cup of tea. I shouldn't wait up for him if I were you."

"But he know I always do, see? That's what's so funny. And to-night he said particular he'd be back, wanted to hear the Frankie Laine records over the wireless at ten-fifteen."

This was interesting as throwing light on the derivation of Ken's vocal style, but not otherwise. How could I put it to his mother that events had led to Frankie Laine being ditched as expendable, that Ken had probably gone into an alley or on to the common with one of the Alton girls? "He probably heard them in someone's house," I said. "There's no need to get so anxious."

"No, I know something have happened, Mr. Lewis. He's never out as late as this unless he's going to a dance, and then he tells me so's I'll know."

"I'm sorry, Mrs. Davies, I'd like to help, but I can't see how I can. I'm rather tired. He'll be back soon, don't worry. Well, good-night."

I went upstairs and into the sitting-room, where I found Jean in her nightdress and dressing-gown (not such a nice one as Mrs. Davies's). Old Probert was in there too, standing on the tiles of the hearth. He was fully dressed, but looked a little bit ill at ease, or so I thought at the time.

SEVENTEEN

"Hallo, dear people," I said, mimicking the generic accent of the Gruffydd-Williamses and their pals. I went some of the way towards Jean and Probert. "Thanks loads for waiting up for me. You really and truly shouldn't have bothered, you know." I thought briefly of what ample warning of my approach must have been given by my chat with Mrs. Davies, then said in my normal voice: "I hope I haven't come back too early. I stayed out as long as I could, didn't I?"

Probert stirred. He was now giving a strong, hairy-eyebrowed stare. He said in his film-Welshman's voice, which recalled to me that of the nut-faced clergyman at my interview: "What are you talking about, John? What's the matter with you?"

"Nothing, really. But there is something rather quaint about this set-up, you must admit. I run into you once at a party. I go and see that lying play of yours, Jean goes and sees it the next night, and then, weeks and weeks later, I suddenly run into you again, here, at one a.m. Wouldn't you feel a bit, well, a bit quizzical if you were in my shoes?"

"I don't know what you mean. I was giving a talk on verse drama to-night at the Cwmhyfryd Library, as you can confirm if you wish to. My bus back to Aberdarcy leaves from just along the street here. I thought I'd stop on my way and look you up. Nothing to be very quizzical about there, is there?"

"Not so far, no, except I don't quite follow why you should want to look me up, as opposed to Jean. But you mustn't get the wrong impression, Gareth. I'm not making any accusations. I'm just intrigued, that's all. I'm intrigued, for instance, about the enormous quantity of looking-up you've done to-night, to last you till now." I still hadn't looked squarely at Jean, but now I heard her mutter something that sounded like "Bloody fool", though I may have been wrong about the second word. Anyway, it added to the notable feeling of relaxed contentment that had begun to grow on me since starting to talk to Probert. Even old Gruffydd-Williams, I thought, could afford to pick up a few tips from me here. It would have been interesting to see what he'd have said if he'd come into their lounge that afternoon when I was having a jolly time on the floor with the cigarette-box.

Probert had narrowed his long eyes more than usual. He came a pace or two nearer, standing on the rug, his arms hanging loosely by his sides. "Whatever is the matter, John? Why are you behaving in such a curious way? If you must know, the reason why I'm still here at this hour is this. I arrived soon after ten. Jean was sitting here waiting for you. She didn't know where you were, and she was getting worried, and I must say I don't blame her. She hadn't seen you since early this afternoon, when you went off to go to your interview. She's been waiting ever since to hear what happened there, and not a word from you all these hours. Well, need I say any more? She was getting anxious and asked me to stay and keep her company. As simple as that. Right?"

The suspicion had been growing on me that among the entities present earlier on the beach had been an occasional rogue mosquito or midge. Having rubbed and pinched ineffectually through my sleeve, I pulled back my shirt-cuff and uncovered three whitish lumps as big as sixpences, witnesses of rabid proboscidiferous greed. Why couldn't they just suck people's blood without having to deposit secretions of their own in exchange? Perhaps they wouldn't get so much fun out of it any other way, and that was quite enough reason, from the point of view of the Great Architect, for things remaining as they were. "What?" I said. "Oh yes, of course. Well, the boys are certainly wandering to-night, eh? And the people at home standing by ready to do something, if only they could think of something to do. Mrs. Davies downstairs waiting for Ken, and you two up here waiting for me. It bloody well makes me feel treasured."

"Take no notice of him, Gareth, he's just a fool. Don't pay any attention. He's half-cut, anyway."

By the way Jean snapped this out I could visualise exactly the look on her face, her chin raised, her eyes half-closed and blinking rapidly, her lips showing their full thickness. So there was still no point in looking at her, although going on not doing so was beginning to give me a bit of a stiff neck. "I'm sorry about all this, Gareth," I said. "There's no sense in going on any longer, I can see that. You're going to stick to your story and I think I probably believe it anyway. But it's too late at night for me to be certain about what I think about this kind of thing. So I'll drop you a postcard. What I mean is, let's pack it in. Only don't come dropping in again, there's a good chap. At least, not when I'm about. Make sure I'm out of the way."

"I've stood enough of that kind of talk," he said, not in his film-Welsh accent, but in the voice that used to bawl down the corridors and across the playground at school. He added one of his favourite phrases of that period: "You shut your gab."

So saying, he came rapidly towards me. I never found out why, because with the second or third pace he fell quickly down, his foot pinioned by one of the many loops Eira had made by knotting the fringe of the rug. I produced a serviceable parody of Whetstone's laugh. "You see," I said to Jean; "I've only got to breathe on them and they've had it." Then I turned to Probert, who was finding it difficult to extract his foot from Eira's gin. "You mustn't be so impulsive, Gareth. All I meant was that I never want to see you. Nothing very offensive about that, eh?"

He got up at last and went to the door. "Will you be all right, Jean?" I noticed he'd had his hair cut, which gave him an adventitious look of meekness.

"Of course she'll be all right, don't you worry. You'd better start walking now. You might get a lift, of course, but I shouldn't build on it if I were you. *The Martyr* is the worst play since *Gammer Gurton's Needle*," I told him finally, ushering him out.

My euphoria lasted until I heard the front door bang and Probert's footsteps die away. Punctually after that a number of disagreeable reflexions presented themselves to me. I went and sat down opposite Jean. There was a lot to be gone through, but this time it surely would be gone through. That, at any rate, was good.

I looked at her, and she looked back at me without expression, indeed without interest. She was obviously tired; there were violet marks under her eyes and the eyes themselves were bloodshot. Her complexion was

roughened. While I was wondering how to begin, she said:
"Well, I gather you didn't get the job."

"No, I don't think I did, but they haven't let us know yet."

"You're pretty sure you didn't?"

"Pretty sure."

"Oh well, that's that, then. I might as well get off to bed."

But she made no move.

"I'm sorry, but it was just the way things worked out."

"How do you mean?"

"I had to more or less turn it down. And anyway I shouldn't think I'll get it after what happened later."

"Thought you said they were going to let you know."

"Well . . ." I sighed; there was so much of this. "I couldn't really tell how I'd done at the interview. Then afterwards I saw Elizabeth. She told me it was all fixed; Gruffydd-Williams was going to see I got the job whatever anyone else said. The whole thing was a wangle, you see. He was just doing it to spite old Rowlands, who doesn't like me apparently. Well, I wasn't going to get mixed up in a business like that. So I told her so." It all sounded staggeringly inept. And surely Gruffydd-Williams, on to-night's showing, wasn't the sort of man who made appointments just to spite people? Not that it mattered now.

"So you turned it down, right?" Jean was sitting there in an attitude that was graceful and uncomfortable at the same time. A hole was worn in the material of her nightdress, under the collar. I wished I had something good to tell her.

"Well, it wasn't quite like that." I told her about the crash and Gruffydd-Williams's attitude to me after it. "So I imagine he'll be revising his views now on who he thinks he'll push into the job," I ended. "I hope it's Ieuan. He needs the money."

"I suppose we didn't need the money," she said flatly.

"Yes, of course, but to get it by a dirty piece of jobbery like that . . . Would you have felt easy about it?"

"I'd have got used to it, and so would you, or you've got even less sense than I think you have." She sat up and grew immediately angry, as if with the movement of her body. "What's all this about, anyway? I don't understand it. What's been going on this evening? What's got into you so you start turning down jobs? I don't know who you think you are, turning down bloody jobs. You make me spew. Now we've got to go on living here with that old faggot downstairs bitching and binding everything we do. What made you tell that Elizabeth you didn't want the job? She'd cook up some story about that smash and so on to satisfy her old man if I know her, don't worry. But she's not going to now you've told her they can keep the job. We're not in the position where we can do that sort of thing, and you know it. It's all right for a lot of other people, but not for us. I know you, though. You've had her this evening, haven't you? That's why you're behaving like this?"

"Yes."

She leant forward, twisting her face up as she spoke. "I knew it, because I know you, see? No need to tell me anything more. You couldn't just do it and forget about it, not you, you had to make a bloody fuss, so you told her what to do with the job she'd landed you. Don't talk to me about Ieuan, you don't care what happens to Ieuan, or his wife. You forgot you were married to me, though, that's what makes me so mad. If it'd just been your job you were turning down, fair enough, you could do as you liked. But it wasn't just your job, it was my job as well, and the kids' too. But you didn't care about that, you'd got to make your stand and be bloody sensitive. Well, I hope you're satisfied."

There seemed little to say to all this. I got up and

226

made to leave the room. My hand was hurting where I'd banged it and I thought I'd bathe it under the kitchen tap.

"Where are you off to?"

"Just going to get a drink. Do you want one?"

"No thanks. I'll tell you something else, too."

"What?"

"I don't care a damn about you and Elizabeth. You needn't think I'm angry because of that. It isn't that at all. I've got to the stage now where I don't care if you sleep with all the women in Aberdarcy and come back asking to be forgiven afterwards. That's not what's got me mad."

"Listen, Jean, I don't mind sounding silly, the only thing I care about is you forgiving me this time. Over Elizabeth, I mean. That's much more important than this job business."

"Oh no it isn't. And as for forgiving you, just forget it. I forgive you all right, it doesn't mean a thing to me. I'll forgive you every time you do it, too. But I'll never forgive you for throwing away that job."

"Don't you really mind what I do with other women?"

"How many more times have I got to tell you? You're the one who minds, not me. Haven't you got that straight yet?"

"Haven't you ever minded, right from the beginning?"

When she looked up at me again, her face seemed to have altered completely, as if she was facing a strong light, but her voice was unchanged, still level, still with the note of deliberate anger: "I don't care what happens now, because it's all over as far as I'm concerned. Whatever you told me couldn't be as bad as what I felt when I realised what you were thinking about that Elizabeth and preferring her to me. That was the worst time, but I've got over all that now. So now you actually come and tell me it's happened, it doesn't mean anything to me, because I've been through all that part. I'd been through it when you started telling me about her before. And you were wondering why you didn't get any change out of me, I could see."

I came over to her. "You mean that's wrecked the whole thing, all our marriage and everything, just because of that?"

"Yes, that's right," she said, leaning forward in her seat. "The whole thing. What do you think it's all about, anyway? Why do you think we got married? I know your rich pals think different, but I didn't know you did. Not then, not when we got married. Or I shouldn't have married you, see? Yes, I know a bit of chasing round after other women now and then doesn't matter, according to you. As long as there isn't too much of it. Well, according to me a bit does matter, a bit's too much. Any at all's too much, so it's over, there's nothing left of the whole bloody issue." She began crying. "Anything at all of that sort matters. According to me."

I bent towards her to take hold of her. She got up, trying to push me away, but I caught her shoulders and, though she twisted her head aside, kissed her near the mouth. When I let her go, she smacked me hard on the cheek. "That's your treatment from now on, man," she said in her normal voice. She brushed past me and started picking up the heaps of children's effects that were littered on the chairs and floor.

I went out into the kitchen and cleared cups and plates out of the washbasin, then turned on the tap and let it run on my knuckles and the back of my hand. The water was warm at first, but soon ran cold. I rinsed out a cup and drank some. I'd been thirstier than I'd realised.

Under the small table by the window was a pile of old newspapers. On the top one I could see a picture that looked familiar and, at the moment only in theory, inviting. Opening and closing my hand slowly, I stooped down and pulled it out. Yes, it was curvesome Marietta DuForgue vacationing at Las Palmas, now rather creased and stained with tea. Marietta DuForgue and her curvesome colleagues had had a bad effect on me. Or was she only a less harmful, and correspondingly less exciting, version of Elizabeth? There was a lot to be said for that opinion, as also for the opinion that the bad effect in or on me was the sort that toted itself around looking for a cause. I put the paper back on top of the pile and got to my feet.

Looking round the kitchen as I dried my knuckles, I caught sight of a plate of dried-up meat and potatoes, no doubt intended for the supper I hadn't turned up to eat. I looked away from it. I went and dried two cups and took the cocoa-tin out of the food-cupboard. There was a nearly-full bottle of milk under the wash-basin in a bucket of water. While I was looking for a saucepan, Jean came in and stood just over the threshold. "What are you doing there?"

"I thought we might have a cup of cocoa."

"Nothing for me, I'm going to bed. And don't use that milk, it's for the kids' breakfast. And I've thought of a couple of other things I wanted to say."

"What are they?"

She watched me for a moment, standing there in her bare feet, her arms full of children's clothes. "What you'd better do is to make up to Elizabeth again quick. Get her to take you away for the week-end or something. I don't care how you do it, but make sure the affair's on again. And then tell her you want the job after all, see? You didn't mean what you said, you acted hasty, something like that. You'll know what to say, I bet. But you get that job back, else I'll stop cooking for you."

"You don't mean that, do you, Jean?"

"Course I mean it, you can get your meals out."

"No, about . . . starting up with Elizabeth again."

"Why not? She's better than me, isn't she?"

"No, she's not."

"Liar. Anyway, you do as I say."

I put down the saucepan I'd picked up at some point and said: "What was the other thing you wanted to say?"

"Can't you guess?"

"No."

"Old Probert, now. Not so bad he isn't, really. Not half so bad as he looks. Bit scruffy, mind, but nothing terrible. He's all right, you know."

"I see."

"Not much to look at, of course. To-night wasn't the first time, by the way. There was that other time you were out with yours. I'm going up now."

"He's so horrible," I said.

"Well, I think Elizabeth's bloody horrible too, but it isn't me who sleeps with her, so it doesn't matter what I think. Doesn't matter what you think about old Probert either, does it?"

"No."

"So long, then. I'll be sleeping in Eira's bed from to-morrow, and you can have her in with you, but I don't want to disturb her to-night now she's settled." She went quietly upstairs.

I stayed where I was in the kitchen for a minute or two, then hurried into the sitting-room. I switched the wireless on, but remembered that the only stations it could get would have closed down by now, and switched it off again. I sat down on the edge of the chair Jean had vacated and began to read the morning paper very quickly, as fast as I could. The door was open and a cold draught was blowing in and making me shiver, but I didn't want to get up and stop reading the paper so as to shut the door. When I was shivering too much to read at all, I went out into the kitchen to fill a kettle for tea. I couldn't find the jug from which we always filled the kettle, and tried to get the mouth of the kettle under the tap, but it wouldn't go under; it never had. Some of the water splashed over my trousers. I turned the tap off, left the kettle in the basin and darted out of the kitchen and downstairs. As soon as I was in the street I broke into a run.

I felt as if something had happened which had made me feel very frightened, and that I must do something which would make me feel even more frightened if I was ever to get rid of the first frightening thing. I felt too as if I couldn't remember what exactly had happened. As for what I'd have to do to get rid of it, it was obvious that I would in fact have to do it, it must come from me, because at this time there was nobody at all about, and so there was nothing that could just happen. I looked to the end of the long street, to where it curved up and sideways; no, nobody there at all. Whatever happened would be something that I did myself, it couldn't be anything else.

After I'd run to the end of the street I stopped for a moment and looked back. There was still nobody there. On each side of the street were the houses, all looking exactly the same under the irregularly-spaced streetlights. Although a window or two was illuminated I couldn't believe there were people in the houses either. I wondered what would happen if I went and knocked on one of the doors. If anybody answered I'd say: "Does Mr. Rigby live here?", just as I used to plan to do when I was a child and hurrying home from Cubs on Wednesday nights in the winter. If I got frightened, I used to say to myself, I'd knock on the nearest door and ask for Mr. Rigby. There wouldn't be anyone called that (if by any chance there was I'd say it was Mr. Johannes Rigby I wanted, so I was quite safe), but while I was talking to whoever came to the door I'd get my courage back. I could do it all the way down the street if necessary, and if the people compared notes afterwards they'd only think I'd been playing some sort of joke, and jokes are all right.

I strained my eyes looking down the street, trying to catch a movement, but there wasn't even any wind to blow things about in the gutter, and there were no clouds in the sky. The stillness made everything unreal and the only thing that would move, myself, unreal in an opposite way. I stood for a moment panting and scratching the mosquito-bites on my forearm until I felt a different kind of fear, different from the one that had made me want to get out into the street, begin to stir and uncoil and move gradually across part of my brain. This, and it had been the same during my childhood, was the moment for Mr. Johannes Rigby.

"Poor old Elizabeth," I said, and started running up the hill. I chose this direction because it would make me more out of breath, but felt that in some other way it was wrong, that I didn't really want to go uphill at all. "Poor old Elizabeth." Making that fuss about the job had just been an excuse. "Excuse, excuse, excuse," I muttered. I hadn't been able to face going on seeing her. "Coward," I tried to call out, "coward." I got so out of breath saying this that I could concentrate all my attention on keeping going up the hill, and on not wasting any energy by letting my foot slip on the smooth paving stones. After a time I found I very much disliked the sound of my own gasping in my ears, and the way something in my pocket kept bouncing against me, and to counteract these things I fastened my eyes on the walls of the front gardens I was passing, noticing how each one made an angle with the pavement so that the walls should be horizontal. I soon managed to make my paces coincide with the moment when each horizontal came to my eye-level. At the crest I stopped again and looked back the way I'd come, but there was an even longer vista this time, again with nothing moving anywhere, so I turned at once and ran at right angles down a gentler slope that led towards Aberdarcy. Almost at once I fell over and grazed the palm of my bad hand and one knee; I was glad of this because the pain would make me concentrate on it. Quite soon, though, it wore off and became a faint throbbing, and by this time the lessening of effort in running downhill, however fast, was allowing me to begin remembering what had happened to make me feel as if I was frightened.

I came to another corner. If I turned here I would, I knew, cut across the long street I'd climbed up from some minutes earlier. Yes, I'd cut across it and go straight on; that was the way to the sea, and I knew now that that was the way I'd wanted to go all the time, even when I turned uphill. This would be down, of course, and would make me less out of breath, but I might be able to make up for that by going as fast as I could, dangerously fast, and so leave myself no attention to spare from the task of not falling over. That would do it. I began racing down the hill, using very long strides. It was working pretty well when I saw, on the pavement by the corner, something moving slightly. It was the figure of a man, and he seemed to be looking up the hill towards me.

At once I slackened my pace to a trot, then to a brisk walk. I didn't want him to start shouting at me, as he was bound to do if I ran past him at full speed. I'd walk till I was well past him, then I'd start running again and make for the sea.

"All right then, what do you want?" the man asked when I got near enough.

My heart was still pounding, bouncing in and out in my chest as if it was made of rubber, but I said clearly "Nothing," and prepared to walk past him. Before I reached him he moved out into my path.

"Wait a minute, you bastard," he said, and took me by the lapels. "Where's Haydn?"

It was Ken Davies. He looked more drunk than anyone I'd ever seen. His normal appearance was one of a rather infamous vitality, but at this moment his face was heavy and pouchy with fatigue of one sort or another. His eyes, which looked as though they might heal over if he allowed them to close, searched my face. I could hear his breath roaring against his palate. "Where's Haydn?" he asked me again, shaking me and forcing me to retreat a pace or two.

With a violent heave I broke free of him and pushed him back against the wall. He bounced slowly forward again, behaving like one moving in water rather than air. "You clear off and leave me alone," I said, and took a pace or two towards the road I intended to cross. Just as my glance was leaving him I saw him spring at me and dodged sideways, but he caught me round the waist from behind and then sank to his knees. I struggled on for a few more yards, until the two of us were halted, locked together, in the middle of the road. I pounded briskly on his hands with my fists. He began protesting more and more loudly as time went by, then suddenly released me. I only just stopped myself from falling on my face, but got clear of him and reached the opposite pavement. Glancing over my shoulder, I saw him on all fours in the middle of the road, his head hanging forward. I walked quickly along to the corner, the turning that led to the sea. Before breaking into a run I again looked back at Ken. He'd gone down on his forearms so that his forehead touched the road; his bottom pointed into the air, giving him a look of a horse stuck half-way through the act of lying down. I could hear him groaning to himself. On the whole he seemed to have entered some state beyond the confines of ordinary drunkenness.

"Oh God," I said, and went back and stood in front of him. It was funny to see him like this, lying so low after the conquests, glories and triumphs of the dance-hall. After the way he'd half-strangled that chap with his own Slim Jim, here he was in the road. It was so funny that I had to laugh for a long time, eventually sitting down beside Ken to laugh better.

An upstairs window creaked up and a woman's voice called: "Joke over, now. Get along home, there's good boyos. You'll wake the baby and she's teething. Only just got her off."

"All right, darling," I said, waving. "We'll be off now. Just got to get him on his feet."

"Good night, boy *bach*."

"What's the matter with you?" I asked Ken in a hectoring tone. "You can't just lie there in the road."

It was clear that he thought he could; perhaps, hearing only my last half-dozen words, he'd taken them as an order. Anyway, without verbal reply, he let his buttocks topple until one hip rested on the ground. I commanded him several times to stand up; then, bending down, made out some streaks of something dark along the side of his neck and round one ear. Mud, I thought at first. No, blood.

It was now that I became aware of the final abandonment of my running-down-to-the-sea project. What had I imagined I could gain by it? I'd have had to go back home some time. For the next few minutes there was a tiring struggle while I pulled Ken to his feet and got him back to the corner of the pavement where he'd originally been standing. It seemed snugger there, somehow. I was afraid I might have caused him to have blood on his neck, and as I saw now, on the back of his head as well.

He half-leaned against the wall here and I half-supported him. He was evidently quite satisfied with this arrangement, making snuggling movements with his head and shoulders, yawning and smacking his lips, as if settling down for the night. He gave a faint farewell belch. "What's the matter with you?" I asked him again. He made no reply.

After a time I found my own eyelids beginning to

droop; if I wasn't careful we might both drop off and be here till morning. One trouble was that I could think of no good reason for hurry. Then I noticed for the first time a pool of fairly fresh vomit a couple of yards away, no doubt voided before I came running down the hill, and this made me wonder just how much of his behaviour could be traced to drink, how much to the bang on the head. I peered again at the wound. At this period Ken was favouring the D.A. cut, which involves, as befits its eponym, the confluence of two wings of hair at the back. I tried to unpeel some of this, but he kept pulling his head away from me and all I could be sure of was that a good-sized patch seemed soaked with blood. I couldn't have done that. I started jogging him about, not too hard in case he got angry again at my failure to produce, or to be, Haydn. "Here," I said loudly, "who hit you, Ken? Who's been bashing you, boy? Come on, now." It suddenly occurred to me that the Slim Jim practitioner and his friend might have chosen to-night to revenge themselves on him. I hoped that wasn't it.

His head was coming up, showing uninquisitive eyeballs. "What you want? Where's Haydn?"

I said quickly: "All friends here, Ken. You've been . . ."

With an efficiency surprising in his state, he hit me in the stomach. I sat down on the pavement, wondering when, if ever, I was going to be able to breathe again. When I could, I went warily back to him. The effort had perhaps taken his last strength; he was on his knees both figuratively and literally, propped against the wall, and his breathing was shallow and noisy. With a strong sense of having done it all before I lifted him up, standing behind him and stepping backwards as he came upright to put my shins beyond range of his heels. He swayed, made a half-turn, and looked at me. This time his eyes were alert. "Christ, it's Mr. Lewis," he said. "How long have you been there?"

"Not long. How are you feeling?"

"Where'd you blow in from? What is this?" he asked in Welsh-American; then, reverting engagingly to Welsh-English: "Bloody terrible head I've got, man. Fell over. Spewed too," he added, seeing the evidence. "*Ach-y-fi*, eh?"

"What about coming home? Can you walk?"

"Aw, can't barge in in this condition, Mr. Lewis. My mam'd half-kill me, you know that. Got to wait till she's gone to bed."

"She's waiting up for you. She won't go to bed till you fetch up, take it from me."

"Seen her, have you? What time is it, then?"

"It must be . . ." I realised I hadn't much idea. "It must be well after two."

"Christ, what am I going to do?"

"Someone slugged you, didn't they?"

"Slugged me?"

"There's blood on the back of your head."

He verified this wonderingly, then laughed. "Fell down outside the Alton Inn after stop-tap," he said. "I remember now. Must have been lying there for bloody hours, man."

"What about your mates? Why didn't they look after you?"

"Only had Haydn Morris with me, and he was taking his woman up the common when I saw him last. Wonder how I made it down here. On my arse, most likely."

"Let's go home," I urged him. "We can say you got hit on the head. You couldn't have helped that. Trying to stop a fight, how would that do?"

He laughed again. "All right, in a minute. Got a fag, boy?"

"Don't smoke," I said, patting my pockets. In one of them was something hard and squarish. Remembering, I said: "Wait a minute, it just so happens . . ." I offered him one of Elizabeth's black fags.

Saying no more than "Christ, what are these?" he took and lit it, and accepted the rest of the contents of the case when I offered them. (I put the case itself back in my pocket; someone might think he'd stolen it if I gave it to him. It could be sent back by post, without covering note, after the precedent given by the Welsh-woman's costume.) Exhaling, he said as if to himself: "Camel-shit, eh?" and spat out a shred of tobacco.

I thought how much I liked him, as he stood there in his mucked-up finery, not inquiring why I had these or any cigarettes on me, not wondering how I'd happened to be out at this time, not thinking there was anything odd about anything, not, above all, knowing or caring anything whatsoever about Elizabeth or Gruffydd-Williams or Whetstone or Theo James or Probert or Gloriana or Stan Johns or Margot Johns or the dentist or the dentist's mistress or Bill Evans. Funny chap, old Bill Evans; it was a pity I'd never got the chance to find out more about his history and status.

After a few more drags at his cigarette, Ken said he'd like to go home now, if I'd give him a hand; he felt a bit shaky on his pins. I was glad of his company back along the street, and with one arm round his shoulder, got him back to the house quite fast. The appearance of unreality in the scene, which had flustered me before, now failed to strike me. "You'd better see a doc in the morning," I told Ken as we reached the house. "You might have a bit of concussion."

Mrs. Davies opened the door to us at once; she must have been standing in the passage. She was ready to listen to my explanations of her son's condition, even appeared to be taking them in. Like him, she evidently found nothing odd in my encounter with him. We helped Ken into the passage, where he started groaning, rather loudly if he cared about allaying his mother's anxiety, but I didn't mind that. I politely tried to conceal my amazement when, so far from managing to blame me for making Ken ill and late (which would have been her typical reaction), she said to me after I'd said good night: "Thank you very much for helping Ken home, Mr. Lewis. Real nice of you it was, and I shan't forget it."

I went upstairs, reflecting that I felt rather tired. I turned out the light in the sitting-room and went into the kitchen, where I picked up in my fingers and put in my mouth the lumps of meat Jean had cooked for my supper. I ate them all, chewing very hard and fast, swallowing all the gristle and fat and even one nameless lump of outlandish consistency. Then I ate all the potatoes. Then I turned to my half-completed preparations for the cups of cocoa. The nylon scourer received employment, pea-liquor was removed from a handy teaspoon, the cocoa-powder was mixed into the statutory smooth paste, the forbidden milk grew warm on the gas-ring. I could slip out early next morning to the nearby dairy. I began meditating on what I was going to do when the cocoa was ready. Meeting Ken Davies seemed at the time to have had a lot to do with making up my mind.

I thought of that upper-class crowd. Why couldn't they be Welsh, I wondered, or since they were mostly Welsh by birth, why couldn't they stay Welsh? Why had they got to go around pretending to be English all the time?—not that there was anything, or anything very serious, wrong with being English, providing you were it to start with. Those who were Welsh to start with should stick to being it. The examples of old Probert, the nut-faced clergyman, and such minor figures as the woman who'd ticked me off on the bus when I was in traditional national dress, were of service in demonstrating the complementary dangers of being too keen on being Welsh.

Then I thought of what I was going to do. Since I seemed to have piloted myself into the position of being immoral and moral at the same time, the thing was to keep trying not to be immoral, and then to keep trying might turn into a habit. I was always, at least until I reached the climacteric, going to get pulled two ways, and keeping the pull from going the wrong way, or trying to, would have to take the place, for me, of stability and consistency. Not giving up was the important thing.

I poured the milk into two cups, feeling a bit nervous, because this not-giving-up business was all very fine and large, but it wouldn't be any good if I tried it on my own, if it only applied to me. That was the one important condition. I took the cups upstairs and into Jean's and my bedroom.

EIGHTEEN

"Well, you should be congratulating yourself," my father said. "An invitation to the home of one of the premier hostesses in this part of Wales. Mrs. Edith Rhys Protheroe requests the pleasure. By God, there's a vocable for you."

"She's always been pretty free with the drink," I said.

"So I understand. Now remember: the main thing to watch when you get there is no laughing at poor old Percy. You'll have a hard fight, mind, if he comes up from the shop to have a drink in his full regalia, and I'm betting you he will. But it's your sacred duty to keep a straight face. Just try and imagine what that man goes through for love."

"And money," I said.

"Oh, good God, I'm with you there, John, we shouldn't forget the financial aspect, granted. Most . . . vital, I agree. But he's safe now as far as that goes. Half-owner of the business. Edie made it over to him early this year. It's easy to underrate old Percy. No flies on him, in spite of his face."

"Well, I never knew that. Just shows, doesn't it? So he lets her put him through the hoop because he likes her."

"You've got it." My father nodded his bald head severely and took his pipe out of his cardigan pocket. "That man is a sacrifice—and a willing one, mark you—on the altar of his wife's desire for social consequence and . . . urbanity." He blew down the pipe, producing a squealing note which he repeated several times for the benefit of the baby, who was sitting next to him on the sofa tearing up yesterday's paper. The baby laughed tolerantly. "In a sense, Edie's position as a leading socialite of Fforestfawr," my father was going on, filling the pipe, but Eira's entry from the garden interrupted him. She was wearing a gorilla-mask cut out of a cereal carton and fitted with string for her by her grandfather, and she was roaring and spreading her arms. After feinting in my direction she threw herself on to my father's lap, took off the mask and asked him in a normal tone why elephants had tusks. Her interest in the border-line of philosophy and natural science showed no signs of abating. A discussion followed, only to be interrupted in its turn by the clacking of the latch on the staircase door and Jean's emergence into the room.

The summer dress she had on, a mainly white affair with red and blue flower-clusters, had been astutely selected—and even more astutely secured on credit—from the stock of Hopkins Gowns, a new and enterprising establishment just round the corner from the Miners' Welfare Hall. She looked very well in the dress and I wondered whether she mightn't have put on a little weight in the last fortnight. A hint of the old sheen had come back to her hair, which as usual rated ten out of ten for profusion. She stood there grinning and blinking while the rest of us stared at her. "My God, girl," my father said, "you'll wipe old Edie's eye in that rig-out."

"Not too kind of informal, is it, Dad?" Jean asked.

"Certainly not. It's what the season requires. You'll probably find old Edie in her taffeta or bombazine or whatever it is, with an Elizabethan collar and six rows of pearls I shouldn't wonder, but that'll only testify to her delusions of grandeur. Now you two run along sharp. Take your time about coming back."

"Sure you don't mind being left with these two?" I said.

"Of course I don't. I'd much rather hear about Edie from you than have another dose of her myself. I'll be interested to see what you make of her these days. And Eira will look after the baby for me, I know, while I have a final crack at the Ximenes crossword. Now, where's the *Chambers*'?"

"On the wireless with your glasses," Jean said. "You're not to start getting the dinner, remember. It's all cold, anyway. And don't let the children get in your way, will you?"

"I'll trample them underfoot if they try to. Come on, now, off to go. But bear in mind: no excess, see? Keep off Edie's cocktails. Sobriety and . . . decorum, let these be your watchwords. Give my regards to Edie and to Mr. Roberts, if he's there. Sobriety and decorum." He waved us good-bye from the step.

We walked off down the road that ran diagonally across the side of the valley and past the small colliery where I now had a job in coal sales. The money wasn't bad: not much less than I'd pulled in as an Assistant Librarian, and likely to increase. At the same time it didn't approach the salary of a Sub-Librarian. I grinned to myself as I remembered the incredible letter from the Committee offering me the job after all, and the absolutely tremendous amount of laughing I'd done while composing my letter of refusal. My grin was the more whole-hearted because it seemed certain by now that my final instruction to the Committee about where to put its job had not been actionable.

Above the pit wall the wheel turned merrily in the gear, twinkling as the sun fell on it. Despite my absence on this Saturday morning, the work of the place was in full swing. Shunting was being executed in the sidings, trams were being pushed about, and a thick pall of coal-dust blew across the road from the screens, only just failing to envelop us. Passing the pit gates gave us a view, in itself unedifying, of the welter of corrugated-iron out-buildings, some of them apparently on the point of collapse. Further away was the 'tip', or spoil-heap, an eminence perhaps 150 feet high with a few patches of grass on one side, and known locally either as the mountain or as Spion Kop[je].

There were quite a few people about, mainly house-wives out for their shopping and children chasing and fighting each other. But the commercial concerns of Fforestfawr were also being pursued: a man in brown overalls and wearing a shiny-peaked cap was carrying a crate of limeade and dandelion and burdock from the Corona lorry to an open front door; a milkman, pencil behind ear, was cackling loudly as he collected his week's money from an old woman with a hearing-aid; the Premier Checks representative, brief-case in hand, stopped at a house just in front of us and set up a great din with the bright brass knocker. While I chatted to Jean I noticed, as I always did, the names of some of these houses: Eureka Villa, Rhosynog, Taliesin's Retreat and Tybach—the last-mentioned a favourite title for small structures in this part of Wales.

Further on, shops began to appear here and there between the houses. Just beyond a wall where someone had painted the words 'FREE WALES', Howell the greengrocer hailed me from his doorway. He was wearing a dark-grey coat and a very light fawn cap. He said: "You're off now, then."

"That's it, boy."

"Where's it to be?"

"Edie Protheroe's for a couple of drinks."

"Ah, the great madam. How's the family?"

"Full of fun."

"Your da's on guard, right?"

"Holding the fort."

"Don't know what to do with myself these Saturdays. Hanging about like a lost sneeze. Only another few weeks, though, and that ball'll be bouncing. Hope they solve the full-back problem this year."

"It's about time."

"I'll be having my season-ticket for the stand as usual. Makes all the difference to your power of enjoying the game. And I'll be having the same arrangement with Handel Preece and the others about the car. There in comfort and back in comfort. Worth twice the money when you get to my age."

"It must be."

"Mustn't keep you, then. Remember me to your da. Tell him I was talking to you."

"I will."

We moved on into the small square at the centre of Fforestfawr. Here we were confronted with the war memorial, the New Palace Cinema, Elim Tabernacle, and the Working Men's Conservative, Democratic and Mutual Dividing Club. Outside Carmel a Wayside Pulpit poster, unchanged since my previous visit in the early spring and now sadly stained, informed me anew that a backward Christian would never make a forward church. Nearby was Rezzi's Café, from which could be heard the hissing roar of one of those steam-jet heater things, boiling up 'coffee' for some idle teen-ager. I laughed a bit. "Do you know what old Rezzi got up to in the war?" I asked Jean.

"No, what?"

"He used to go out and flash his torch at the Germans . . ."

"Flash his what?"

"Now then. Flash his torch. He used to go up on the mountain when he heard them coming over and flash his bloody torch into the sky. No good to anyone, of course. Though I suppose they might have been glad to know they were still over land." Laughing again, I moved over to the mail-slit of the Post Office, which was next door to Rezzi's, and dropped a letter through it. It was addressed to Ieuan Jenkins, Esq., The Sub-Librarian Elect, c/o The Public Library, Aberdarcy.

"Is that the one to Ieuan?" Jean asked as we walked on.

"Yes, what about it?"

"Nothing. John, I'm sorry I lied to you about old Probert that time. Christ, I'd never have let him come near me, let alone . . . I shouldn't have lied to you, though."

"Don't start that again. It's all right, honestly."

"I really am sorry."

"Rubbish, I keep telling you it did me a power of good at the time. It was just what the doctor ordered."

"John."

"Yes?"

"You are glad we came here, aren't you?"

I nodded to a man I knew, a behinder from the local pack-mill, and said: "Of course I'm glad, aren't you?"

"Yes. Don't you feel you're running away, though?"

"Yes, I do, thank God. This isn't like you, angel, getting all tied up with the word; Ieuan's the one for that. You want to forget about 'running away' being what people say about armies retreating and deserters and so on. This isn't like that. Our kind of running away was a stroke of bloody genius. It's always the best thing to do in that kind of situation, provided you can do it. We were lucky there. Now, here we are. I hope we do get a look at Percy. Edie tends to keep him in the background when she's feeling really hostessy."

. We'd come to a large butcher's shop outside which two or three cars were parked. None of them, I noted with absent-minded satisfaction, was large or of amphisboenic appearance. The door adjoining the shop-front was open and, at Jean's request, I led the way in and up the steep stairs. A growl of conversation indicated the right door.

Before we were fairly inside the room a large blonde woman with earrings that would have been just right for a Zulu came striding tenaciously towards us over the heavy carpet, her hand, well reinforced with rings, held out in front of her as if paralysed. When it actually came to it, she didn't shake hands after all, but gave first me and then Jean a lovely warm hug, saying, during the intervals when her face wasn't muffled: "Well, my dears, this is . . . most delightful; it's been such a . . . horrid long time since we . . . all had a real get-together." Her devotions completed, she took our arms and towed us round the room, declaring her belief that we knew everybody. This wasn't quite accurate: Edwin Pugh, a local schoolmaster who did a bit of sporting journalism on the side, was a familiar figure; so was Gaynor Harries, a doctor's dispenser some years older than myself and still on the look-out for a husband; and so was Roberts, the colliery manager, a short thick-set man who looked very much like a colliery manager, and who was accompanied by his silent wife. Two other persons, however, were unknown to Jean and me, a deficiency at once remedied by Edie Protheroe (that's right, the big woman with the Zulu earrings). These two were a married couple called Watkin; he, it transpired later, taught social science at Aberdarcy University College; she, it could be seen straight away, was blonde like Edie, but smaller and paler, as she could hardly help being. A nice-looking girl, I thought, if you liked that type.

Glasses inlaid with representations of tropical fauna and containing very dry sherry indeed were handed to us. To my palate the stuff tasted rather like the brine those pickled herrings are bottled in, plus a scintilla of dish-cloth, but I swigged it manfully and let myself be taken round the room either by my own whim or under Edie's direction. Jean soon got haled off to chat to Pugh, the schoolmaster, and Gaynor Harries, the dispenser. I saw Gaynor give Edie a resentful glare as the junction was effected. Poor old Gaynor, I thought, she was hoping to get Pugh to herself at this do and impress him with her talents, which weren't inconsiderable, though for a girl who wanted to get married as badly as she did they weren't the right ones, either. Then I thought, more feelingly this time, poor old Pugh. Twenty years of living in lodgings might make him consider it after all.

I talked to Roberts and his wife for a few minutes. When he wasn't giving me looks of caricatured appraisal and when I wasn't responding with the demeanour of a smart lad from whom great things, or at any rate things, might be expected in the future, we were agreeing that while England's batting left a good deal to be desired, particularly as regards the vexed question of a partner for Len Hutton, her bowling was in a healthy condition and indeed recalled the great days of Larwood and Verity, which I, of course, would be just too young to remember. Roberts went on to give a long account, notable for much self-correction and interim recapitulation, of an epic bowling performance against Australia, witnessed by him in its entirety at Lord's, or was it the Oval? At any rate, the heroes had been Larwood and Voce, or was it Gubby Allen? Although nodding my head almost without respite,

I took the chance of seeing what Edie'd had done to the place since my last visit. At first glance there didn't seem to be much that was new apart from the illuminated fish-tank behind the television set, but intenser scrutiny revealed a green-and-mauve-checked shawl kind of affair draped along the back of the sofa, a 'contemporary' chair upholstered in shaggy yet quilted stuff, a pair of oak hands holding an oak head in them on the mantelpiece, and, right under my nose, the latest Graham Greene and Angela Thirkell lying, still in their jackets, on a copy of *Vogue*.

While Roberts was still explaining to me that none of these youngsters of to-day had the pace off the pitch of old Maurice Tate, whom I, of course, came along too late in the day to have seen, Edie appeared and pinioned me by the arm. I had time to give Roberts my father's respects and my own kindest regards before being toted round the room in a semi-circle and brought to a halt in front of the Watkins, the university couple. Jean, I saw, was still with Gaynor and Pugh. The latter's great shallow lower jaw was wagging crazily and a flush had embrowned his lean cheeks. Sherry, dry or not, wasn't something he saw very much of as a rule.

The male Watkin plunged without preparation into an account of his doings at the College. He wore a brown suit with wider tan stripes than I thought was prudent. He somehow looked as if he was older than he looked. "We're trying to find the social switches," he said.

"The social switches?" I said.

"That's right. Now: when you switch on the light, what happens? The light comes on, doesn't it?"

"Yes, if the lighting system's in order."

"Agreed, yes, agreed, a very fair point. But if it is in order, then the light must come on, mustn't it? It's got to, hasn't it? Simple cause and effect. That's all it is."

"Well . . ." I said.

"Right, well we want to find the social switches, that's all. We're after the points of contact, if you like, such that if you do *a*—pressing the switch—then you get *b* and nothing but *b*—the light coming on. *B* being in this case the social effect of your policy *a*, got it? There's nothing very mysterious about it, is there?"

"Supposing . . ." I said.

"Of course, we've got a long way to go yet. But when we've acquired the requisite knowledge then society will in fact be an object of scientific study, got it?"

I was wondering rather foggily how he could think that this was conceivable, and was glancing at Mrs. Watkin, who'd been watching her husband without once blinking her eyes, when the door opened and Percy came in. He was wearing his full-dress butcher's uniform—blue-and-white apron, yellow straw boater, dazzling black leather leggings, black tie and hard white collar—and looked as if he was about to step on to a float exhibiting, in some guild procession, the costumes of meat purveyors from the Middle Ages to the present day, himself coming about the middle of the nineteenth century. He carried a large steel in his hand, and with it he beckoned petulantly to his wife. "Edie," he said hoarsely, "I want you, girl."

Despite my father's warning I let a laugh through. I managed to keep it down to a grinding sound at the back of my nose, but its identity was clear, at least to Mrs. Watkin, whose eye I caught at that moment. She responded with a noise of the same kind, and went rather red. Her husband kept his gaze fixed on Percy, who now said with champing emphasis, but still hoarsely:

"Edie, Mrs. Hall's come in downstairs and she says you gave her change for a ten-shilling note yesterday afternoon instead of for a pound note which was what she gave you, she says. What shall I tell her, pet?"

"Tell the old bag to try it on at Probyn's if she feels like it but she can bloody well stop trying it on here because we've rumbled her and she's tried it on once too bloody often, tell her," Edie bawled.

Her earrings whirling, she turned back to Pugh and went on describing, Jean told me later, how once, when 'plastered', she'd broken the glass tops of two glass-topped tables in Porthcawl. Percy stood there a moment longer, swinging his steel and looking rather dashed. No one would have taken him for the ex-War Reserve constable he was. Then he nodded his head, adjusted his boater and plunged out of the door. His boots thundered on the stairs.

"Well, as I was saying just now," Watkin went on, "once these switches are located we can arrange them into some sort of pattern, can't we? A world-picture, got it? It . . ."

I glanced again at Mrs. Watkin, whose face was still rather red. She looked very pretty like that, and even more so when she turned down the corners of her mouth in what might have been half smile, half suppression of smile. She raised her eyebrows about a tenth of an inch.

Hardly had Watkin really got going with a series of unsupportable predictions about his world-picture, before Edie, the Porthcawl anecdote rounded off, came up and carted him away. "Sorry, darling, can't have any of this husband-and-wife stuff at these little get-togethers of mine. Come along," she said. As she swung him round I fancied that his feet left the floor for an instant.

Mrs. Watkin did the smile again. She was certainly a very fine little thing, shy on a quick look, but the smile and an ability, now demonstrated, to do things with the muscles round the eyes hinted that perhaps she wasn't really very shy after all. A glance at her beetroot-coloured blouse showed, without me much wanting to be shown, that she wasn't really very thin, either. After another lift of the eyebrows, which were unplucked and unusually straight at the outer corners, she said: "Well, this is a queer old place, isn't it?"

"Haven't you been here before?"

"No, we haven't been living in Fforestfawr very long, you know. We only came down here in the spring. We were in Oxford before then. This is all rather . . . new to me."

"You don't know Wales, then? I take it you're English?"

"Yes, I've lived near Oxford all my life until now. But I've already found out a bit about Wales, believe me. Yes, sir, there isn't much you can teach me about what goes on down here, or perhaps I should say what doesn't go on. Yes, that's more like it."

She said the last bit rather loudly. Her face seemed to have stayed flushed after the laugh at Percy and I realised she was probably a little drunk. "This is my home town," I said stiffly. "I was born here."

"Well, if you'll excuse my saying so, you don't look it. Not that I want to run the place down, of course. After all, it's my husband's part of the world." She tipped her head over towards where Watkin was standing with Gaynor, Pugh and Jean. "He insisted on getting a job down here," she added. "So naturally we had to come. Do you know something?"

"Try me and see."

It was an innocent come-back, but the eyebrows went up again and the shoulders wiggled. "Why not?" she said. "Have you got a cigarette?"

"I'm sorry, I don't smoke."

"I do, all the time. Never mind, I can stand it for once."

"What was it you wanted to know if I knew?"

"Oh yes. I was just going to say you were the first person I've met down here who looks as if he knows the score. You know, knows his way around."

251

"Oh, I look as if I know that, do I?"

"I'm telling you you do. Do you live here?"

"Yes, I work here. In the colliery."

"What, not down that horrid mine?"

"No, on top of that horrid mine. The office."

"Well, that is a relief, I must say. I shouldn't like to think of you getting all black."

"Why not?"

"One of these days I'll tell you why not. What's your name?"

"John Lewis."

"Mine's Lisa. Watkin. But you know it's Watkin. I never thought I'd have a name like that."

"Lisa?"

"No, Watkin, you fathead."

I hadn't really thought she meant Lisa. I said it because it fitted in with the role of heavy-lidded insouciance that had been growing upon me. Another manifestation of it was the faint smile I was allowing to 'play' round the corners of my mouth. It was like old times, back with my roles again. I said lazily: "Well, you've certainly impressed both your names on my memory."

"Have I? I'm glad. Do you go dancing?"

"Sometimes."

"Do they have dances here in the winter? I suppose they do, in the church hall and worked in with a sewing meeting?"

"No, they aren't all like that. The Police Ball's usually quite good fun. Bags of drink, if you like that sort of thing."

"Oh, I do." She proved it on the spot by picking up somebody else's glass from next to Graham Greene and draining it. "Are you going to the Police Ball this year?"

"Oh yes, I expect so."

"Taking your wife? Never mind, I'll be taking my husband. We'li be even, Stephen. You'll dance with me if

252

I ask you nicely, won't you, John? And I ask very nicely when I feel like it."

"Yes, we'll have a dance all right."

"That's right. But we'll see each other before then, won't we?"

"I shouldn't be at all surprised." I let the smile play a bit more strenuously.

"Neither should I. Any idea when it'll be?"

"None at all at the moment."

"I tell you what, I'll get hubby Watkin to ask you round one evening. Would to-night be too soon?"

"Well, I think perhaps . . ."

"To-night would be lovely, wouldn't it? I'd love it to be to-night." With a jerky movement she shifted her position so that I was between her and the rest of the room. She drew in her breath, opened her mouth and put the tip of her tongue out at me, moving a little closer.

I took it all in, then said: "Will you just excuse me a moment? I want to have a word with Edie." Crossing the room, I said: "I'm hellish sorry, darling, but I've just remembered something. I've got to catch Dyfnallt David when he comes off shift. Very important. Lovely party, Edie, dear. I must rush now. You stay on, angel," I added to Jean, who'd heard most of what I'd said to Edie. "See you back home. Good-bye all, got to rush," I ended in ringing tones, waving to all the company except Lisa Watkin, and left the room. My feet made an almost continuous drumming as I shot down the stairs. In the street I stopped for a moment to get my breath. I seemed to have been deprived of a lot of it in the past fifteen seconds.

Someone else came down the stairs. I got myself all squared up for instantaneous flight, but it was Jean. She was grinning a bit. "Well, what was all that about? Who's Dyfnallt bloody David?"

"A bass-baritone with the Welsh National Opera

Company, most likely. It was the first name I thought of. Let's get going, eh?"

"Come on, now. Let me in on it."

"That woman. I had to get away from that woman. So I got away from her. Crude but effective, you know. We'll have a couple at the Foresters on the way home. Not dry sherry, though. It isn't my drink at all."

I took Jean's arm and we moved across the square. The shift at the pit had just emerged and colliers in their neat suits and caps were walking past us or towards the pub. I waved to an overman I knew. An ancient bus half full of more colliers chuntered by. At the pub door we had to wait for a moment until the way cleared ahead of us. To anyone watching it might have looked as if Jean and I, too, were coming off shift.

MORE ABOUT PENGUINS, PELICANS, PEREGRINES AND PUFFINS

For further information about books available from Penguins please write to Dept EP, Penguin Books Ltd, Harmondsworth, Middlesex UB7 0DA.

In the U.S.A.: For a complete list of books available from Penguins in the United States write to Dept DG, Penguin Books, 299 Murray Hill Parkway, East Rutherford, New Jersey 07073.

In Canada: For a complete list of books available from Penguins in Canada write to Penguin Books Canada Ltd, 2801 John Street, Markham, Ontario L3R 1B4.

In Australia: For a complete list of books available from Penguins in Australia write to the Marketing Department, Penguin Books Australia Ltd, P.O. Box 257, Ringwood, Victoria 3134.

In New Zealand: For a complete list of books available from Penguins in New Zealand write to the Marketing Department, Penguin Books (N.Z.) Ltd, Private Bag, Takapuna, Auckland 9.

In India: For a complete list of books available from Penguins in India write to Penguin Overseas Ltd, 706 Eros Apartments, 56 Nehru Place, New Delhi 110019.